THE MASTERSINGER FROM MINSK

THE MASTERSINGER FROM MINSK

AN INSPECTOR HERMANN PREISS MYSTERY

MORLEY TORGOV

DUNDURN
TORONTO

Editor: Sylvia McConnell
Copy Editor: Cheryl Hawley
Design: Jennifer Scott
Printer: Webcom

Library and Archives Canada Cataloguing in Publication

Torgov, Morley, 1927-
The mastersinger from Minsk : an Inspector Hermann Preiss mystery/Morley Torgov.

Issued also in electronic formats.
ISBN 978-1-4597-0201-1

1. Wagner, Richard, 1813-1883--Fiction. I. Title.

PS8589.O675M38 2012   C813'.54   C2011-906597-5

1   2   3   4   5   16   15   14   13   12

We acknowledge the support of the **Canada Council for the Arts** and the **Ontario Arts Council** for our publishing program. We also acknowledge the financial support of the **Government of Canada** through the **Canada Book Fund** and **Livres Canada Books**, and the **Government of Ontario** through the **Ontario Book Publishing Tax Credit** and the **Ontario Media Development Corporation**.

Care has been taken to trace the ownership of copyright material used in this book. The author and the publisher welcome any information enabling them to rectify any references or credits in subsequent editions.

J. Kirk Howard, President

Printed and bound in Canada.
www.dundurn.com

Dundurn
3 Church Street, Suite 500
Toronto, Ontario, Canada
M5E 1M2

Gazelle Book Services Limited
White Cross Mills
High Town, Lancaster, England
LA1 4XS

Dundurn
2250 Military Road
Tonawanda, NY
U.S.A. 14150

To Anna Pearl, Sarah Jane and Douglas,
Carrie, Benjamin, Sydney Allison, Rebecca, and Marshall

And in memory of Alexander Penn Torgov

PROLOGUE

It must have struck the composer, the conductor, the cho-
rusmaster, the stage director, the house manager, even
the old impresario Mecklenberg who thought he'd seen and
heard everything in his time — all of them solemnly assem-
bled side-by-side in red, plush seats in the front row of the
orchestra section — that what they were about to witness up
there on the bare stage was nothing short of a medieval duel:
two titans prepared to face each other at full tilt in mortal
combat. Each combatant was a tenor; even in the dimness
of the place (the house lights were only partly on) there was
about each of them the enviable radiance of youth, physical
strength, ambition, and readiness. Each hoped and silently
prayed that when this was over he would be the one given
the sign — an imperial nod from the man seated at the centre of that stern-faced company down there in the front row.

To the tenor so touched by fortune would go the leading
role in the composer's new and long-awaited opera. To the
other, the loser (if one could be said to be a loser in such aus-
picious circumstances), would go the secondary role, that of
the character doomed to an ignoble downfall at the opera's
tumultuous climax. At the composer's insistence, for this
occasion the audition pianist had been discharged; the two
tenors were to sing without the benefit of accompaniment,
the better to test their ability to thread their way through

the unconventional vocal twists and turns and changes of key which made the song assigned to them for this occasion unlike any other they had ever sung or dreamt they would be called upon to sing.

The older of the two singers was stocky and broad-chested. Barely thirty, he was a bit on the portly side for a man of his years, but there were compensations: flaxen hair down to his shoulders, silvery-blue eyes, a light-skinned and fresh complexion. Almost perfect. Almost exactly what the composer envisioned when he conceived the part.

The other candidate was taller, his figure carved like that of a Roman statue. Dark hair and blackish brown eyes set in an olive-skinned face were certainly the opposite of what the composer had in mind. His brief resumé gave his age as twenty-six; it contained only scant details of his career to date.

Both singers performed with supreme confidence, even brilliance, the older of the two singing first in recognition of his seniority. Each exhibited the voice of a true *heldentenor.* Given the peculiarities of the music, the few flaws that were heard — the odd flatness or sharpness, perhaps a wrong inflection — were understandable (though to be sure the composer would have made a mental note of each slip, no matter how minor).

So it would be close. Less than a heartbeat would sepa-rate the two when the choice was made.

When the audition concluded, all eyes quickly turned to the composer. By his own tyrannical decree it was he and he alone who had the final word on every detail from the buckles on the choristers' shoes to the colour of the sky on the painted backdrops to the most important detail of all — the casting of the principal roles and, in particular, the principal tenor role upon which the success, or failure, of the new opera would depend.

The conductor, seated closest to the composer, dared to lean toward him to offer a whispered suggestion, only to be stifled with a dismissive wave of the composer's hand. The others in the front row knew better than to venture their opinions. On the stage stood the tenors, maintaining a respectful and somewhat cautious distance from each other, their bodies rigid, their expressions tense.

For a moment or two there was nothing but dead silence.

Suddenly, startling everyone, the composer sprang from his seat. He was beaming, even ecstatic, as though he'd seen a miracle. "Henryk Schramm! Henryk Schramm!" He shouted the name over and over again, his voice echoing across the vast empty auditorium. Motioning excitedly for the young singer to advance to the apron of the stage, he called out, "You ... *you* are my Walther von Stolzing, Schramm! Why have I not heard of you before? Never mind, Schramm, God Himself sent you here!" Still excited, the composer turned to the stage director. "The hair's too dark, of course; he'll need a blond wig. The eyes we can do nothing about, but the skin tone must be lightened. His height is just right, so the heels of his boots won't need building up. And no padding in the shoulders of his costumes. The man's got the physique if not the face of a true Franconian knight!" The stage director did not bother to agree or disagree. After all, what was the point?

The composer shot a steely glance at the impresario. "What are you waiting for, Mecklenberg?" he demanded. "I want a contract for this man ready for signature before I leave for lunch."

The victorious tenor took a step forward. "Maestro Wagner?" His voice was timid, a far cry from the voice with which, only minutes earlier, he had won the coveted lead role. The composer didn't appear to have heard him, so he repeated, a bit more forcefully, "Maestro —?"

The composer swung around to glare at the singer. It occurred to Schramm that the man he was looking down at from the stage — a man considered (grudgingly by some, admiringly by others) the musical giant of the century — was anything but a *physical* giant. If anything prominent stood out, it was, of all things, his chin, a sharp outcropping of skin and bone which, combined with the fierceness of his eyes, was enough to discourage any form of challenge to his authority, even from men who towered over him in body or in rank. His mouth was a simple slit unsoftened by lips. Everything converged around a hawk-like nose. Taken together, the features of his face left a large question as to whether he had ever been a child, or laughed, or made love.

"Well, what is it, Schramm?" the Maestro snapped. That was something the young tenor would have to learn: Maestro Richard Wagner was not accustomed to being interrupted. "Well, speak up."

"I just wanted to thank you for —"

Wagner cut him off. "You can thank me by singing the 'Prize Song' on the night of the premiere the way you sang it here this morning; only *better*, of course."

To the other tenor, the older and shorter one, now waiting awkwardly off to one side of the stage, Wagner announced, "You will do nicely for the role of Beckmesser, Grilling."

Wolfgang Grilling was not pleased, nor was he able to conceal his displeasure. "But Maestro," he said, coming forward, "with all due respect, may I remind you that you yourself chose me to sing the role of Erik in *The Flying Dutchman* just two summers ago in Dresden. Surely —"

"Surely *what*? Do you want the part of Beckmesser or not, Grilling? Yes or no?"

"But the simple fact is —"

Again Wagner cut in. "The simple fact, Grilling, is that I have spent sixteen years of my life giving birth to this opera. It is *my* career, not yours, that is at stake. Do you understand? For the last time, then, yes or no?"

Grilling replied with a sullen yes, then glared at his manager cowering in the shadows. The manager responded with a hapless shrug as if to say *One might just as well argue with the wind.*

It was an effort for Wagner to climb the half-dozen steep steps to the stage. The early spring dampness which seeped into Munich's ancient buildings, including the opera house, also found its way into Wagner's bones, moving him to mutter curses as he completed the ascent and hobbled to centre stage. Once there, however, he was every inch in command.

What followed had all the pomp and import of a royal proclamation. "I want everyone's attention," he began, pausing until he was satisfied that the hall was as quiet as a tomb. He continued: "I have concluded all the necessary arrangements with management. The first performance of *Die Meistersinger von Nürnberg* will be given here, in Munich, on the evening of June twenty-first —" He paused again, then added "in the year of our Lord 1868," as though somehow this mention of the divine lent extra significance to the scheduled date. "This means we have barely three months to prepare for the premiere. I will be putting the finishing touches to the libretto

and score over the next several days, following which rehearsals will commence promptly at nine o'clock in the morning
one week from today. Of course the solo and choral parts will
rehearse at first with piano accompaniment only, but in the
meantime I shall expect the orchestra to be thoroughly prepared by the beginning of the second week of May."

Wagner planted a pair of gold-rimmed pince-nez onto
the narrow bridge of his nose and squinted down at Hans
von Bülow, the conductor. "Is that understood, von Bülow?"

The conductor edged forward in his seat and seemed about
to question the feasibility of Wagner's plans; then, obviously
having second thoughts, he sank back, resigned. "Understood,
Maestro," von Bülow replied, sounding as though he were an
ordinary foot soldier about to die for king and country.

Like a field marshal, Wagner barked, "Schramm, stay, I
want a word with you. The rest may go. Remember ... one
week today, here, nine in the morning ... sharp. That is all."

Wolfgang Grilling, clutching the music for the 'Prize
Song' in one hand, used the other to scoop up his cloak
from a nearby stool. Passing in front of his rival he paused
long enough to murmur, "Good luck, Schramm. Believe me,
you're going to need it!"

Once the others had departed, leaving Wagner and
Schramm alone on the stage, everything about the composer seemed suddenly to soften, his face, even his voice.
Clearly intrigued by the young tenor, he asked: "Why am I
not in the least familiar with you, Schramm? Your resumé
states that you've sung in several foreign cities ... Prague,
Budapest, even Moscow of all places! I cannot imagine that
it stops snowing long enough in Moscow for a singer to utter
a sound! How did you manage in Russia?"

"Alas, Maestro," Schramm said, pretending to be crest-fallen, "like Napoleon, I retired half-frozen and fully defeated."

For the first time the composer broke into a laugh, reminding Schramm of the sudden collapse of a stone wall. Just as suddenly, Wagner's expression tightened into a serious scowl. "You know how much the success of *Die Meistersinger* means to me, Schramm. There were one or two rough edges in your performance of the 'Prize Song' this morning … nothing serious, mind you … but we'll work on it together, you and I, until it's perfect. I trust you appreciate how much depends on you now." Laying a fatherly hand on the tenor's shoulder, Wagner issued his final order of the day: "Now go rest that golden voice of yours, Henryk Schramm."

He had nothing to eat prior to the audition and was starved. After lunch (his first experience with sauerbraten … these robust German midday meals would take some getting used to) Henryk Schramm wrapped himself in a heavy woollen cape and, feeling restored, strode briskly from the restaurant to his lodgings in the nearby artists' quarter of Munich, a distance of only a few short blocks but long enough for the April winds to penetrate the dense weave of the cape. He should have been accustomed to this kind of weather, given where he was born and raised. Nevertheless, twenty-six harsh winters had strengthened his resolve: as soon as he was famous enough and rich enough, he would restrict his appearances to opera houses and concert halls in cities where palm trees lined the boulevards and gentle breezes blew only from the south the whole year round.

At a small writing table in his modest room, he set out paper and pen and began to write:

My dear Peter:

You will no doubt be pleased to learn that the audition this morning went well, in fact, better than either you or I could have expected. Who would have imagined that W. (my God, what a formidable presence he is!) would make up his mind on the spot! I thought surely I would be kept in suspense for several days at least, especially bearing in mind that my competitor for the role of Walther was himself a tenor of exceptional talent whose Nordic features are obviously more appropriate for the part of a German knight than my own. So I was fully prepared to be sent packing (in which event this entire gamble of mine would have come to nothing). Instead, the role is mine!

You were right, of course, about the "Prize Song." It is so different and so difficult to sing. Yet, as you pointed out when you played it through and I heard it for the first time, it is incredibly beautiful … all the more astonishing when one considers the personality of its creator. Your coaching stood me in good stead; without it my voice would not have been up to the task nor would I have fully grasped the meaning of the song.

Do I dare, Petya, to believe that the gods are smiling favourably upon my plan? My course is now set, and I am steadfast in my resolve. The premiere of Die Meistersinger is scheduled for June twenty-first here in Munich and I will try to keep you posted as we progress.

Do write to me soon, dear Petya, but for the moment the less said to my mother the better if you happen to see her.

My fellow contestant this morning is a tenor from these parts by the name of Wolfgang Grilling. He made no secret of his bitterness about having been relegated to the secondary role of Beckmesser and I anticipate some difficulties with him along the way. If he turns out to be troublesome … well, I will deal with him if it should become necessary.

How I long for an early return and the resumption of our long-standing arguments about the relative merits of Verdi, Mozart … and of course W. himself!

Your devoted —
H.S.

CHAPTER ONE

Beneath Munich's polished surface of culture and prosperity and good manners, evil burrows its way through a thousand subterranean passageways. And because evil has no sense of time or timeliness, I find myself intensely engaged in my work at all hours of the day and night while men living more conventional (should I better say sensible?) lives are enjoying a Sunday afternoon stroll with their families, or an evening of cards at their favourite coffeehouses, or a middle-of-the-night spontaneous moment or two of lovemaking, matrimonial or otherwise. Being in demand around the clock, I am like a sentry on endless guard duty and dream of uninterrupted slumber the way a gambler dreams of an uninterrupted winning streak at roulette. (Indeed, the gambler stands a better chance than I of realizing his dream, I'm sure.) And yet even a policeman absorbed in the very down-to-earth business of crime and punishment is entitled to indulge in the occasional fantasy, is he not? Which is what I was doing on this April night. Winter was leaving its harsh aftertaste on the deserted streets in the form of a bitter wind, giving me the sinking feeling that if spring were to occur at all it would be on some planet other than our own. I was experiencing fatigue unlike any I had previously experienced, fatigue so profound that, though I hadn't had time for a decent meal in the past three days, the thought of food was the furthest thing from my mind. My fantasy consisted of a warm bed, and eight hours at the very least of pure unadulterated sleep.

Let me explain: Earlier in the day I had concluded a marathon effort to seek out and capture the perpetrator of a series of vicious rapes in the area around Friedensplatz, a small square in the south end of Munich frequented by prostitutes and, of course, by men seeking their favours. Posing as a pimp (a role I found uncomfortable not only because of its inherent odiousness but because I was obliged to wear such outlandishly tasteless attire) and under the generous guidance of an acquaintance, Rosina Waldheim, a madam of remarkably high principles given the nature of her enterprise, I carried on almost without pause a seventy-two hour surveillance which resulted in spotting the culprit as he was stalking an intended victim. The details of his arrest needn't be spelled out. Suffice to say that word of my success spread quickly throughout the ranks of women who made their living in and around Friedensplatz. As I made my way by carriage back to my apartment for some much-needed peace and quiet, it occurred to me that I might soon be seriously considered for sainthood by a group of happily relieved (though unrepentant) sinners. Oh well, I told myself, one takes one's rewards wherever one finds them.

I must explain, too, that this triumph of detection and arrest was not without its sour side. The mission had originally been assigned by my superior, Commissioner von Mannstein, to Detective Franz Brunner. What ensued was either the result of a fit of zeal on Brunner's part, a shabby attempt to enhance his record of service, or downright incompetence. Whatever the reason, Brunner, with almost lightning speed, apprehended "the culprit" who turned out to be a member of the Norwegian delegation to an international conference in Munich held to discuss improved standards for the manufacture of dairy products. The unfortunate fellow was entirely innocent, a classic instance of the wrong man at the wrong street corner at the wrong time. True, he had ventured down to Friedensplatz for an hour or so of recreation (the work of a food scientist, after all, can be deadly serious) but his only crime, if it can be called a crime, was to get into a heated dispute over the question of price with one of the prostitutes during the course of which the prospective customer flung several insults at her. That this was conduct unbecoming of a Norwegian delegate is undeniable, but Brunner, who happened to observe the argument, saw it as sufficient evidence that the man was the sought-after rapist. Repercussions from the false arrest carried out by my colleague Brunner were felt at the highest diplomatic levels both in Norway and Germany, and the commissioner found himself bearing much of the blame for what the press headlined as "the Friedensplatz Fiasco."

This, then, is how I came to be involved in the case. "Preiss," said Commissioner von Mannstein, rocking back and forth on the heels of his polished boots (a habit whenever he was agitated), "Germany expects that you will restore the reputation of our nation ..."

Restore it I did. But less than a year before the Friedensplatz affair I had been imported from Düsseldorf to take up the post of chief inspector in Munich, a post Franz Brunner, then a fifteen-year veteran of the city's police force, had expected to be awarded. In a hundred different ways,

Brunner has ever since demonstrated his deep resentment at having been passed over by an out-of-towner. My having caught and arrested the real villain of Friedensplatz, I was certain, would stoke the fire of Brunner's animosity toward me into white-hot flames. It had been difficult enough all these months living and working side-by-side with Detective Franz Brunner. Now it would be impossible.

By the time I reached my apartment I was too exhausted to feel the elation that normally follows a successful arrest, and too exhausted to worry about my relationship with Brunner. Without bothering to remove my clothes I threw myself down onto a divan and swore that even if God were to come knocking at my door I would not answer.

Of course that is precisely the kind of resolution I should have known better than to make. If my experience as a policeman has taught me anything it is that, as my Jewish friends say, Man plans and God laughs. Sure enough, just as my eyes, heavy with fatigue, were beginning to close there came a knock at my door.

It was gentle at first and I heard myself groan and call out in a weak voice, thinking it was the concierge delivering a message, "Please leave it under the door." But the knocking continued, firmer and louder this time. "I said please leave it under the door," I called out again, angry and ready to strangle the fellow. The next series of raps sounded as though the person were using brass knuckles. Flinging myself up from the divan I marched to the door intending to take years off the caller's life.

Opening the door I began to shout "Why the devil can't you —" and then I saw that it was not the concierge after all.

"Detective Preiss?" the caller cautiously said.

"*Chief Inspector* Preiss," I replied. So what if I was rude; if the man had the gall to seek me out at my lodgings, and at this hour of the night, the least he could do was address me by my proper title.

The caller glanced at a small card in his hand. "It says here *Detective* Hermann Preiss."

"It says *what*?"

"Here, see for yourself —" He handed me the card.

"Who gave you this?" I demanded.

"A detective by the name of Brunner … at the Constabulary."

Brunner! That bastard! Trust Brunner not only to pawn this fellow off on me but to understate my position in the department.

"Did Brunner not take the trouble to mention that I'm off duty at the moment?"

"He said nothing about that," the caller said. "He simply assured me that you are best equipped to deal with this kind of case. In fact, he went so far as to say there wasn't a detective in the whole of *Europe* who is better equipped. It must be exceedingly gratifying to hear that you are held in such high esteem by your colleague."

Making no secret of my impatience, I asked, "What sort of case are we talking about? Somebody make off with your prized Dachshund?" I wouldn't have put it past Brunner.

"Please, Chief Inspector," the man said, "I would not dream of disturbing you were it not that a serious threat has been made and I desperately need your help."

A serious threat? It was difficult to imagine a serious threat being made against this fellow. He was at least a head shorter than I. So short was he, in fact, that had I passed him in the street for the first time I would have turned swiftly about in disbelief for a second look. The climb to the second storey where my rooms are located had left him breathing heavily, but it was only after he removed his tall hat and wiped his brow with the sleeve of his coat that I realized how old he was. His hair — what there was of it — was pure white and matted with perspiration. Drooping jowls and patches of loose skin under his eyes gave him the look of a worried bloodhound.

"I wonder if I might trouble you for a glass of water, Inspector?" he said, his lungs now issuing a wheezing sound.

I had no choice. "I suppose you'd better come in," I said.

Watching him down the glass of water under the stronger light in my sitting room, I could see now that he was clean-shaven and that his clothes, which because of his small stature would have had to be custom-made, were well cut and carefully put together. He had removed his gloves to accept the glass of water, revealing a diamond ring on the index finger of his left hand (the hand holding the glass), the stone a good two carats if not more. Only after he had finished off a second glass of water did he introduce himself. "My name is Otto Mecklenberg. Your colleague Brunner did not seem to be familiar with my name but —"

I said, "*The* Otto Mecklenberg … the impresario?"

The old man's face suddenly lit up. "You flatter me, sir. I wasn't certain if —"

"Of course I'm familiar with the name. Whenever music is spoken of in Munich your name is spoken in the same breath, especially when the subject is opera."

"Then Brunner was right," Mecklenberg said. "He told me you're the one policeman in the whole of Europe who takes an interest in opera. I have to add, Inspector, that Brunner pronounced 'opera' as if it were an incurable disease."

"*Detective Brunner* is an incurable disease," I said. "Now, please tell me … why would anyone want to threaten *you* of all people?"

"No no," Mecklenberg said quickly, "*I* am not the one threatened, it is my client who's the potential victim."

"And your client is —?"

"Richard Wagner."

"Someone is threatening to kill Wagner?"

"Worse, Inspector."

"What can be worse than a death threat?"

"You have to know Richard Wagner as I do in order to answer that question," Mecklenberg replied. Reaching into an inside pocket of his coat the old man extracted an envelope. "Here," he said, handing it to me, "open this please and read the note."

The envelope was addressed in crude block letters to Richard Wagner. It turned out to contain a single sheet of inexpensive stationery upon which in the same crude hand a one-line message appeared:

JUNE 21 WILL BE THE DAY OF YOUR RUINATION

I read the message aloud several times. Something about it made no sense to me. "If someone were truly out to do serious harm why would he give advance notice of his intention? I mean, since when does a criminal announce his *schedule* for the commission of the crime?" I shook my head. "I'm sorry, Herr Mecklenberg, but this has all the marks of a prank … granted a nasty prank, but nevertheless a prank and no more. Besides, the note speaks of ruination rather than death, which sounds to me like some kind of petty revenge is what the writer has in mind."

I started to hand back the envelope and note but Mecklenberg raised his hands in a gesture of refusal. "If you're as knowledgeable about opera as your reputation suggests, then you must know all there is to know about Wagner. The man's notorious. Let us be honest about it. There is no other way to describe him. Anyone who reads the newspapers surely is aware that Richard Wagner engages simultaneously in two professions: the first is music, the second is getting into all sorts of trouble."

"You're referring to his political activities?"

"You call it political activities," Mecklenberg said with a cynical smile. "Unfortunately, our government calls it treason. And Wagner's denunciation of the church has the Archbishop of Munich labelling him a blasphemer. And that's not all, Inspector. I would not be the least surprised if somewhere at your headquarters there is a file as thick as your fist filled with charges brought against the man by his creditors. Fraud, cheating, issuing bad cheques … Wagner's done 'em all. You know, of course, that he was only recently permitted to return from Switzerland where he was in exile."

"But Herr Mecklenberg," I said, "governments don't deliver threats hand printed on cheap slips of paper, nor do princes of the church. As for victims of petty crimes, and even creditors facing significant losses, hints of revenge are not their typical *modus operandi*; prompt acts of brutality are more popular forms of retribution. Take my word for it."

"With all due respect, sir, this is not what you would call a typical situation. June twenty-first is the date for the premiere of Wagner's new opera, you see."

"New opera? I must have missed the announcement in the newspapers."

"Ah, Inspector Preiss, that's the point. There was *no* announcement in the newspapers. The date for the premiere is known at the moment by a mere handful of people … people who are directly involved in the production. In fact, the June twenty-first date was disclosed by Maestro Wagner only yesterday following auditions for the principal male role."

"And the new opera is —?"

"Die Meistersinger von Nürnberg," Mecklenberg replied in a hushed voice, as though he was afraid that the very mention of the opera's title might invite some sudden calamity.

"Well, sir, if indeed the date is known by a relatively few people at this point, then it stands to reason that the number of possible suspects is very limited. If I am correct in this assumption, then my job should be quite simple. No need to cast a broad net here; the fish, so to speak, are all close to the boat. At any rate, June twenty-first is some two months off which gives me plenty of time to —"

"On the contrary, Inspector, whoever wrote this note must be sought out and brought to justice immediately! There's no time to waste!" The old man's small bony fingers, gripping the brim of his hat, began to tremble.

"Please, Herr Mecklenberg, this is not a life-and-death matter," I said. "Trust me, sir. I've had years of experience —"

"But you have never been exposed to the likes of Richard Wagner, have you?"

"Of course I will need to interview him. Perhaps in a day or two. You might bring him round to my office at the Constabulary, Herr Mecklenberg. Say, uh, the day after tomorrow, at ten in the morning?"

"I don't think you understand, Inspector," Mecklenberg said. "He must see you now ... *tonight*. The note was slipped under the front door of his house late this afternoon and the man is beside himself. Please, Inspector Preiss, I have a carriage waiting —"

CHAPTER TWO

A man was striking the keyboard of a piano with his fists as though it were an anvil, sending clusters of notes flying discordantly into the air, while crying aloud in a high-pitched grating voice over and over, "No no no!" the cries of a man at his wit's end, yet plaintive at the same time, a man desperately wanting something beyond his reach.

Mecklenberg and I had just taken our first steps into the entrance hall of Richard Wagner's house, admitted by his housekeeper, her hands protectively pressed against her ears and shaking her head as if to let us know she'd been through these upheavals many times in the past. The clamor came at us even louder now, penetrating the closed doors of the drawing room beyond. Again "*No no no!*" followed this time with "That is *not* what I want! You are *not* singing a national anthem, for God's sake! You are supposed to be *lovers!*"

"I'm afraid we've caught your man at an inconvenient time," I whispered to Mecklenberg. I had begun to unbutton my coat but stopped short. "Perhaps we should put this off until tomorrow."

The old man seized my arm. "Please, Inspector, it's only a private rehearsal. Nothing out of the ordinary, I assure you. He prefers these intimate sessions; it's just that he becomes a little irascible at times." He shrugged and gave a weak smile. "You know how geniuses carry on, I'm sure."

I expressed surprise that Wagner would be in a mood to rehearse with singers given the threatening note left earlier in the evening. "He's under extraordinary pressure," Mecklenberg explained. "The new opera opening soon, auditions, rehearsals, revisions and more revisions, financial arrangements, and so on." Clearly Wagner's long-time impresario was accustomed to making excuses for his client's conduct.

"But how does anyone survive these tantrums of his?" I asked. "Come to think of it, how does *he* survive his tantrums?"

"Believe me, Preiss," Mecklenberg said, smiling as much as his aged jowls would permit, "in the end it's worth all the fuss and bother."

"Fuss and bother? You call what we've just heard 'fuss and bother'?"

Before Mecklenberg could respond, the doors of the drawing room were thrust open. "Mecklenberg, where the hell have you been? Why are you standing there like a piece of furniture?"

Then Wagner's eyes landed on me like grapeshot. Lowering his voice he said to Mecklenberg, "Is this the policeman we sent for?"

Nervously Mecklenberg replied, "Maestro, allow me to —"

"Can't the man speak for himself?" Still eyeing me, Wagner said, "And you are who?"

"Chief Inspector Hermann Preiss, Maestro." I took a firm step in his direction and offered my hand.

"I never shake hands when I'm working," Wagner said without so much as a flicker of apology. "I don't know why it is, Chief Inspector, but too many men nowadays seem under some kind of compulsion to prove their manliness by crushing the living daylights out of you when they shake hands.

My hands are my life, Chief Inspector."

I couldn't resist a smile. "I assure you, Maestro Wagner, I would have been as timid as a virgin."

Wagner stared at me for a moment with what I took to be disapproval, then suddenly smiled (though cautiously). "Well, Mecklenberg," he called over his shoulder, "at least he's got a sense of humour. Are you quite sure he's a policeman?" His eyes narrowed again. "Wait ... Hermann Preiss? ... weren't you the detective back in Düsseldorf some years ago ... yes, of course! ... involved with the Schumanns. Am I correct?"

"You are, sir."

"Pity about the poor idiot. Schumann, I mean. Died young, didn't he? Some asylum near Bonn, as I recall. That wife of his ... Clara ... *there* was a witch if ever I met one. Never had a decent word to say about me and my music. Still doesn't, damn her. Brahms ... Johannes Brahms ... now *there* was a man more to her taste, in every sense of the term, if you know what I mean." Wagner frowned, as though struggling to recall something. "There was talk about whether or not Schumann did away with some journalist ... something scandalous about Schumann's past that this writer threatened to expose. They say Schumann literally got away with murder." Looking me straight in the eye, Wagner snorted, "Doesn't say much about the quality of police work in Düsseldorf, does it ... people getting away with murder."

I had two choices here: to agree with him, as a good public servant should do, perhaps even going so far as to bow and scrape; or to reply in kind and to hell with the consequences. I chose the latter. "It occurs to me, sir, that you must be a genuine connoisseur of police work, having been involved much of the time with justice systems here and abroad."

Wagner glared at me for a moment, then turned to Mecklenberg, the old man looking as though he wished the floor would open and allow him to disappear. "Well, Mecklenberg, at least he's not spineless, which is more than I can say about most people with whom I'm forced to deal these days, isn't that so?" Returning to me, Wagner said, "I'm not sure we're going to get along, you and I, Preiss. I've been confronted with a serious threat. I need a man who will be at my service, nothing less."

"And that is exactly what I'm prepared to do, be at your service," I said. "I am not, however, prepared to be your *humble* servant."

I won't flatter myself by claiming that this retort had the effect of putting the Maestro in his place; whether one knew Richard Wagner by reputation only, or was a personal acquaintance over many years, or was meeting him for the very first time as I was, one thing was incontrovertible: nothing short of the voice of God could cause this man to go weak at the knees. Still, my refusal to humiliate myself at least managed to establish a ground rule that would govern my relationship with Wagner if only for the time being. As far as I was concerned, Richard Wagner needed me more than I needed Richard Wagner.

"Very well, you two. Come!" Wagner stood to one side, motioning for us to move into the drawing room. He pointed to a sofa in a remote corner of the large room and ordered us to be seated there. "We're nearly finished, these two young people and I. There's not much more we can accomplish, not tonight at any rate."

I had expected to be introduced to the pair of singers posted close to an enormous Bösendorfer, waiting in silence,

like soldiers anticipating their next orders. But no intro-
ductions were forthcoming; instead it was back to business.
Wagner took his seat at the piano and, sounding more like a
military commander than a musician, he delivered the following lecture: "I remind you once again that this scene is crucial
between Walther and Eva. Act Two succeeds or fails depending on how you relate to each other at this point. You are planning to elope; you are frustrated by conventions that constrain
your emotions, your love for each other. Walther has been
treated like an outcast by the Mastersingers Guild; Eva is being
used as a pawn in what will be an arranged marriage. Both of
you are challenged now to defy narrow conventionalism. So
passion ... *passion!* ... you must not only sing, you must *act!*"

What followed for the next thirty minutes was some
of the most sublime music and singing ever to fill my ears.
Indeed — and I admit this without shame — I could feel tears
forming in my eyes and I was forced to blink hard at times to
clear my vision. If the person responsible for this was a monster (and already I'd formed an opinion that he was) then let
him be monstrous, I thought. As for the two singers, despite
the fatigue evident in their faces, they were carrying out the
monster's orders above and beyond the call of duty.

At last, Wagner removed his hands from the keyboard,
signalling that the session was ended. Nodding brusquely,
all he said to the singers was "We're getting there. Go home.
Get some rest. Tomorrow morning, ten o'clock sharp."

Rising from the sofa, I approached the three at the piano,
calling out, "Maestro, I should like an introduction to your
singers, if you don't mind."

"Why? Is it essential for some reason that you meet
them?"

"No, not essential," I admitted, somewhat taken aback, "but it would be a privilege ... for me, I mean." Addressing the singers, I said, "I'm Inspector Hermann Preiss, of the Munich Police."

The tenor, without waiting for Wagner's approval, stepped forward, his hand outstretched. "I'm Henryk Schramm." He beckoned the soprano to come forward. "And this ... this is Karla Steilmann!" Schramm said this with such enthusiasm that I wondered whether it was her voice or her beauty that elicited such a show of warmth and admiration from her collaborator.

Visibly annoyed that these two young people hadn't waited for him to manage the formalities, Wagner addressed them gruffly, insisting that they depart without further delay given the demands of tomorrow. "Now get home, the two of you. Go! Out!"

"I do hope we meet again, Herr Preiss," the young woman said, reducing me with her smile to a mound of wet clay.

Wagner stood watching with undisguised impatience as his singers made their exit. Then, satisfied that they had left the house, he turned on me and said in an angry voice, "That was most imprudent of you, Preiss, if I may say so. I am not eager to announce to the entire world that my career — maybe my life itself — is so threatened that I require the protection of the police. Do you have any notion at all about how much comfort and joy such a revelation would bring to my enemies? My God, man, a little discretion!"

"I think you're overlooking something, sir, with all due respect," I replied. "It was *your* idea ... *your* sense of urgency ... that brought me here tonight. It was *you* who invited me to be in this room when I would have been perfectly content to wait in some other part of the house until your rehearsal was finished."

Wagner did not take kindly to this response, which was no surprise. To Mecklenberg, who was by now a living portrait of misery, he called: "Is *this* the best you could secure for me?"

In a weak voice the impresario answered, "I was assured, Maestro, that Inspector Preiss is the finest in the Munich Constabulary. None better."

"He certainly doesn't impress me as having the attributes of a conventional policeman. Considering the threat made against me, one would expect at least a modicum of sympathy, of respect."

"If you are looking for a 'conventional' policeman," I said, "then look elsewhere, Maestro. To borrow your little sermon to your singers a few moments ago ... or at least part of it ... I have always felt challenged to defy narrow conventionalism."

"Is that so, Preiss? Well, then, perhaps that explains the stories about your involvement with the Schumann case a few years back in Düsseldorf."

"Stories?"

"Yes. About how you were apparently so blinded by Schumann and that wife of his that —"

"You needn't repeat it, Maestro. What was mere gossip has unfortunately grown into a legend."

"Ah, so Franz isn't telling tales out of school after all."

"Franz? You mean Franz Brunner?"

"*Brunner*? Who the devil is Franz Brunner? I'm talking about Franz *Liszt* of course."

"Ah yes, the father of the woman with whom you are having an affair ... a rather notorious affair."

"That is none of your business, Inspector," Wagner shot back.

"*Everything* is my business, Maestro Wagner," I said. "Your lady friend —" I began to say.

"I have many lady friends, Preiss."

"Your *lover*, then ... Cosima von Bülow, wife of the conductor. I, too, have ears that pick up tales out of school, tales to the effect that your former friend Franz Liszt is appalled that his daughter has left her husband and become your mistress. Maestro von Bülow can hardly be thrilled by these events."

"These are personal matters, Preiss," Wagner shouted. "I repeat: they are none of your business."

"The threatening note you received ... could it not have been written by Liszt, or von Bülow, or some government official, for that matter? Any one of these persons, it seems to me, might have a powerful desire to bring about your downfall."

Wagner fell silent and stood studying me for a few moments. Quietly he said, "I see that you are indeed not a conventional policeman. You seem to know a great deal about what goes on in the musical world, at least here in Munich."

"And elsewhere," I said. "But, to be frank, your activities, Maestro, extend far beyond the boundaries of the musical world. Politics, revolution, creditors and the avoidance of creditors ... the very name 'Richard Wagner' conjures up as much discord as harmony throughout Europe. I have just mentioned three people who would have ample cause to write that note, but there could be thirty, or three hundred, or even three thousand!"

And with that, I reached for my coat and hat. "It is late, sir. You must excuse me. If you want me, Mecklenberg knows where to find me."

Without another word, I turned and made a brisk exit, leaving one of the most vocal men in Germany speechless.

CHAPTER THREE

The Munich Constabulary is located at the east side of Karlsplatz, facing the Palace of Justice on the opposite side of the square. With good reason, the Constabulary is looked upon as the ugly cousin of the Palace. While the Palace shines as a tribute to the noblest of Renaissance style, in sharp contrast the Constabulary is an angry-looking edifice, its grey stone façade frozen into a permanent scowl that menaces passersby and forces them to avert their eyes. Even citizens who are entirely innocent pass through its guarded portals feeling they must be guilty of something.

If the Constabulary's exterior is forbidding, the interior is even more so. A century of hard use has left its woodwork scarred and blackened. Coats of dark green paint applied slapdash every few years to the corridors have made the place as inviting as a shelter for the insane. Every surface — floors, walls, ceilings — is as unyielding as stone, so that people's voices and the staccato clacking of officers' boots on the bare marble floors resound as in a huge hollow cavern.

My own office, alas, offers nothing exceptional to its stern surroundings: in size and furnishings it suggests that my daily occupation is that of a monk (an irony considering that for the life of me I cannot recall the last time I visited any room or building that has anything at all to do with faith). My "cell" has only one attribute — privacy. Thanks to my seniority, I need share it with no one. In the midst of all this architectural ugliness I at least have the comfort of my own company.

How odd, then, that whoever a hundred years ago concocted this four-storey pile made certain to provide space on the uppermost floor for a common room (or "lounge" as Commissioner von Mannstein prefers to call it) for senior police personnel. Not that it is elegant, this so-called lounge: a scattering of chairs with straight unforgiving backs and under-nourished upholstery; a half-dozen small simple wooden tables whose tops bear numerous hieroglyphics carved by irreverent off-duty policemen. (One such carving is a rudimentary depiction of two dogs copulating, an obscenity that would earn any ordinary civilian a year behind bars but which here, in the common room, is a source of constant amusement, even pride!) A collection of oversized oil portraits of past commissioners decorates the walls, each stern face staring down at us with an expression of extreme contempt. One can peer out at a restricted landscape of Munich through three narrow windows that serve unfailingly to restrict light and air and to keep the city at a safe distance. All in all the room brings to mind the ancient Greek motto: *Nothing in excess.*

It was here, in the common room, that I encountered Franz Brunner the morning after my initial exposure to Richard Wagner. Slouched in his chair, feet resting on another chair he'd drawn up, he held half a sandwich in one hand while munching the other half. "Well well, good morning, Preiss," he called out, his voice thickened by a mixture of bread, cheese, and some garlicky variety of sausage. "Or should I say good afternoon? Isn't this what they call 'bankers' hours' … in by noon, out by four?"

I responded with what had become in recent weeks my standard greeting to the man, "Go to hell, Brunner." The fact that I was still feeling the effects of the last few grinding days and had therefore arrived for work three hours later than usual was none of his damned business.

Brunner pretended to be hurt. "And here I was certain," he said, "that you'd show up this morning with — what? — a magnum of Champagne? A flask of Napoleon brandy? Or at least a handful of decent Dutch cigars, Preiss." The petulance in his tone made him sound like a rejected ingénue instead of a forty-five-year-old detective whose girth stretched the buttons of his waistcoat to their limit.

"And why would I want to shower you with gifts, Brunner?" I knew the answer, of course, but was nevertheless curious to hear it from his mouth in order to fuel my loathing for the fellow.

Brunner didn't disappoint me. "I thought you'd want to show your gratitude, Preiss."

"Gratitude for what?"

"For putting that little man … what's his name —?"

"Mecklenberg —"

"Yes, Mecklenberg … for putting him on to you. I mean, it's common knowledge that Chief Inspector Hermann Preiss is the darling of artists of all stripes."

I knew what was coming next. Detective Franz Brunner never passed up an opportunity to remind me of the city where my career had its beginnings and where one case in particular in which I was deeply involved ended in an unsolved murder that has haunted me ever since. "Wasn't it Düsseldorf? There was that madman, uh, Schumann, some sort of crazy musical genius. Murder, attempted suicide; you must have had your hands full. None of that nonsense ever got solved, did it, Preiss?"

In a calm unruffled way that I knew was bound to irritate him I replied, "Allow me to congratulate you, Brunner. If nothing else, you *are* blessed with the gift of consistency." I paused for a moment to let the insult sink in, then said, "Look here, Brunner, whether or not you choose to believe me, I *am* sorry about what happened, I mean that business at Friedensplatz. I give you my word; I had nothing whatever to do with the commissioner's decision to remove you from the case."

Still slouching in his chair, Brunner eyed me with disdain. "Well, Preiss," he drawled, "not only will your name presumably become hallowed in every whorehouse in Munich; I imagine your many friends in the artistic community, knowing *their* moral standards, will similarly toss rose petals in your path, especially an upstanding citizen like Wagner."

"You've heard of Wagner, Brunner?"

"Don't look so astonished, Preiss," Brunner said. "The man's notorious. His music's outrageous too."

"I wouldn't have dreamed you're a music-lover, Brunner," I said.

"I'm not," Brunner said flatly. "Wouldn't give a pinch of snuff for the best of it, if you want the truth."

"Then I really am astonished," I said. "I could swear I saw you dancing with some woman —" I made a gesture indicating grossly oversized breasts "— one day during Oktoberfest. Yes, a Saturday it was. A street dance. I think you were wearing lederhosen. I must say, Brunner, you showed a rather pretty leg, as they say."

"Damn you, Preiss!" Brunner said, sitting up and slamming the uneaten half of his sandwich onto a nearby tabletop.

Jabbing an index finger in the air in my direction he repeated, "*Damn you!*"

"Please, Brunner, a little restraint. We *are* officers of the law, brethren on the side of the righteous."

"Brethren my ass!" Brunner shouted. "I will go to my grave, Preiss, and still not understand why that bastard von Mannstein saw fit to import a man like yourself — a police-man from the backwaters of Düsseldorf — into Munich. I've given fifteen years of my life —"

"Oh please, Brunner," I interrupted, again deliberately keeping my voice even, "not this conversation again." We had been through this subject several times before and each time I'd been obliged to remind Brunner that both of us, along with several others, had submitted written applica-tions stating our credentials and our visions of the future of law enforcement in Munich; both of us had been sub-jected to lengthy, even gruelling, interviews with the Police Commission Board; and in the end it was I who emerged with the appointment of chief inspector. "You may whine and wail all you like, Brunner," I said, "but I won this post fair and square and I'll be damned if I'll allow you to saddle me with guilt because of your failures."

An unswallowed portion of sandwich spewed forth from Brunner's mouth. "Failures! Failures! You arrogant son-of-a-whore, Preiss!"

This brought a slight smile to my face. "How did you know, Brunner? Yes, I *am* arrogant, unabashedly arrogant, as it happens. And what's more my friend, I am also a son of a whore … or so I was told. I'll be honest with you. I will go to *my* grave someday and not be sure who sired me. Permit me, Brunner, to congratulate you on your perspicacity."

Brunner eyed me with suspicion. "On my what?"

Before I could define perspicacity for Brunner the doors of the common room were thrust open and in strode Commissioner von Mannstein, followed by a heavyset man whom I immediately recognized as the mayor of Munich (his handlebar mustache and chest-length beard were more renowned than his record as the city's chief magistrate). Brunner and I automatically shot to our feet and stood to attention. In unison (for once) we said, "Good day, gentlemen."

Von Mannstein gave us a stiff smile. "At ease, gentlemen," he said, then stood aside and made a polite gesture in the direction of the mayor. "It is my high honour," the commissioner said, "to introduce to you our distinguished mayor, the Honourable Klaus von Braunschweig."

I offered my hand first. "I am honoured, sir," I said.

Brunner hastily wiped his right hand, which only moments ago had borne visible traces of bread, cheese, and sausage, on the side of his trousers, then he too offered his hand and acknowledged the honour.

The commissioner turned to Brunner. "Brunner, you needn't trouble yourself to stay, thank you. Oh, and when you leave would you be so good as to lock the doors behind you. We require a few minutes of absolute privacy up here with the chief inspector."

Bile is said to be an aid in the digestive process, but when a malfunction occurs — as it was now occurring somewhere within Franz Brunner — the result is frightening to behold: redness of face; profuse perspiration on forehead and upper lip; twitching of veins in temples, eyes fiery. Clicking his heels, Brunner responded, "As you wish, gentlemen." Each step on his retreat from the room was like the blow of a hammer against the uncarpeted floor, the slamming of the doors behind him like a rifle shot.

Pausing first to make certain Brunner was well away, the commissioner spoke up. "Preiss, Mayor von Braunschweig and I have a matter of utmost importance to discuss with you. Please understand that this discussion must be kept in the strictest confidence. Indeed, there will be no written record unless and until His Honour the Mayor expressly authorizes such a record, in which event I and I alone shall open and have custody of the file. Do I make myself clear, Preiss?"

"Absolutely, sir," I said.

"Good. I know we can depend on you, Preiss. Now then, I will ask the mayor to lay certain facts before you, describe the problem those facts present, and inform you as to what is required of you. I suggest the three of us be seated."

There must be a special school, or perhaps conservatory, where politicians learn how to clear their throats in order to add portent to what they are about to say. If that is the case, then Klaus von Braunschweig, mayor of Munich, must have graduated with highest honours. What seemed like a full minute went by before his vocal passages were sufficiently clear to permit the utterance of words, during which I found myself leaning forward in my chair in a state of suspense, as though I was about to be dispatched on a mission in outer space.

"Chief Inspector Preiss," he began solemnly, "our fair city has in its midst an abomination, a thorn in its side, an agitator, a subversive, a disease who must be rooted out, eradicated, driven from the gates of Munich for all time." There followed a brief dramatic pause, then he continued, "Does the name Richard Wagner mean anything to you, Preiss?"

I frowned, pretending to rack my brain, my eyes fixed on the ceiling. Slowly I replied, "I suppose that, like many people, I've heard the name mentioned from time to time, usually in connection with music … you know, opera, that sort of thing. He's reputed to advocate some rather radical ideas about music that have raised quite a few eyebrows."

"Yes, but the trouble is," von Braunschweig said, "that his radical ideas are not confined to music and the eyebrows he raises are not those of his fellow musicians alone. Maestro Troublemaker fashions himself an expert on social and political issues. Writes these damned articles in newspapers here and abroad about freedom and the necessity to revisit and revise laws and regulations that are well-established and are the very fabric of German society. What's even worse, Preiss, is that the man has the gall to suggest that *art* is what German culture is all about. Art! My God, when was the last time an artist led an army to victory on a battlefield, I ask you?"

"You appear," I said, "to take this entire Wagner business very personally, sir."

"And with good reason, Preiss," the mayor said. "You see, the eyebrows that have been raised by Wagner's activities belong to the highest government officials in Bavaria. And they have made it all too plain to me that if Munich is to continue to enjoy the blessings of tax contributions from the state treasury, money that is urgently required to maintain our fine institutions, our magnificent boulevards and parks, then we must get rid of this man Wagner or at least silence him once and for all. You say I take it personally, Preiss? That is an understatement."

Commissioner von Mannstein gently laid a hand on the mayor's arm. "I have to mention to the chief inspector another troublesome aspect, Your Honour … that is, if you will permit me —"

Von Braunschweig looked annoyed. "I thought I had covered the subject fully," he said.

In a low voice, the commissioner said, "There's the matter of Wagner's outspoken anti-Semitism, Your Honour. His attacks on Jews and their effects on German culture, to say the least, are vicious."

Looking even more annoyed, the mayor shot back, "Who the devil cares about the Jews, von Mannstein? They are nothing but pimples on our backsides. If there's a problem with our Jews it's purely secondary. In fact, it's less than secondary."

"With all due respect, Your Honour," the commissioner said, "there are Jewish bankers in Frankfurt who are very vital to Germany's economy. I'm sure you are aware of that. They can scarcely be regarded as 'pimples.'"

"Then let the citizens of Frankfurt wrestle with that particular problem," von Braunschweig said with a dismissive wave of his hand. "My concerns are for my own constituents here in Munich."

And for your own comfort and welfare as the highly paid, handsomely housed, and soon-to-be-generously pensioned mayor here in Munich, I added in my own mind. I had expected that, having raised the issue of Wagner's anti-Semitism, von Mannstein might pursue the matter further. The mayor's brusque dismissal, however, was enough to discourage him. Turning his attention to me, the commissioner said, "What His Honour wishes now, Preiss, is that you, being the officer most fitted for the task, should find a way to insert yourself into Wagner's circle, become somehow as close to him as one can become, keep a keen eye on

his activities ... not just musical, you understand, but gener-
ally. We need to know what he's up to, who are his allies. In
short, Preiss, we need to build a strong enough case against
this man Wagner so that once again he can be sent into exile
never to be allowed back into Germany ... *never.*"

"And when am I to begin this assignment, Commissioner?"

The commissioner extracted from his vest an exquisite
gold pocket watch. "The time is now twelve minutes before
noon, Preiss. You have just begun."

CHAPTER FOUR

Foreign visitors to Munich are often amused (and frequently distressed) by the penchant on the part of local restaurateurs to give their establishments exotic French and Italian names — for example Café Paris or Trattoria Venezia — when a quick glance at the menus reveals that the cuisine is strictly German. This happens to be the case with my favourite eating place in Munich, Maison Espãna, whose proprietor makes no apology for fraudulent misrepresentation and brazenly serves the best Wiener schnitzel in Europe in a large room filled with dark woods, plenty of polished brass, and the golden glow of gaslight. The owner, Sigmund (Ziggy) Bolliger, greets me always in French or Spanish whenever I enter his restaurant, both of us knowing full well that beyond his simple greeting he speaks not a word of either language. (What would life be without these charming little illusions?) On this particular evening, however, seeing that I was accompanied by two very attractive young people, Ziggy forgot himself and welcomed me in German, all the while fixing his eyes on the female in our group.

"Herr Bolliger," I said, "I've assured my guests that they haven't lived until they've tasted the Wiener schnitzel at Maison Espãna. Let me introduce you to Fräulein Karla Steilmann and Herr ... or should I say Heldentenor? — Henryk Schramm."

"Did you say heldentenor, Inspector?" Bolliger looked impressed. "Then these must be opera singers!"

"How clever of you, Ziggy," I said. "In your next life you should consider a career in the police force. Now give us a nice quiet table where we can talk, please, and a bottle of your finest Riesling."

At a corner table away from the hubbub of other diners, I offered a toast, the three of us raising our wineglasses. "To a successful premiere of — what is the name of the opera again? —"

"*Die Meistersinger von Nürnberg*," Schramm said.

"Of course," I said. "You must forgive me. Opera titles with more than two words give me trouble every time. Here's to *Die Meistersinger von Nürnberg*."

Each of us took a sip of wine.

"And here's to Richard Wagner!" I added with a little too much enthusiasm.

Schramm and Steilmann looked at me as though I were mad. "Are you *serious*, Inspector?" Schramm asked.

Steilmann seemed to be struggling to avoid bursting into laughter. I put down my glass. "Have I said something amusing?"

She said, gently chiding, "Surely you're being disingenuous, Inspector Preiss. You *did* see him in action the other night, did you not? And you expect us to toast this ... this terrorist? When I was a young girl I witnessed my mother giving birth to my baby sister. Believe me, Inspector, her agony was nothing compared to what it is like preparing an operatic role under Maestro Wagner's tutelage."

Schramm nodded vigorously in agreement.

"Then tell me this," I said, "if he is, as you put it, a terrorist, why are you subjecting yourselves to such torture? After all, Wagner is certainly not the only composer of operas in Europe. There's no shortage, thanks to Mozart and Beethoven, though both are long gone now. And then we have Verdi and Berlioz and Rossini and —"

"Yes yes, of course, Inspector," said Schramm. "But the answer to your question can only be answered with another question. Why does the moth seek the flame and why do sheep follow their leaders fatally over steep cliffs?"

"Oh come now, Schramm, do you want me to believe that opera singers have something in common with moths and sheep … that all of you share some inexplicable death wish?"

Schramm laughed. "All right, Inspector, I admit I've exaggerated somewhat. I do have a habit of answering a question *with* a question. I suppose it's part and parcel of my upbringing."

"And where might that have taken place … your upbringing, I mean?"

Schramm looked down at the glass of wine in his hand. "Oh, my family lived in a number of towns. It's really not very interesting, Inspector, I assure you. Let's just say the Schramms lived a very itinerant life."

I said, trying not to belabour the matter, "It sounds to me as though your father was a man of religion, Schramm. Perhaps a minister of the church or some such occupation. They do tend to travel about."

Schramm looked up at me. "Yes," he said, "something like that … you know, travelling about."

I thought I detected a faraway look in Schramm's eyes, a hint of distance to his voice, that suggested this was a topic he preferred not to pursue. I turned my attention quickly to Karla Steilmann. "And you, Fräulein Steilmann, you are from?"

"I am a dyed-in-the-wool Viennese, I'm afraid," she said, smiling apologetically. "You see, Inspector Preiss, I know immediately what you're thinking. You're thinking that, unlike you Germans, we Austrians are a frivolous lot. Too much whipped cream, too many cherries, too much music in three-quarter time. Yes?"

I feigned disappointment. "I could have sworn that you were pure German. Perhaps we should order dinner before sorrow overwhelms me." To make sure she didn't take me seriously, I took her hand in mine, but as enchanted as I was at that moment I did not fail to catch a flicker of jealousy in Schramm's eyes.

To me he said, "Did I hear correctly something about ordering dinner? Please don't think me rude, Inspector Preiss, but I *am* famished. We've been rehearsing most of the day with only a short break for lunch and another for coffee mid-afternoon."

Just then Ziggy Bolliger passed near our table. "I say, Innkeeper —" I called out.

Bolliger drew close. Addressing my guests he said, "This is the only man in Munich I permit to call me Innkeeper. But then, what choice does a humble citizen like me have, eh? When the Chief Inspector calls, we come running."

"Bolliger, stop complaining and let us have three Weiner schnitzels with plenty of red cabbage on the side, also enough potato salad for three hungry people. Oh yes, and another bottle of Riesling, Ziggy. By the way, why is this Riesling so much better than what you usually serve?"

In a half whisper Bolliger replied, "Because it was stolen

from somebody's private collection." Without waiting for my reaction Bolliger spun round and disappeared into the kitchen. A minute later he was back at our table, his expression remorseful. "I cannot apologize enough," he said. "Chef tells me because we were so busy earlier this evening we are totally out of veal. We *can,* however, offer you a pork schnitzel which, I promise, will be equally delicious."

I turned to Schramm and Steilmann. "Take my word for it, even if Ziggy's chef were to use cardboard the result would be marvelous. Shall it be three with pork instead of veal, then?"

Karla Steilmann had no problem with the proposed change. "And you, Schramm," I asked, "the same?"

"I'm sorry," Schramm replied, "but I have an allergy to certain foods and pork happens to be one of them."

Bolliger brightly came to the rescue. "Chicken then! Chef does a roast chicken basted in a wine sauce fit for a king, with spätzli and some country-fresh greens."

Schramm nodded agreeably. "And please, the skin? I like it left on and very crisp."

Bolliger beamed. "Ah, a true connoisseur! I wish more Germans had your understanding of poultry, sir. You must be from the east where people know the proper way to cook and eat a chicken. Prussia, perhaps?"

This brought a wry smile to Schramm's face. "The Inspector is right, Herr Bolliger. You have a natural talent for police work. Yes, I'm from the east, you might say."

After Bolliger, looking happy, left us to return to the kitchen, I replenished our glasses, then said, attempting to maintain a casual air, "So tell me, you two, how long have you been involved in the world of opera and how did you come especially to be involved with this fiend Wagner?"

Karla Steilmann spoke up first. "I began singing when I was about nine or ten years of age. I sang in a children's chorus at school, but once I reached my early teen years it became apparent that I had the makings of a soprano, and one of my music teachers took me under his wing until I reached sixteen, at which point I was ready for more serious training. For the next three years I lived the life of a nun at the Music Academy in Vienna. At twenty I was offered the role of Pamina in *The Magic Flute*. That ended any possibility that I would spend the rest of my life as a hausfrau. My parents — my father was a customs officer, my mother a part-time seamstress — were distraught, of course. In their minds a life on the stage represented everything that was wicked. I swear, to this very day, Inspector, they regard what I do as the work of the devil." Suddenly she threw her head back, laughing. "It has just occurred to me: they are absolutely right! I *am* working with the devil himself, Richard Wagner!"

"And you, Schramm," I said, "you feel the same way, I suppose."

"You've now had some exposure to the Maestro, Inspector, albeit brief. How would *you* feel?" Schramm said.

"Ah, Schramm, there you go again, answering a question *with* a question." I wagged a finger at him. "When a policeman asks a question, you must give an answer. That's the law, you know." I said this with an amiable smile which was met with an equally amiable smile from Schramm, but silence. I decided not to press him further on the point. "And were your parents similarly unenthusiastic about a musical career for their son?" I asked.

"Do you have children, Inspector?" Schramm replied. Breaking into a laugh he added, "I know, I know, another question followed by a question. I apologize, I really do."

"I have never been married," I said, "and have no children. At least none that I'm aware of. Why do you ask?"

"Because Karla's experience with her parents is all too typical. I, on the other hand, was lucky. As a boy I demonstrated a good voice and a good ear. Fortunately I lost none of my potential when I went through a voice change. Like Karla, I underwent rigorous training, and was ready at twenty for my first major role. But I was encouraged throughout by my parents, both of whom were musical. Father played the violin and Mother loved to sing. It's a pity that you've never had children, Inspector. I think you would have made a very good father, one who would not have been horrified to discover a singer among your brood."

"I'm afraid you're quite wrong, Schramm," I said, topping up his wine glass again. "Truth is, I would have made a terrible parent. You see, Schramm, I've got where I am because my most basic instinct is suspicion. I am suspicious of everything and everyone. Even a newborn babe is an object of suspicion as far as I'm concerned."

Karla Steilmann patted my arm. "Now now, Inspector, you must not put yourself down so. I'm sure you're joking."

"On the contrary," I said, affecting a severe look, "I'm perfectly serious."

Schramm turned to his companion. "In that case, Karla, say no more. Obviously our host is not the genial fellow he appears to be. We mustn't even *hint* about our criminal pasts or we're liable to find ourselves being led out of here in irons. And worse still, without having eaten a morsel of food!"

"I'm not quite so heartless," I said. "I'd let the Fräulein have her schnitzel and let you finish off your roasted chicken, skin and all. Speaking of which, I see we are about to be served by the innkeeper himself."

Ziggy Bolliger, accompanied by a waiter bearing an enormous tray of food, carried a second bottle of wine which he deposited on our table with the kind of flourish one would expect from a prophet presenting the Holy Grail. "*This* is stolen from *my* private collection," he declared as he uncorked a fresh Riesling whose label was unfamiliar to me. "King Ludwig himself does not have access to this particular vineyard," Bolliger boasted, splashing a bit of the pale gold liquid into a fresh crystal goblet and offering it to me. The expression on my face, after I had taken a sip, told him it was superb. "You see," he said, addressing Schramm and Steilmann, "nothing is too good for Chief Inspector Hermann Preiss … or for his guests!"

The entrées, which were also superb, were followed by slices of warm apple strudel whose wrapping was as delicate as butterfly wings, coffee strong enough to fortify a regiment of infantry, and tiny glasses of Armagnac.

Schramm leaned back in his chair and let out a pro-longed sigh. "I haven't felt so relaxed in ages. Everything inside me seems suddenly to have unwound. Maestro Wagner has a way of tightening the screws that hold a person together until you think you're going to split apart like a piece of dry wood."

Karla Steilmann nodded in agreement. Touching my hand, she said, "Thank you, Inspector. Dinner has been like a tonic for us."

"And for me as well," I said, making certain not to disturb her hand, enjoying its soft touch on mine. "You must under-stand, both of you, that an occasion like this is a very special pleasure for me. It is blessedly far removed from the grimy habitats of crime I'm forced to visit day and night in my work. My colleagues, of course, are convinced that my interest in the arts, especially in music, is pure snobbery. Between you and me, they're right. I wouldn't miss an opportunity to hobnob with two attractive and talented young people like you for all the sauerkraut in Germany!"

Steilmann cast a sly glance at Schramm. "Ahah! So that explains it, Henryk. That's why we are being wined and dined so generously tonight." She turned to me, her hand still resting atop mine. "You're not the only person who possesses a suspicious nature, Inspector Preiss. Henryk and I had this strange feeling that there was some ulterior motive behind your invitation. I mean, you show up at Wagner's house at a strange hour of the night; the Maestro is obviously very uncomfortable about your arrival while Henryk and I are still present; you meet us fleetingly; and the next thing we know, Henryk and I are drinking wine that's too good for the king as your guests. Be honest, Inspector; wouldn't a string of circumstances of this sort arouse *your* suspicions?"

"Well, you may put aside your suspicions. This little dinner tonight is merely one more step in the rise of Hermann Preiss from peasant to poet, and nothing more. So let us have another round of Armagnac and drink to innocent pleasure." Bolliger had left the bottle of Armagnac at our table, a gesture not customarily extended to other patrons of Maison España and not lost on my appreciative guests.

Schramm raised his glass. "To Ziggy Bolliger!"

Steilmann and I joined him. "To Ziggy Bolliger!"

We sat for a moment or two in contented silence. Then, in an offhand manner, I said to Schramm, "By the way,

Schramm, you didn't mention what you performed in when you made your first major appearance. Was it in an opera?"

"Yes, *Nabucco*. Are you familiar with it?"

"Giuseppe Verdi, right? I've never heard the entire opera, but the chorus 'Va pensiero' I've heard several times. Very stirring, I must say. Has to do with freeing Hebrew slaves during some invasion or other of Judea in biblical times."

"Very good, Inspector! Needless to say, Wagner despises it. Says it's the kind of tune gondoliers sing in Venice. Besides, anything that has to do with freeing Hebrew slaves would never strike a favourable chord with the likes of Richard Wagner, as you're no doubt aware."

"It doesn't bother you?" I asked, directing my question at Schramm.

"You mean his views about race?" Schramm was looking me straight in the eye. "Not in the least. Singing is my life, Inspector. I live to sing. The only thing that bothers me is an off-key note."

"And you, Fräulein Steilmann … I suppose your outlook is the same?"

"One does not lightly turn down an opportunity to work with a genius like Maestro Wagner," she replied. "What you heard the other night was only a small sample of the music he's composed for *Die Meistersinger*. Only an idealistic fool would refuse a part in this opera."

I reached for the bottle of Armagnac. "Then let's have a final toast," I said, filling our glasses again. "To the future of opera, and may all your dreams come true and your plans succeed!"

Schramm raised a hand as if to halt the proceedings. "Dreams coming true, yes. But plans succeeding, no. You know what they say, Inspector: Man plans and God laughs. So I'll drink to dreams only, if you don't mind."

It turned out that Schramm and Steilmann had lodgings within a short distance of one another and were able conveniently to share a carriage. I on the other hand preferred to return to my apartment on foot despite the late hour. I was counting on the bracing night air to clear my mind of all the wine and brandy I'd consumed, and indeed the long stroll through the dark quiet streets left me feeling fully awake by the time I reached my residence. Settling myself at my desk, I took a small notebook and pen and jotted down the following:

> *Henryk Schramm does not eat pork (claims*
> *to be allergic)*
> *His first operatic role is in Nabucco, about*
> *Hebrew slaves*
> *Father was — is? — a violinist*
> *Has a habit of always answering a question*
> *with a question*
> *Says Man plans and God laughs*

I sat for a long while reading and rereading what I'd written. At last, I picked up the pen and added a final note:

> *Henryk Schramm ... or whatever his real*
> *name is ... is a Jew.*

CHAPTER FIVE

The first object that caught my eye when I entered my office early on the morning following dinner at Bolliger's was a note propped up at the centre of my desk, as though daring me to ignore it. The handwriting, as always, suggested the author was on the back of a runaway horse. The message, however, was clear and concise. "Preiss — I need to see you at once on a matter of urgency!" The signature, of course, was that of Commissioner von Mannstein. I let out a long loud groan (one of the privileges that comes with occupying a private office). Having spent yet another restless night (too much wine, too much rich food, too many lingering thoughts about Karla Steilmann), I regarded the prospect of beginning this day on a matter of urgency with the commissioner as less appealing than a march to the scaffold. Besides, I continued to be nagged by questions about this man Henryk Schramm. Detectives and cows have one thing in common: we are ruminants; we chew and chew again what has already been swallowed. The more I recalled fragments of our conversation over dinner, and turned over in my mind how at times he would look me squarely in the eye while at other times diverting his gaze when responding to a question, the more I doubted that Schramm was who he said he was.

Von Mannstein wasted no time getting to the point. "I have here a copy of an entry made in the daily log of Detective

Brunner," said the commissioner, waving a sheet of paper but not offering it to me to examine. "The entry records that Brunner was approached by one Otto Mecklenberg concerning a threat made against Richard Wagner. I gather, Preiss, this fellow Mecklenberg is what is known in musical circles as an impresario, one who manages the day-to-day business affairs of artists. Sounds like a nursemaid, if you ask me. At any rate, apparently this matter has fallen into your hands, Preiss. Correct?"

I hesitated, observing the deep scowl on the commissioner's face. How to answer: yes? no? maybe? Perhaps all three? Rashly I chose the truth. "Yes, Herr Commissioner, that is correct."

I was not prepared for what followed. Von Mannstein's scowl vanished. "What a stroke of luck, Preiss! What perfect timing!" The commissioner was exultant. "It's as though the gods had somehow intervened and ordained that you, Preiss, should come to the rescue of Munich!"

"I'm afraid I don't quite understand, sir —"

"Don't you see, Preiss? Thanks to your involvement with Wagner … I understand he counts on you to find and arrest whoever is threatening to ruin him … you are in an ideal position to keep an eye on what the man's up to. I don't mean musically; frankly I don't give a damn if Wagner composes operas or lullabies. Come to think of it, far as I'm concerned *both* kinds of music put people to sleep."

The commissioner took a moment to chortle at his own wit, then carried on: "It's Wagner's *political* activity the mayor and I are concerned with. Also certain aspects of his social and personal life which are infelicitous to say the least. Bear in mind, Preiss, it is imperative that we amass sufficient

grounds to rid Munich of Richard Wagner once and for all."
Von Mannstein paused and gave me a quizzical look. "Tell
me, Preiss, when von Braunschweig and I met with you, why
did you not disclose that you'd already become engaged in
this Wagner affair? Frankly, I was distressed at first to learn
about it from Brunner. No doubt he brought it to my attention because he was concerned about a possible conflict of
interest; you know, the kind of thing that might have proved
embarrassing to us, eh?"

"I'm certain Brunner acted with the best of intentions, sir,"
I said. (At the same time I made a vow to myself. Someday,
preferably in the very near future, I would see to it that Munich
saw the last of Detective Franz Brunner once and for all.)

Von Mannstein shook his head reassuringly. "Well, Preiss,
have no fear in that respect," he said. "I set Brunner straight,
of course. I know you to be a man of exquisite discretion. In
all likelihood you did not consider it prudent to reveal such
confidential information in the presence of the mayor."

The commissioner was certainly correct in one respect.
With good reason he knew me to be a man of exquisite discretion. It was his bad luck, and my good luck, that during
my lengthy vigil to catch the Friedensplatz rapist I happened
to come across von Mannstein as he was departing the off-
limits establishment of Madame Rosina Waldheim. Despite
the black wide-brimmed hat pulled down over his brow
and the turned-up collar of his civilian greatcoat, I had recognized him immediately. Besides he retained the bearing
and swagger of a cavalry officer (which he indeed was in his
earlier days) and his stride, as he took leave of that elegant
whorehouse, left not a shred of doubt in my mind that the
man was none other than my superior at the Constabulary.

We exchanged quick but meaningful glances, said not a word to each other, and he took off in a waiting carriage. Neither of us ever spoke of this afterwards; however, this fleeting and accidental encounter, later enriched by Madame Waldheim's revelation that he was a frequent and generous patron, created a silent bond between von Mannstein and me.

I returned to my office relieved on one hand that Franz Brunner's sly attempt to scuttle my career had not only failed but might have actually contributed a gold star to my service record. On the other hand I had to face an uncomfortable truth: Just as Henryk Schramm and Karla Steilmann were drawn to Richard Wagner like moths to a flame, so too was I caught up in that irresistible force.

Walking a thin line is not new to me. I've broken a law or two in my time, and stretched moral judgment to the point where it snaps like a dry tree branch, all for the sake of catching a criminal. I've learned to accomplish this with a minimum of agonizing about it before, during, and afterward. But the thin line now lying before me was one I was not accustomed to tread. I wondered: would this prove to be *my* ruination?

CHAPTER SIX

The studio of Sandor Lantos occupied the ground floor of a two-storey house that squatted in the overpowering shadow of the Opera House. Lantos's living quarters took up the second storey. One wall of the studio consisted almost entirely of windows, which not only admitted natural light much needed for Lantos's line of work but afforded a view of the façade of the Opera House that must have served as a daily inspiration to him. Noticing that I was struck by that view, Lantos said, "Hardly a day goes by that I don't pause and stare at that sight, Inspector. Just imagine: Mozart's *Idomeneo* had its premiere in that very place. And Maestro Wagner has had five — *five* — of his operas introduced there!" He gave a deep sigh. "Alas, Inspector Preiss, you and I … yes, and Wagner too … will be long gone and that edifice will still be standing. If only God, when He was creating Man, had made us as enduring as brick and stone."

"Oh, but He did," I said, "only He did it in the form of music."

Lantos looked at me with astonishment. "Pardon my frankness," he said, "but I was not expecting a philosopher to respond to the note I sent you. I mean, after all, as a police inspector —"

With a reassuring smile I said, "I'm not the least offended. Nor, I hasten to add, do I consider myself a philosopher. As for God and music, I'm not certain whether God invented music or music invented God. Most of the time I believe they're one and the same. Which is why I attend concert halls but not churches. And now that I've bared my soul to you, Lantos, perhaps you'd satisfy my curiosity. I've never before been in the studio of a costume and set designer. If you will pardon *my* frankness —"

"You were expecting more romantic surroundings, eh? Well, I'm sorry to disappoint you."

"Oh, I'm not disappointed at all," I lied, unable to ignore the pockmarked plaster walls where Lantos habitually pinned or nailed his sketches, the stained floorboards, the strong smell of oil paints and turpentine, an easel and adjoining worktable spattered with every colour and mixture of colours known to man. It was difficult to imagine that the grandiose productions staged so close by owed much of their splendor to what was created in this stuffy and unruly place.

Lantos, reading my mind, said, "You see, Inspector, I am a humble man doing a humble job in a humble location." There was not so much self-pity as ruefulness in Lantos's voice. No doubt in his youth he had ambitions to be another Rembrandt and was forced, by limitations in his talent, to settle for set and costume design. A man I judged to be in his late fifties, he was spending whatever years were left to him in the service of one patron, Richard Wagner, not a pretty fate for any artist.

"Your note said you have something of extreme importance to tell me," I said, glancing at the same time at my pocket watch.

"I'll come directly to the point," Lantos said. "Here, please look at these sketches, if you will —" Lantos reached behind him, then handed me a dozen sheets of heavy art paper which had been lying on the worktable. "These are my designs for costumes for a character called Beckmesser in Maestro Wagner's new opera *Die Meistersinger*. I believe you already possess some knowledge of the work." Lantos gave me a look as if to say he knew more about my involvement than I suspected. Knowing that gossip is as much a part of the world of music as notes and time signatures, I didn't bother to question the source of his information. "What do you think of them, Inspector? Please be honest, sir."

"Why would you seek my opinion?" I said. "I'm a policeman, not an art critic."

"Humour me anyway," Lantos urged.

I thumbed through the sketches. "Very colourful, very professional. I'm not surprised that Maestro Wagner has retained you all these years as his principal designer."

"Ah, but that's the point I'm getting to. These are *his* designs, based on *his* ideas and his alone. I am merely the instrument that puts them on paper."

I shrugged. "So what's the problem, Lantos?"

"The problem is that the singer hired to play the role of Beckmesser, a tenor by the name of Grilling, Wolfgang Grilling, took one look at my work and reacted so violently that I was frightened to death. He threw the papers on the floor and if I hadn't bent down quickly to pick them up I swear he would have trampled them. 'I'll be the laughingstock of Munich!' he yelled. Oh my God, Inspector, the man was furious. Said the costumes would make him appear like the village idiot. Worse still, he claimed the audience would take him for a Jew! You see, the Maestro insists that the Beckmesser character must have this somewhat prominent hooked nose. Which is precisely how I've depicted the face in the sketches."

"You explained to him that you were simply carrying out Wagner's orders?"

"Yes yes, of course. But Grilling was in no mood to listen to reason. So I appealed to his manager —"

"His manager was present?"

"Yes. You know how most opera singers are, Inspector; they must have their lackeys in attendance at all times, like valets and footmen are to royalty. Grilling's manager is Friedrich Otto, a man I've known for years. A gentle, decent man, really. Poor fellow was terribly embarrassed by Grilling's outburst, especially when Grilling began uttering threats and curses. Otto suggested a meeting with the Maestro to request alterations in costume and make-up."

"Is that a possibility?"

"You mean will Richard Wagner consent to changes? Ask me if palm trees will ever grow in the Alps, Inspector."

"But if Grilling was Wagner's choice to sing such an important role, one would think the Maestro would be eager to placate the fellow."

"Wrong, Inspector. Firstly, Richard Wagner placates nobody … nobody except where there's money to be borrowed. And even *then*, Wagner manages to convince the lender that he, Wagner, is doing him a great favour! Secondly, you must understand that the role of the loser, Beckmesser, is as vital in a way as the role of Walther von Stolzing, the winner. After all, Beckmesser is a scoundrel, a thief, an imposter, and, yes, more than a bit of a fool. In every respect he is the opposite of Walther. So it's absolutely essential that a strong contrast between the two be made clear right down to their stockings. No, Otto may have the best of intentions but he'll be wasting his time."

"And if, as you predict, Otto fails, what will Grilling do?"
I asked.

"He said … and these are his exact words, Inspector … he
said 'The world will never hear a single note of *Die Meistersinger*.
I'd rather burn down the Opera House than walk onto that
stage looking like this!'"

"But Lantos," I said, "you of all people must be familiar
with artists' temperaments. All fuss and bother. How did
Shakespeare put it: 'Full of sound and fury – '"

"Signifying nothing," Lantos cut in. "Ah, but that's not
the case here. I heard the anger in Grilling's voice and saw
it in his eyes. There was enough fire there to burn down
Munich, I tell you!"

Lantos paused and I could tell there was something else
on his mind. I said, "Is there another point you wish to make,
Lantos? If it's a matter of strict confidence, you can trust me."

Suddenly Lantos took a step forward and gripped my
arm. It was the kind of physical gesture that normally would
have caused me to shrink back (I dislike being a captive
audience). And yet there was a look of such desperation in
Lantos's face that I resisted the impulse to remove his hand.
"You must help me, Inspector Preiss. This is a terrible situation for me."

"For you? How so?"

"I have invested all of my time and energy for months
now to create designs for the new opera. I'm speaking literally of dozens of costume designs because *Die Meistersinger*
calls for a huge cast and chorus. Sets too, I've completed
several thus far and several others are nearly complete. And
to date I've not been paid one pfennig. Not one pfennig! I
have a wife and five children. If this production fails to go on,

well, Maestro Wagner is not famous for recognizing financial obligations nor is charity a compelling part of his life.
That is why I need your help, Inspector."

"My help? I told you before, my dear man; I'm not a philosopher, I'm not an art critic, and I'm *not* a bill collector.
Believe me, I deeply sympathize with you, but —"

"But you are in a position to do more than sympathize,
don't you see?" Lantos said, releasing his grip on my arm,
much to my relief. "You are Chief Inspector of Munich. Your
reputation is well-known. Go to Wolfgang Grilling. Go
to Friedrich Otto too. All you have to do is warn them —
warn Grilling in particular — that nothing must be done
that would interfere with the premiere of *Die Meistersinger*.
Warn him that you are aware of his threat —"

I shook my head. "Lantos, listen to me. My business is
crime. If I had to arrest every foul-mouthed hothead who
uttered a threat, there wouldn't be a prison in Germany large
enough to hold the crowd."

"And if Grilling carries out his threat, how will you feel,
Inspector? What will be your answer then?" Lantos cast his
glance upward to the second storey, where his wife and five
children presumably were staring at an empty larder as we
spoke. "When was the last time you sat down at a supper
table that had no bread, Inspector?"

I wanted to tell Sandor Lantos that a breadless table was
a routine occurrence throughout my childhood. Instead, I
said, "Very well, I will go to Grilling and to his manager."

At these words, Lantos did it again; gripping my arm,
and looking intently into my eyes, he said in a quiet voice,
"If Wolfgang Grilling does anything to stop this opera, I will
kill him with these hands."

CHAPTER SEVEN

Munich's hotels that cater to the upper class, like Munich's better restaurants, go to desperate lengths to distance themselves from their stolid German roots, but in a different manner. Where local restaurateurs take liberties with French and Spanish names for their places of business, local hoteliers, with a kind of presumptuousness that knows no shame, christen their edifices with the names of foreign royalty — kings, queens, emperors and empresses, as well as lesser ranks — stopping short only when it comes to popes, cardinals, and archbishops (although why the nobility of the church are excluded from such honours is beyond my comprehension).

The Eugénie Palace is no exception to this tradition. If anything, it has elevated the tradition to heights other hostelries in the city cannot hope to attain. Its public areas are paved with more Italian marble than Caesar's eyes ever beheld; its French crystal chandeliers and mirror-backed wall sconces fill each room with sunshine even on the dullest days. Rumours abound, of course. It's said that the crimson carpets were dyed in the blood of a thousand slaves a century ago in Constantinople. A printer is said to have been shot dead for negligently omitting the *accent* in "Eugénie" on the hotel stationery. True or not, such rumours have lent an aura of grandeur to the Eugénie Palace which its guests acknowledge with proper respect when paying extravagant bills at the end of their stay. I swear that I do not have a socialist bone in my body and yet, whenever for some reason or other I find myself a visitor, I cannot resist being repelled by the unabashed hedonism that oozes from every pore of the place.

I was in the midst of expressing these deep-seated feelings to Helena Becker when, giving me a look that told me she'd had enough of my self-righteousness, she pressed a finger to my lips and said, "Hermann, darling, do shut up!" Following which she rather forcefully removed my hat and coat and pushed me in the direction of a generously pillowed four-poster complete with satin canopy. In a while, after we had finished testing the limits of that fine piece of furniture and lay catching our breaths, Helena whispered into my ear, "There now, Hermann, the Eugénie Palace isn't *all* bad, is it?"

"I know it's none of my business," I replied, "but how can a cellist — even a successful cellist like you — afford the rates here? You must have a patron back in Düsseldorf. Come clean, Helena; who is subsidizing this lavish lifestyle of yours?"

Her voice low and resonant like the low notes of her instrument, Helena said, "I have a lover in Düsseldorf, Hermann. I perform for him privately. He lies back in his bed and sighs with satisfaction every time I embrace my cello, and when I begin to play, no matter what the piece, he closes his eyes and lies there with the sweetest smile on his sweet face. Alas, Hermann, you will never know what it is to be adored, but I must tell you it is a sublime experience."

"And does this sweet man know about you and me?" I removed Helena's arms from around my neck. "Or are you playing a cello with eight strings, so to speak?"

I thought the coldness in my voice would take Helena aback, but instead she threw her arms around my neck again. "He is eighty-three years old, Hermann, bedridden, probably dying —"

"But rich, eh? And who is this angel of yours, may I ask?"

"An old friend of yours, Hermann. In fact, more than a friend; a man who did much to advance your career when you were a member of the Düsseldorf Police."

"You don't mean —?"

Helena sat up in bed, a hint of triumph in her smile. "The Baron himself. Baron von Hoffman." She fingered a slender gold chain that encircled her neck, smiling even more broadly at me, awaiting my next question, knowing what it would be.

"From him? From your eighty-three-year-old lover?"

"And more, darling. Much more. A chest full, in fact."

"The baroness … how does she view all this?"

"From the grave, I suppose. She passed on not long after you left Düsseldorf for Munich. They had no children, you know."

"So you're the daughter the Baron always wanted. How convenient. The recital you're giving tomorrow night at the concert hall … I understand it's sold out, but even your fee can't possibly cover the bill here. Let me guess, Helena: the Baron showers you with his wife's jewels; you then sell them to —"

"To another old friend of yours in Düsseldorf."

"Not that scoundrel Thüringer! Please, Helena, tell me it's not true."

"The old bastard drives a hard bargain but so do I, Hermann. The pattern is always the same. I take a piece of jewellery to his shop. He starts off by offering me half of what I know it's worth. We fence back and forth and then I move in for the kill. I remind him that you managed to keep him out of prison for years even though you were aware he was more often than not selling stolen goods from his shop."

"That's not quite fair, Helena. After all, Thüringer did fulfill a useful role. He was my most reliable informant. I've lost count of the number of thieves and fraud artists I was able to apprehend thanks to Thüringer's eyes and ears."

"Nevertheless, *he* knows that *I* know enough about him that one word from me to the right person at the Düsseldorf Constabulary and he'd be behind bars dining on bread and water for the rest of his days."

I sat up in bed now and held Helena by the shoulders. "My God, Helena, what happened to the sweet innocent young cellist I found so enchanting back in Düsseldorf?"

"The sweet innocent young cellist made the mistake of falling in love with a certain police inspector. Or have you forgotten that fact, Hermann? Whenever I so much as whispered the first syllable of the word 'marriage' you fled to the other side of the planet. And you still do. Sweetness and innocence and youth have a tendency to disappear when that kind of rejection occurs often enough. So yes, you're absolutely right, my dear. The woman you are holding so firmly has become a tough old bird."

"But a *beautiful* tough old bird."

Helena pulled away from me. She sat eyeing me suspiciously for a moment or two. "All right, Hermann, out with it. What is it you want?"

I tried very hard to appear insulted. "Me? What do I want? I was only —"

"You were only flattering me. Don't try to fool me, Hermann Preiss. I know you better than you know yourself. 'Beautiful old bird' indeed. I've never yet received a compliment from you that didn't have some slime-covered motive attached to it. Out with it, Hermann!"

"You are absolutely right," I confessed. "You do know me better than I know myself. Beauty, brains, intuition, you have them all, Helena. Which is why I need your help."

Helena shook her head, looking at me more in sorrow than anger. "Just as I thought. Please tell me it isn't about that Schumann business back in Düsseldorf. Don't tell me that case has come back to haunt us."

"No, Helena, it's over and done with as far as I'm concerned. But I've got myself involved with another bunch of musicians, here in Munich this time. Does the name Richard Wagner ring a bell?"

Helena said, "You must be pulling my leg, Hermann. Of course the name Richard Wagner rings a bell. Rings a lot of bells, in fact. Let me guess: in addition to the many crimes he's been accused of, he has now murdered somebody. How delicious! Who, Hermann? Who's the victim? One of his lovers? An unpaid creditor? Wait, I know who: a soprano, one of the many young virgins Wagner ravages before hiring them."

"Sorry to disappoint you," I said, "but this is one of the rare times when your intuition fails you. Fact is, somebody has issued a threat against Wagner, a rather vague threat but one which must be taken seriously."

I followed this with a complete account of my involvement thus far in the Wagner case, including my introduction to Henryk Schramm, Karla Steilmann, and Sandor Lantos.

I explained as well my dilemma, my duty on one hand to carry out the orders of the commissioner and mayor, and my obligations on the other hand to seek out and apprehend whoever had issued the threatening note.

When I'd finished, Helena frowned. "It's all fascinating, Hermann, but I've never met any of these people. Except for Wagner, of course, I know nothing about any of them. So why would you want *my* help?"

"After your recital tomorrow evening, I've arranged for a small dinner party at a favourite restaurant of mine, Maison España —"

Helena clapped her hands. "Wonderful! I *love* Spanish food!"

"Sorry to disappoint you again, dearest, but Maison España is about as Spanish as Johann Sebastian Bach. The proprietor's name is Ziggy Bolliger, a charming fake if ever there was one, but in fairness his schnitzels are the finest in Europe. Now then, Helena, I have to be honest with you. This is not intended to be purely a culinary treat. You see, I've invited two singers who have the leading roles in *Die Meistersinger*, the tenor Henryk Schramm and the soprano Karla Steilmann. I need your special feminine insights about these two after you've had an opportunity to spend some time with them, even if it's only over dinner."

"Why?" Helena wanted to know, frowning again. "Surely you don't suspect *them?*"

I replied as patiently as I could, "Helena, darling, how many times must I tell you? A detective suspects *every*body."

"You mean even *I* could be a suspect?"

"I mean even my own *mother* could be a suspect."

"Your mother has been dead for years, Hermann."

"That's entirely beside the point."

"Be serious, Hermann. What am I supposed to be discerning during this late supper you've arranged? I'm always famished after a recital. I hope I can at least dine on your friend's famous schnitzel before I have to go to work, so to speak."

"I'll come to the point," I said. "This man Schramm … there is something about him that —"

"That what —?"

I paused. "No, Helena, I'm not going to say anything more. I don't want to say anything that might influence your opinion of him."

Helena gave me one of her carnal smiles. "Is he handsome and young?"

"Devilishly so."

"Tell me more, Hermann."

"No."

"*Please —*"

"Absolutely not."

"You're jealous of him, aren't you, Hermann?"

"Teasing me won't work," I said. "I'm not saying another word about Schramm. I want your impression of him without being tainted in advance."

"Tainted? You mean there's a dark side to this tenor?"

"Enough, Helena." I got out of bed, got dressed while Helena watched in silence, and reached for my hat and coat. "Good luck tomorrow night, my sweet," I said, planting a kiss on her forehead.

Pouting, Helena said, "I think it's positively beastly of you not to at least give me a hint of what I'm to look out for at this little supper of yours."

I moved to the door, turned and blew her a kiss, then let myself out, calling back, "Sweet dreams, Helena." Closing the door behind me, I heard something strike it. Whatever Helena threw, I hoped it wasn't too valuable.

The hour was late and the night air sharp but I decided a walk from the Eugénie Palace to my rooms, a distance of a little over a kilometre, would condition me for a good night's sleep.

No sooner had I stepped from the ornate front entrance of the hotel onto the deserted sidewalk than I heard a voice call out, "Inspector Preiss, thank God I've found you!" I turned to see a small figure hobbling toward me like a piece of fragile old crockery. "Thank God I've found you!" he repeated.

"Mecklenberg! What on earth brings you here?"

He appeared and sounded short of breath, which I was beginning to think was his natural state. "Your colleague Brunner was right, Preiss. He informed me that your cellist friend was in Munich. I learned that she is a guest at the Eugénie Palace, and here you are! I've got hold of you just in time."

"Just in time for what?"

"There's been a murder, Inspector ... a man by the name of Sandor Lantos."

CHAPTER EIGHT

"Sandor Lantos has murdered someone?"

"No, no," Mecklenberg wheezed, clutching his chest as though he were in pain. "Lantos is the *victim*. He ... uh ... he —"

I hooked an arm through one of Mecklenberg's arms, fearing he was about to collapse. Though he was a small man, his weight, such as it was, anchored me to the sidewalk. "Come with me into the hotel," I said. "You could use a comfortable place to sit and a good strong cup of coffee."

Huffing and puffing, and waving his free arm impatiently, the old man responded, "There's no time, don't you see? Besides, I haven't even told you who Sandor Lantos is ... or rather was."

"There's no need to," I said. "I happen to know."

"Then you will understand that Maestro Wagner is beside himself, poor man. This is tragic for Wagner. Tragic!"

"Excuse me, Mecklenberg," I said, "but aren't you missing the point here? Tragic for *Wagner*? What about Lantos's wife and children?"

Abruptly the old man shook loose and stared at me as though I were out of my mind. "His wife and children? What about them? Who gives a damn, Preiss? It wasn't *their* opera Lantos was working on. It was Wagner's. That is what matters."

Recalling for a moment my one and only conversation with Sandor Lantos and his concerns for his family, I was appalled by Mecklenberg's utter lack of compassion, but for the moment police business came first. "How did you learn of Lantos's death?" I asked.

"Earlier this evening," Mecklenberg replied. "I was to meet the Maestro at the opera house. We had some urgent business to discuss. I found him in a terrible state of upset. I have to explain, Inspector: The final scene of *Die Meistersinger* takes place in a public square. The entire cast is on stage for the competition about to begin ... the principal characters, a large chorus of townspeople, my God the entire population of Germany! In typical fashion, Wagner was busy with a tape measure; he was actually measuring the space available for this crowd scene, right down to the last millimetre. It turned out that the set designed by Lantos would not accommodate all these people and Wagner was having a fit, yelling, cursing, vowing to skin Lantos alive. He insisted we proceed straight to Lantos's studio which, as you perhaps know, is no more than a stone's throw from the opera house."

"But wouldn't Lantos's studio be closed for the night?"

Mecklenberg gave me a sardonic smile. "Closed? That would mean absolutely nothing to Wagner. When you work for Richard Wagner there is only one time zone on this earth — Wagner Standard Time. Twenty-five-hour days and eight-day weeks. So off we went. When we reached the studio we found the front door slightly ajar. Wagner of course took this as an automatic invitation to enter without so much as a polite knock. I followed after him. None of the lamps had been extinguished and I took for granted that Lantos was working late. The place was a mess, papers strewn all over, many of them in shreds."

"Yes yes, but what about Lantos?"

Shuddering, Mecklenberg replied, "You won't believe your eyes, Preiss."

"So it's true after all," I said, muttering to myself, "the pen *is* mightier than the sword —"

"I beg your pardon?" Mecklenberg called, making certain to keep a respectable distance behind me and well away from Lantos's body which lay sprawled in a chair behind his worktable.

"It's nothing, Mecklenberg. I was just talking to myself."

Lantos's throat had been pierced by one of his sketching pens, pierced so deeply its long steel nib had obviously penetrated the man's windpipe. His eyes were open, staring, as though he couldn't believe this was how he was about to die.

Two young constables had arrived on the crime scene before me, dispatched by the night duty officer to stand guard and make certain nothing was disturbed. Fortunately two other constables had already ushered Lantos's wife and children away from the premises. "They were screaming and carrying on something awful," one of the guards reported, adding that an older man also had to be escorted out of the studio. "Kept shouting 'Who could do this to me?'" the guard said. "I wrote down the man's name here in my notebook. Wagner, Richard Wagner, or something like that." The blank look on the constable's face indicated Wagner's name meant nothing to him.

Careful still to maintain a safe distance from the corpse, Mecklenberg called to me again. "What kind of monster could have done this?"

"No monster," I said, "just a human being with inhuman strength."

"But why? Lantos was an artist, a quiet decent hardworking man. I can't imagine he had an enemy in the world."

"I can," I said quietly, again speaking to myself, not thinking old Mecklenberg could hear me.

But hear me he did. "You can?"

"Forgive me, Mecklenberg," I said. "It's just the cynic in me. A meaningless remark, the result of too many years of seeing this kind of thing."

For the moment this lame excuse seemed to satisfy Mecklenberg's curiosity.

I made certain that the next thing I said to myself could not possibly be heard by anyone in the room. "Wolfgang Grilling. Who else?"

CHAPTER NINE

I had stayed on at Sandor Lantos's studio late into the night examining everything from the man's corpse, with its face frozen in an expression of open-mouthed astonishment, down to the tiniest scraps of sketching paper flung about the room as though by a furious wind. Though anything but an accomplished artist myself, I made a number of drawings of various parts of the crime scene that were at least serviceable, and fleshed these out with copious notes. By the end of that long night the thought which had first flashed through my mind — that this was the work of Wolfgang Grilling — was now deeply engraved. Not only would Grilling, a robust and powerfully strong man, have had the strength, he would have had the motive, given the rage he directed at Lantos after he'd viewed the sketches for his costume and make-up as Beckmesser. In all likelihood there had been an altercation between the singer and the designer; perhaps at some point Lantos, his own temper flaring, might have made threatening moves against Grilling, though the seated position of Lantos's body made this possibility remote and suggested that Grilling must have attacked suddenly and with great speed and deadly precision.

One other fact convinced me the murderer was Wolfgang Grilling: the only sketches left undamaged were those of the Beckmesser character. One would have thought these would have been the first to be destroyed. Instead, though crumpled a bit here and there, they were not only intact but had escaped being strewn about with all the other papers. To me, this was the sign of a consummate amateur. *If I destroy these sketches they'll know for certain it was I who killed Lantos; therefore I'll leave them more or less untouched and they'll think someone else with a grievance did away with Lantos.*

The following morning I arrived at my office at the Constabulary to be greeted by a remarkably elated commissioner and a smirking Franz Brunner.

"Well, Preiss, our man Wagner seems to have handed himself over to us on a silver platter," he crowed. "As if his other crimes aren't enough, he's now added murder to his résumé."

At this, Brunner's smirk expanded into a smile of satisfaction. "To save you the trouble, Preiss," he said, "I interviewed the stage manager and his crew at the opera house last night. To a man they all agreed: it had to be your man Wagner who murdered Lantos. When he discovered that Lantos had botched the measurements for the scenery, Wagner stormed out of the house uttering threats against Lantos. They said it was as though all hell was about to erupt right here in Munich! Not a shred of doubt about it, Preiss; Richard Wagner is our killer." Turning to the commissioner, Brunner said, "With all due respect, sir, I think no time must be wasted. Wagner has a reputation as an escape artist. I would be prepared to arrest him within the hour if you will permit."

Commissioner von Mannstein looked gravely at me. "Well, Preiss, it seems Brunner here has done you a favour. I see no point in agonizing over this. Brunner's absolutely correct, you know; Richard Wagner is a genius at disappearing when it suits him. I want the two of you to bring him in without delay. I'm dispatching both of you in case the man makes a fuss. As a matter of fact, better take an extra couple of constables to make sure we do the job right. Last thing in the world I need at the moment is to have to inform the mayor that we had Richard Wagner where we wanted him and bungled. Off you go then, and Godspeed."

I made no move and, seeing this, the commissioner frowned. "Well, Preiss, I thought I made myself perfectly clear —"

"You did, sir. There's only one problem —"

"Problem? Brunner's done his homework very efficiently I would say. I see no problem."

"The problem is this, sir: Richard Wagner did not murder Sandor Lantos. Richard Wagner could not possibly have murdered Sandor Lantos."

"And what makes you so sure?" von Mannstein demanded, obviously displeased.

"It's true that Wagner was furious with Lantos and made straight for Lantos's studio to vent his rage," I replied, "but he was at that point in the company of his manager, the impresario Mecklenberg, and it was the two of them who, upon arrival at the studio, discovered that Lantos had already been murdered. No, Commissioner, Richard Wagner is not our man."

Chewing his lower lip, a habit whenever he was unhappy, the commissioner glared at me, then at Brunner. To Brunner he said, "You failed to mention that Wagner was accompanied by this fellow Mecklenberg when he fled the opera house, Brunner." Without waiting for Brunner's explanation von Mannstein returned to me, still glaring. "Then who the devil *is* our man, Preiss? Do we at least have a suspect?"

At moments like these I rely upon an unfailing rule of conduct: *When in doubt, lie.* Looking my superior straight in the eye, I answered, "I have no idea, sir." The commissioner's face turned into a hairy mask of disappointment, the bushy eyebrows seeming to merge with the oversized moustache, which in turn became one with his generous sideburns and beard. Seeing this sorry expression on his face, I was overcome with pity, if only for a second or two, and quickly added, "However, I did engage in a careful survey of the murder scene and am confident that before this day is out significant clues will emerge."

Hardly had these words escaped my lips than I knew I'd made a serious mistake. Von Mannstein's eyes narrowed sharply. "Clues? Such as?"

"Well, to be frank, Commissioner —" I paused, desperately trying to think up an answer that would satisfy the man. The news he most wanted to hear — that Wagner was somehow implicated in Lantos's murder — was something I could not bring myself to fabricate, yes, even I who am not above shaping and reshaping truth now and then depending on circumstances. "To be frank, we find ourselves in a milieu far different from what one might call run-of-the-mill people, you know, citizens of a lower social order. We are dealing here with, shall we say, subtler forces."

This brought another smirk to Brunner's face. "With all due respect," he said, directing his remark to the commissioner, his tone sarcastic, "that is nonsense. Criminals are criminals. I, for one, am not dazzled by these 'subtler forces.' There's nothing subtle about murder."

Ignoring Brunner's comment, the commissioner said, "See here, Preiss, you seem to have had more than a little involvement over the years in Düsseldorf as well as in Munich with people of that ilk ... I'm referring of course to these peculiar musical types with their temperaments and their idiosyncrasies. Of course, I myself have little or nothing to do with them; in fact, it's a point of pride with me that I avoid their company as I avoid what you so aptly call citizens of a lower social order —"

I wanted to interject, "Except prostitutes," but held my tongue.

"So here is my decision," the commissioner continued. "I want a full report by tomorrow morning, first thing, concerning your findings at Lantos's studio, following which you have until the first of next week ... that gives you five full days from today ... to put two and two together and arrest the perpetrator of this crime. I hope you're a good navigator, Preiss, one who knows his way among the shoals and shallows of these so-called artists. It certainly sounds to me as though somebody in that strange crowd has to be the guilty one."

"But, sir," I began to protest, "five days —"

Von Mannstein's hand directed me to halt. "Five days, Preiss. Not a minute longer. And remember, if there is anything — *anything* — even a mere grain of sand, which connects Richard Wagner to this ugly affair then I want him brought in as well. I'll see to it that Brunner is free to work with you, of course."

Franz Brunner gave me a dry smile. "Of course," he chimed in. "I look forward to the experience, as a matter of fact."

"I'm sure you do, Brunner," I said, returning an even drier smile. "After all, it's not often that you get to come in contact with people who speak in words of more than one syllable."

Observing that both Detective Franz Brunner and I were smiling at one another, Commissioner von Mannstein chuckled. "Nothing like a bit of humour between comrades, eh? Well, splendid! Now let us to our work."

CHAPTER TEN

The supper party I had arranged to follow Helena Becker's recital was meant to be a quiet intimate affair, and I thought I had made this perfectly clear to Ziggy Bolliger, the proprietor of Maison Espâna. I suppose I ought to have known better, given Bolliger's fondness for ceremony. Meeting us as our carriages pulled up, Bolliger paraded us into the restaurant as though we were courtiers showing up for a grand ball. With measured steps he ushered us along a deliberately circuitous path to a table reserved at the very centre of the place, all the while smilingly acknowledging the attention of his patrons as if he himself were the arriving celebrity. At surrounding tables, diners who had attended the recital broke into genteel applause (the men more enthusiastic than the women in appreciation of Helena's somewhat revealing gown) while I, as shameless now as Bolliger, basked in her limelight. Besides Helena, my party comprised Henryk Schramm, Karla Steilmann, and a fourth guest, the pianist Madam Olga Vronsky, whom Helena had brought from Düsseldorf as her accompanist, the same endlessly patient and suffering Madam Vronsky who some years earlier had valiantly struggled to teach me to play the piano and who, in her sweet-natured way, taught me that nothing cures vain ambition as effectively as a healthy dose of truth. (Nowadays I play for a critical audience of one

— myself.) Earlier that evening both women had performed two Beethoven sonatas for cello and piano followed by Franz Schubert's *Arpeggiona*, and the adoration that flowed upward from the audience to the stage when they took the last of many bows was almost palpable, not the least my own for, despite my aversion to public displays of affection, I found myself throwing kisses to both cellist and pianist as though I were some starry-eyed Romeo.

Of course Helena could not wait to call attention to my behavior even before the cork in the first bottle of Champagne was popped. Addressing my guests she said with a sly grin, "I trust everyone noted how our host abandoned his habitual reserve at the conclusion of the recital. If I'm not mistaken, I believe I even heard a bravo or two coming from his direction." Wagging a finger at me she said, "You must watch yourself, Hermann. That's conduct unbecoming a police officer."

Gruffly I replied, "Nonsense! You wouldn't catch me shouting 'Bravo' in a hundred years. Far as I'm concerned there's solid reliable military band music; all the rest is just so much whipped cream."

"Liar," Helena said, squeezing my hand.

"Which brings up an interesting subject," Schramm said. "Speaking of police officers, tell us, Inspector, any word yet on Sandor Lantos's killer? There are as many rumours flying around the streets as there are seats in the opera house, but of course you must be aware of that."

I was not at all prepared for this sudden change of topic, yet not surprised that it was Schramm who brought up the subject. I had not at this point succeeded in identifying what there was about Schramm's character that gave me the distinct feeling there was more to him than met the eye and ear. The plain fact, however, was that a tiny seed of unease had planted itself under my skin and was growing steadily with each exposure to the man. Better, therefore, to answer his query by falling back on standard police issue. "I hope you won't think me rude," I said, "but the investigation into Lantos's murder is at a very delicate stage and I'm naturally bound to exercise absolute discretion."

Schramm's face took on a troubled look. "I hope you won't think *me* rude, Inspector, but with all due respect I have to point out that poor Lantos may only be the first victim. What I mean is, there is no secret about the number of enemies Maestro Wagner has accumulated. Suppose someone, let's say someone with a profound grudge, or perhaps some homicidal lunatic, has decided to wreak vengeance on Wagner by eliminating all of us one by one, starting with Lantos and eventually ending with the Maestro himself. Maybe this strikes you as farfetched but still —"

I leaned back in my chair smiling with what I hoped was an air of smug self-confidence. "My dear Schramm," I said, "in my line of work nothing is ever farfetched. Nevertheless, one mustn't let one's imagination run away with itself. 'Murder may pass unpunished for a time, but tardy justice will o'ertake the crime.'"

Karla Steilmann said, "I didn't know you're a poet, Inspector."

"I'm not," I said. "That was written by an English poet by the name of Dryden. I'm particularly fond of that little couplet, needless to say."

"Let me offer another rhyme," Schramm said. "'Unless the crime is solved by winter's freeze, the evil deed will fester like old cheese.'"

Madam Vronsky's face suddenly brightened. "Wherever did you pick up that saying?" she asked Schramm. "I haven't heard it since I was a child. My uncle Alexander Vronsky was a police official in St. Petersburg and used to quote it often, in Russian of course. But I must say your translation into German is impeccable, Herr Schramm."

Quickly Schramm said, "It's not *my* translation. I must have read it somewhere."

"But have you been to Russia then?" Madam Vronsky wanted to know.

"I sang in Moscow ... once," Schramm replied.

"You must let me teach you how to say it in Russian. Somehow it sounds more authentic in my native tongue," said Madam Vronsky.

"I'm sure it does," Schramm said, giving her a gracious smile, "but perhaps another time when this stomach of mine is not rumbling with hunger."

As Schramm said this, a waiter miraculously appeared and stationed himself next to me like a soldier reporting for duty. "You see," I said to my guests, "this proves the wisdom of an old French saying: 'Always choose a table near a waiter.' Shall we order?"

I had made a point of seating Helena Becker next to Henryk Schramm hoping this would encourage more direct conversation between the two while I would try to preoccupy Karla Steilmann and Madam Vronsky. Throughout a course of appetizers followed by entrées my plan worked beautifully so that by the time the dessert cart arrived, Becker and Schramm appeared thoroughly engrossed in one another. For me then, the challenge was to keep one ear devoted to conversation with Steilmann and Vronsky while straining with the other ear to catch snippets of dialogue between the other two, no easy trick given that, as supper progressed, both Helena and her new tenor friend began lowering their voices until they were speaking almost in whispers. At first I found this annoying and frustrating, but on second thought I told myself this was probably for the best. After all, it was I who had enlisted Helena and cast her in this position, and if she were carrying out her mission a little more ardently than I required then at least the end would justify the means. Helena Becker was a shrewd judge of people, often more so than I; if her obvious enchantment with Schramm and his with her was the price I had to pay for the benefit of her impressions, well, so be it.

I was not the only person at the table annoyed and frustrated. Karla Steilmann, despite my efforts to keep her and Madam Vronsky engaged, from time to time shot glances across the table at Helena and Schramm that grew chillier as the meal went on, and I became increasingly aware that, in response to my questions to her, which were becoming longer and longer, her answers were becoming shorter and shorter to the point where a "yes" or "no" or curt nod of the head was all she managed.

The atmosphere turned more to my taste with the arrival of liqueurs, at which point Helena and Schramm became unlocked and joined the group for a toast, all of us raising our slender crystal glasses. As host I took it upon myself to offer the toast. "To the Fatherland," I said, "and to German culture! May they continue to flourish!" After a first sip, I raised my glass high again. "A second toast, if I may," I said with forced cheerfulness. "Here's to a smashing success for the new opera ... *Die Meistersinger von Nürnberg* ... and to a long and productive life for its creator Richard Wagner!" Out of the corner of my eye I observed that Henryk Schramm was the only one whose response was less than enthusiastic. His lips had curled into a thin smile and when he set down his glass it was apparent that he'd barely tasted its dark amber contents. I had intended a third toast but before I could do so Schramm brought the supper party to an abrupt close. Glancing at his pocket watch — a splendid heavy gold timepiece with an ornately engraved cover — he announced, "I don't know about you fine people, but I've been sentenced to a day of hard labour tomorrow at the Richard Wagner Center for Delinquent Tenors —"

Immediately Karla Steilmann chimed in, "Yes, I too have a punishing day of rehearsals ahead." Pointedly she said to Schramm, "Henryk, it's very late, I know, but I'm going to hold you to your promise to see me home."

With a knowing smile Helena said, "You see, Herr Schramm, time waits for no woman."

Schramm asked, "But what about you, Fräulein Becker?"

I jumped in. "Oh, don't worry about Helena and Madam Vronsky, Schramm. They're in police custody for the evening."

I should have known this would bring out the mischievous side of dear Helena. "Now Hermann, aren't you being a little presumptuous? I cannot remember the last time a handsome tenor was concerned about my welfare. God knows even if *you* don't; the streets of Munich are not the safest places in the world at this hour of the night."

"I'm sure you will be in good hands with Inspector Preiss," Karla Steilmann assured Helena, rising at the same time from her seat and advancing firmly toward Schramm. "Come, Henryk, time to bid goodnight to these lovely people."

Before departing, Henryk Schramm kissed the hands of both Helena and Madam Vronsky, murmuring to each of them "Be well."

Later, back at the Eugénie Palace, after seeing to it that Madam Vronsky was comfortably settled in her room, I followed Helena to her suite where, once the door was closed behind us, without so much as a split second's hesitation she said "He's Jewish, you know."

"Who? Who's Jewish?"

"Don't be cute, Hermann. Schramm. Who else would I be talking about?"

"What makes you so sure, Helena? Did he say so?"

"Of course not. Don't ask me how I know. *I know.* Trust me, Hermann. Henryk Schramm is a Jew."

CHAPTER ELEVEN

As Helena described them to me, the telltale signs that convinced her Henryk Schramm was Jewish were subtle. Producing a flask of brandy that was a routine part of her accoutrements whenever she was on tour, she filled two small glasses, offered one to me, took a sip from the other, and began: "He has a way of using his hands when he talks. Not animated, mind you, Hermann, but expressive. If he's making a point he uses his index fingers, moving them from side to side as though he's saying maybe yes, maybe no." Helena seemed to be smiling to herself. "Rather charming, really, when I come to think of it."

Dryly, I said, "I'm sure, Helena. What else?"

"Before he takes a first bite of a slice of bread he sprinkles a pinch of salt on it. It's a habit of his; I noticed he did so several times."

"Maybe he's simply superstitious. I believe that particular habit is common among Eastern Europeans."

Helena shook her head. "This man is not a superstitious type, Hermann. But he *is* a pessimist. So many of his views of things are stitched together by a dark thread of pessimism."

"For instance?"

"He's quite convinced that German culture will fall victim eventually to all the industrial activity that's consuming our people, that we'll become a nation of crass materialists.

As for himself, he predicts that, as wonderful as Wagner's new opera is, it will fail and that he, Schramm, will therefore suffer an early end to his career as a singer."

"Pessimism is not the exclusive territory of Jews, Helena," I said.

"Of course not," she agreed, "but they seem to visit that territory more than most tourists, at least in my experience. One other thing, Hermann: did you observe something when he said goodbye to Olga and me?"

"Yes. He kissed your hands. Nothing unusual about that. Even *I* occasionally stoop to such endearing gestures ... that is, when I'm too weary to try something more energetic."

"Ah, it's not what he *did*," Helena said, "but what he *said*. A thoroughgoing German would look into my eyes and whisper *auf Wiedersehen* at such a moment. *He* looked into my eyes and whispered 'Be well.' Those were his parting words."

"And you're saying that's typical of those people?"

Helena said, sounding sure of herself, "I've lived much of my life with 'those people.' I *am* one of 'those people.' Remember? I know what I'm talking about, Hermann. My father changed his name from Gershon Bekarsky to Gerhardt Becker after my mother persuaded him he was better off with a new name. But one thing a new name can't do ... it can't change old habits. So yes, pessimism remained in his bones. And yes, he used his hands a great deal whenever he was involved in some deep discussion. Loved salting his bread. Never said goodbye to anyone without adding 'Be well.' I repeat, Hermann, although Schramm never said a word to me during our conversations tonight about being Jewish, he is, he definitely is."

Without asking permission, I reached for Helena's flask

and helped myself to a second brandy. "That's not like you," Helena said, watching as I downed it in a single draft. "You seem to be trying to drown out something."

"On the contrary," I said. "In wine there's truth, but in brandy there's clarity. Not answers, but at least *questions* begin to make sense ... one question, at any rate."

Helena teasingly brought the brandy flask to the lip of my glass. "If you're wondering about making love tonight, Hermann, perhaps a third?"

Gently I pushed the flask aside. "Listen to me, Helena. Given Richard Wagner's renowned hatred of Jews, why would he engage a Jew to sing the leading male role in one of his operas? It stands to reason Wagner hasn't the slightest suspicion about Schramm. But there's an even more intriguing question, isn't there? Why would a Jewish tenor take the trouble to conceal his background and, of all things, want to sing in an opera composed by one of the most virulent anti-Semites on the face of the earth?"

Once again Helena took up the flask, this time with a serious expression. "Maybe you should have a third drink after all —"

"No, no, thank you. Enough is enough. You must be exhausted after such a full evening, Helena. And as for me, I have an early appointment tomorrow morning. Between you and me, it's not going to be very pleasant. I've summoned another tenor for questioning at the Constabulary. Name's Wolfgang Grilling. It's in connection with the murder of Wagner's designer Sandor Lantos."

"Do you think Schramm has a point ... I mean about some enemy of Wagner setting out to —" Helena cut herself short. "That's simply too preposterous."

"Not at all," I said. "Crime and preposterousness are blood brothers. Sometimes they are even blood sisters." I rose from my chair, moved to where Helena was seated, kissed her on the forehead, and whispered "Goodnight, my sweet. Be well."

"You're leaving me up in the air like this?" she asked, full of indignation.

"Yes, Helena," I replied, "but with a word of advice. Whatever you decide to throw at the door as I'm closing it behind me … make sure it's not too expensive."

CHAPTER TWELVE

Before attending Helena Becker's recital I had dispatched one of my young constables, Emil Gruber, to the residence of the tenor Wolfgang Grilling bearing a summons to appear at my office at ten o'clock the following morning. I gave, as the reason for our meeting, my need to obtain as much background as possible into the character and work of Sandor Lantos from people who were in contact with him either socially or professionally, all in the hope of forming a picture of Lantos's killer. I made a point of stating my reason innocuously, even humbly ("… your insights and experience would be of incalculable assistance, Herr Grilling …"), avoiding even the slightest hint that, for the moment, I considered him the prime suspect. Knowing that most artists and entertainers are not what are known as "morning people," I planned to make this session as comfortable and informal as I could despite the fact that my office, like all offices in the Constabulary, can only be described as a formidable collection of unrelieved squares and rectangles. I would deliberately sit next to Grilling, rather than sitting in my usual place behind my desk; I would keep the conversation at the level of a chat rather than an interrogation. I even went so far as to order a pot of coffee to be delivered from the commissary, a demand so rare that the steward who took the order, when he thought I wasn't looking, shook his head as though questioning my sanity.

Ten o'clock arrived, but not Wolfgang Grilling. Very well, I told myself, allowances must be made. God knows, I should have grown accustomed to a certain amount of tardiness among musicians; Helena Becker, for example, was notoriously late for every appointment she and I made, and I had come to regard this habit as part of her charm — the profound and totally insincere apology accompanied by a sweet smile and the brush of her lips on my cheek. On the other hand, word was that if an artist were late for an appointment with Richard Wagner the fires of hell flamed up through the floor while lightning flashed through the ceiling. Face it, I said to myself, I am not Richard Wagner. Grilling will therefore make his entrance a quarter of an hour late and offer a profound and totally insincere apology. (No kiss of course.) I helped myself to a cup of coffee from the steaming pot (which did arrive on schedule) and sat back awaiting Herr Grilling.

Fifteen minutes past ten and no Wolfgang Grilling. I helped myself to a second cup. Half past ten. Still no Grilling. Coffee no longer steaming, lukewarm, barely drinkable. Eleven o'clock. No sign of Grilling. Coffee cold. My temperature beginning to rise.

I sent for Constable Gruber. "Gruber, I want you to go round to Grilling's rooms," I said, "and I don't give a damn if he's still in his nightshirt or in his bath, I want the bastard here! And no excuses, do you understand? I don't care if he's *dying*, Gruber!"

One hour later, at the stroke of noon, Constable Emil Gruber stood before me removing his helmet and wiping his sweaty brow. "Sorry, Inspector," Gruber said, his voice hoarse with excitement, "but this fellow Grilling —"

Impatiently I said, "Well, what about him, damn it —"

"He won't be keeping his appointment."

"And why the hell not?"

"He appears to be dead, sir."

"*Appears*? You mean he's *playing* dead?"

"Oh no, Inspector, in my opinion he is genuinely dead," the young constable said with such earnestness that for a fleeting second I regretted my sarcasm. "I have to report," he went on, "that upon arriving at the subject's premises I proceeded to make my presence known by knocking several times, each time with increased vigour, on the door of his apartment, whereupon, failing to achieve a response I sought the assistance of the concierge and immediately upon gaining entry with the master key I discovered the body of a scantily attired male person lying in a position consistent with —"

At this point I'm afraid I exploded in the face of the well-meaning constable. "For God's sake, Gruber, *please!* Enough police terminology! Tell me in plain language!"

"The subject … sorry … Herr Grilling … was lying on the floor. I immediately checked his pulse and determined that he was deceased."

"Other than feeling for his pulse, you touched nothing?"

"Nothing, sir, absolutely nothing."

"And you instructed the concierge to touch nothing?"

"I not only instructed her —" Here Gruber produced a key. "I made certain by relieving her of the master key." Gruber seemed about to add something but stopped himself.

"Well, Gruber, speak up. What is it?"

"I have to warn you, sir," Gruber said, "it's not a pretty sight. I mean the body, and the place itself. The concierge, poor woman, nearly fainted. As for me —"

"Gruber," I said, "I was investigating crime scenes and mutilated bodies when your mother and father were still wondering what they had to do to conceive you. Now be so good as to order a cab at once."

CHAPTER THIRTEEN

I should not have dismissed Constable Gruber's warning so curtly. The sitting room where Wolfgang Grilling's lifeless body lay looked as though it had been invaded not by a single intruder but by an army of intruders, so violently was everything strewn about. Underfoot lay a veritable stew of broken glass and crockery intermingled with crumpled bits of newspaper obviously swept from a large table used to hold books and periodicals which occupied a prominent spot near the fireplace. Someone, either the victim or his assailant, had desperately grasped the curtains covering the set of windows in the room, bringing down not only the thick green velvet draperies but the brass rod on which they hung as well as the wall fittings. Streaks of blood crisscrossed the curtains, stained the light grey upholstery of the armchairs on either side of the fireplace, and defaced in a particularly grotesque way a pen sketch of Grilling lying within reach of his body, its frame and mat bent out of shape. Every lamp in the room had been knocked over, every chair upended, every rug left askew.

Central to this disorder was the corpse of Wolfgang Grilling, lying face up, the head close to the fireplace, arms outstretched and wide apart as though held down by a superior force, legs similarly positioned. His throat, just below the Adam's apple, had been deeply pierced. Left carelessly across Grilling's chest was a sharply pointed iron poker, part of the fireside implements that stood in the overturned stand nearby, its shaft wet with Grilling's blood.

I removed my greatcoat and hat and handed them to Gruber. "Find a place to hang these. And better do the same with yours, Gruber. Looks like we're going to be here for quite a while."

Opening my notebook to a fresh page, I prepared to make a rough sketch of the position of Grilling's body when the door to the apartment opened and in strode my colleague Franz Brunner.

"I came as soon as I heard the news, Preiss —" Brunner stopped short. "My God," he said, looking about, "it looks like the Battle of Waterloo!" Then his eyes fell on Grilling's body. "Well, Preiss," Brunner said, shaking his head as though some extraordinary wisdom was about to be imparted, "one thing is for sure: this man will never sing again."

"Thank you for that insight, Brunner," I said. "Now then, right off I need you to interview the concierge. Did she see anybody arrive or leaving? Did she hear anything? There's a suite of rooms directly below this one. Did the occupants see or hear anything?" I turned to Constable Gruber. "It appears I won't require you after all, Gruber. Detective Brunner is on hand to assist. What I want you to do is this: find Maestro Richard Wagner."

Wide-eyed, Gruber said, "*The* Richard Wagner?"

"Yes, Gruber, *the* Richard Wagner. You have some acquaintance with the man?"

"My older brother sings in the chorus at the Opera House."

"So much the better, then. Find Wagner. You may inform him that Wolfgang Grilling has been killed, but he's not to be told any other details. Understand? Tell him

I must meet with him, preferably at his residence no later than four o'clock."

"What if —"

"No 'what ifs,' Gruber. Four o'clock. At his house."

Fervently Brunner asked, "You think Wagner may have done this, Preiss? The Commissioner will be thrilled!"

"Not so fast, Brunner," I said. "All I know at the moment is that Grilling was extremely unhappy about his role in Wagner's new opera and made no secret of it. He certainly made Sandor Lantos aware of it, and I believe Grilling's manager Friedrich Otto brought the situation to Wagner's attention."

"What could possibly make Grilling unhappy? I'm no opera lover, but one would assume that a singer would sell his soul to the devil for an opportunity to work with a famous composer, even one with Wagner's reputation."

"This is what I've managed to learn thus far, Brunner: At the audition for the leading tenor role in Wagner's new opera, Grilling lost to a virtually unknown singer by the name of Henryk Schramm and dared to express his displeasure to the Maestro very openly in front of a number of people who were present. The role he was forced to accept is that of a despicable secondary character, the foil for the hero. To make matters worse, Grilling loathed the costume Lantos designed, based of course on Wagner's instructions. And, heaping discontent on top of discontent, Grilling complained bitterly that his facial makeup would make him look like a Jew. Grilling went so far as to threaten to burn down the Opera House. He said so in no uncertain terms to Lantos."

"You knew about Grilling's threat, Preiss?"

"Yes. The information came from Lantos himself."

"And yet you did nothing about it?"

"In case you've forgotten, Brunner, the next time I had occasion to see Sandor Lantos, which was the day after my visit to his studio, he was as dead as your memory appears to be."

"Now hold on, Preiss!" Brunner said, taking a step toward me, his hands tightening into clenched fists. "You may be my superior but that doesn't entitle you —"

"Shut up, Brunner. I know exactly what's on your mind. My God, you *are* so terribly obvious, aren't you? You'd like nothing more than to run back to the Commissioner and have him cite me for dereliction of duty. I can hear you now, Brunner: 'Yes, Commissioner, Inspector Preiss knew all about the bad blood among Lantos, Grilling, and Wagner, did nothing about it, and now two of them are dead while that devil Wagner remains free!'"

Turning petulant, Brunner protested that I was being grossly unfair, that all he was attempting to do was assess the facts, that he hadn't the slightest intention of impugning my reputation behind my back. For a split second I was almost convinced Brunner meant what he was saying. But then he added, almost throwing the sentence away, "Of course, Preiss, you do seem to have lost the primary focus —"

"*What* primary focus —?"

"Well," Brunner began cautiously, "the Lantoses and the Grillings of this world come and go, and while it's unfortunate that their lives ended the way they did, life still goes on without too many ripples in the water, doesn't it?"

"Get to the point, Brunner."

"The point, yes, Preiss. The point is that we … you and I, that is … are charged with a serious responsibility —"

"You mean, to deliver up Richard Wagner to von Mannstein and the mayor on a silver platter, preferably bound and gagged and ready for summary trial, execution, and burial at sea."

Returning to petulance, but this time in a voice so quiet I wanted to throttle him, Brunner said, "You misconstrue everything I say, Preiss. I am absolutely committed to seeing that justice is done, as I'm sure you are —"

"Don't patronize me, Brunner. And understand this: so long as I am in charge, our primary focus, as you put it, will be as much to find and arrest whoever is threatening Richard Wagner as it is to satisfy the commissioner's and mayor's agenda."

"In other words," Brunner said, "you seriously insist upon viewing Wagner as a *victim* in all this?"

"I continue to view him as a genius."

"A *corrupt* genius —"

"A genius nevertheless —"

"— who believes that, being an exceptional man, he is permitted to do exceptional things even if he breaks laws that ordinary men are bound to obey. Come now, Preiss, aren't you too forgiving? You do have a reputation for being overly attracted to so-called creative types, even dazzled, one might say. Look here, Preiss: you say Wagner was furious with Lantos, and that he treated Grilling badly. A moment ago you gave instructions for Wagner to be available for interrogation at four o'clock and at his own residence. If it were up to me —"

"Which it isn't —"

"— Wagner would be arrested within the hour and the interrogation would take place where it ought to take place, at the Constabulary. What you are doing is tactically wrong, Preiss!"

"Brunner, this is not a debating society. I consider your remarks impertinent. If you're interested in rescuing your career you would do well to get below and interrogate the concierge without further delay."

"I fully intend to make a note of this conversation, Preiss, I warn you."

"Brunner, please feel free to write a complete memoir and publish it in tomorrow's edition of the *Munich Times!*"

With both Constable Gruber and Detective Brunner out of my way, I was at last free to complete my sketch of the room, its furnishings, Grilling's death position, and the general disorder surrounding his body. I tried not to think about Brunner's criticism of me although, in truth, he was not entirely wrong, and I had to admit to myself that if one can be blinded by sound, then I had probably had my vision (not to mention my good sense) clouded by the music of Richard Wagner the night I witnessed, albeit it briefly, the rehearsal in his house with Schramm and Steilmann of an aria from *Die Meistersinger*. Years earlier, in Düsseldorf, I had made the mistake of allowing my enchantment with the famous Schumanns, and particularly with Clara Schumann, to taint my investigation into a murder in which they were suspect. Was I about to make a similar mistake here in Munich? *Enough introspection, Preiss,* I lectured myself, bearing in mind the parting advice of one of my mentors at the Police Academy. "Remember, Preiss," he said, "examine the lives of others, but live your own life *un*examined."

My rough sketch completed, I surveyed the room one more time to make certain I'd included the important details. And then one thing struck me: If whoever killed Grilling had accomplished his purpose, why then were dozens of papers, mostly letters and envelopes, deliberately torn, many to shreds, and scattered about in a frenzied manner? I randomly inspected a number of these. Bills, a few personal letters apparently received from Grilling's parents and a sister, several invitations to forthcoming social events, a wedding announcement. Nothing worthy of special attention. If anything, it seemed that Wolfgang Grilling, despite what some would regard as his exotic profession, lived a rather unexciting life.

I was about to give up on this aspect when my eye caught a portion of an envelope lying not more than an arm's length from Grilling's body. It consisted of the upper right-hand corner and bore a cancelled stamp that was unfamiliar to me. With the aid of a magnifying glass, I recognized the crowned head of Catherine the Great beneath which appeared words that I could not read, printed in the Russian alphabet. Of the address only the letters "amm" were visible but the placement of these suggested they were part of the name of a person to whom the letter was sent rather than part of his or her street address. On the reverse side again Russian words, these handwritten, presumably part of a return address.

Why would Wolfgang Grilling be in possession of a letter from Russia seemingly addressed to someone other than him? I began to scour the room hoping to find a match for the portion of envelope but none was found. Nor could I find a letter written in the Russian language that might have been delivered in the envelope.

And then I thought of my Russian friend Madam Vronsky. She and Helena Becker were scheduled to return on the three o'clock train to Düsseldorf and it was now half past two. Carefully I tucked the envelope portion into an inside pocket of my jacket, seized my coat and hat, rushed to the street, and hailed a cab. "To the railway station," I ordered, adding, "and there's double the fare if you can get me there in ten minutes."

CHAPTER FOURTEEN

With only minutes to spare before the train for Düsseldorf was due to depart, I arrived at the railway station to find a jumble of humanity filling the platform: travellers dressed in their finest attire as though bound for Sunday church, powerful baggage men nimbly wheeling heavily laden luggage carts through the crowd; the air thick with the excitement of travel and the acrid smells of overheated oil and iron from the cars. Clouds of steam worked back along the platform from the engine that stood puffing and heaving like some gargantuan beast impatient to be let loose.

I began to panic. Where, in all this chaos, could I possibly find Helena and Madam Vronsky? And if they had already boarded, in which of the dozen coaches would they have settled?

As luck would have it, one person on that overstuffed platform stood out from the others. She was carrying a canvas and leather cello case. Of course it had to be Helena. Though she was far ahead of me I called out and miraculously both she and Madam Vronsky turned, having recognized my voice despite the din. Pushing my way through the crowd (and ignoring the odd "How rude!" and "Who does that man think he is!") I reached the two women quite out of breath. "Thank God for your cello," I blurted out, "otherwise I might never have found you."

Helena broke into a smile. "Why Hermann, how sweet of you to go out of your way just to say goodbye to us!" Smiling still, but with a shrewd look in her eyes, she said, "All right, Hermann, what really brings you here?"

The conductor in charge of Helena's and Madam Vronsky's coach interrupted. "Sorry, ladies, but the train leaves in a few minutes." He gestured toward the entrance. "Please."

I removed my police identity card and flashed it in the conductor's face. "I'm here on urgent police business," I said. "This train does not budge until I'm finished, is that understood?"

Looking shocked, the conductor sputtered, "But if they are under arrest —"

"They are *not* under arrest. I only need a minute or two."

"My God, Hermann," Helena said, "what are you up to?"

From my notebook I extracted the fragment of envelope I had found at Grilling's lodgings and handed it to Madam Vronsky. "Please look carefully at this," I said to her. "The return address on the back, can you read it?"

Madam Vronsky brought the fragment almost to the tip of her nose, then drew it away almost to arm's length. "I'm sorry, Inspector, my eyes are beginning to play tricks with me —"

"Here, Madam Vronsky," I said, and gave her my magnifying glass. "Try this, please. Take your time, it may be important."

Again the conductor interrupted. "Sir, I'm getting a signal from the engineer. We have a schedule which must be kept. These ladies must board without delay."

Ignoring him, I pressed Madam Vronsky. "Look closely … can you read whatever's there?"

"The handwriting is Russian. But I can only make out the word 'Minsk,' you see, on the back where the return address would be." Turning to the other side, she added, "The name of the person to whom the letter was addressed is incomplete, of course. I can only make out the letters 'amm.' Oh, and look here. *Srohchnoy pohchtoy*, which means special delivery. I'm sorry, Inspector, if that's not much help to you."

"It's an excellent start. Thank you, Madam Vronsky. I won't detain you further. Thank you again." I gave her a respectful kiss on the cheek.

Several cars back another conductor, apparently the senior one of the crew, pierced the air with a shrill blast of his whistle followed by a shouted warning that the train would leave in exactly one minute.

Helena gave me a wistful smile. "Both cheeks for me, Hermann."

Warmly I obeyed.

She touched my face with her gloved hands. "When will we see each other again?"

"This case I'm working on ... when it's over ... I know a spot near Lucerne. It's particularly beautiful in June."

"June of what year, Hermann?"

It was my turn to produce a wistful smile. "Be patient with me, Helena. I'll do my best."

"That seems to be my role in life," Helena said, "playing the cello and being patient with Hermann Preiss."

"Look at it this way, Helena: how many women can carry on two careers at the same time? Lucerne in June; that's a promise."

I waited for the two women to hustle aboard their coach. Then, with the station clock showing a quarter of four, I made a quick exit, hailed a cab, and gave the driver the address of Richard Wagner's residence.

CHAPTER FIFTEEN

I arrived at the Wagner residence precisely at four o'clock to be greeted, not by the Maestro himself, but by a woman whom I had never before met or even seen from a distance but whom I recognized in an instant. And why would I *not* recognize her? Probably no woman in Germany was the object of as much gossip as the woman now offering — with unexpected cordiality — to take my hat and coat. "You are Inspector Preiss, of course," she said. This led to an awkward moment or two for me. What to call her? As though reading my mind, she said, smiling wisely, "I'm sure you're well aware of our circumstances, Inspector Preiss ... I mean Richard's and mine. Despite the fact that we're — how should I say? — betwixt and between? — I refer to myself now as Cosima *Wagner*."

"Madam Wagner it is, then, thank you. The Maestro? We have an appointment —"

"Ah yes, Inspector. Richard is terribly occupied at the moment in his study. The pressures of his new opera, you understand. It is like giving birth not to a single child but to triplets. He begs your forgiveness and promises he will be along shortly."

The pressures of his new opera? Not a word about the murder of his set designer and one of his leading singers? But why bother this woman about such questions.

It was said that Cosima's love for Richard Wagner bordered on outright hero worship, that she had fallen under his spell when, as the sixteen-year-old daughter of Franz Liszt, she was present during Wagner's visit to her family home and heard him read selections of his poetry that would, years later, become part of his *Ring Cycle*. Recently she had left her husband, the eminent conductor Hans von Bülow, after thirteen years of marriage in order to devote her life to Wagner. In fact, the two had already had a child together, a daughter Eva, and there were rumours that she was pregnant by the composer once again. The flow of adoration was mutual, according to people close to them. Wagner's wife Minna had done him the favour of dying two years earlier thus bringing to a convenient end an unhappy marriage and leaving him free to live openly with his beloved Cosima.

Given the kind of blind faith Cosima was said to have in her hero, would she be expected to show concern for the two men associated with him who had suffered violent deaths? "The pressures of his new opera" … that was all that seemed to matter.

As for the "betwixt and between"? Well, living under the same roof as man and wife but without the supposed benefit of a marriage certificate gave cause for much scorn in German society. But who was I to scorn? The union of my own parents — a history of mismatching, poverty, frustration, and recrimination — was proof that a marriage certificate was no guarantee of wedded bliss.

"Please join me for tea," Cosima Wagner said, motioning me to follow her into the sitting room. "You know, Richard and I spent some time in England, and while he has mixed emotions about the British — not everyone in London loved his music — he did admire their daily ritual of four o'clock tea and those silly little sandwiches they like to nibble." Holding an almost paper-thin sandwich daintily, she laughed. "See, this is how the English eat them, as though they're eating flower petals. And this … *this* Inspector … is how these people manage to accumulate an empire! Can you believe it?"

She was tall and slim, plainly dressed but immaculately groomed. Her facial features and complexion resembled those of her father — a strong but attractive Roman nose, skin fair and flawless. Even in serious conversation she spoke with a half-smile which, in this starched and formal sitting room, contributed a much-needed touch of warmth.

"I hope and pray," she said, beginning to pour tea into two of the three fine china cups arranged on a silver tray before me, "that you're here to assure Richard that the threatening note he received is a mere hoax. I've done my best to allay his fears but he needs to hear it from someone in an official capacity, such as yourself, Inspector."

"I hate to disappoint," I said, "but an honest question deserves an honest answer, Madam Wagner. I am here because two men closely connected to Maestro Wagner, and indeed to his new opera, have been murdered."

Abruptly she ceased pouring tea. Her grey-green eyes were staring at me. "Surely you're not suggesting … I can't bring myself to say it —"

"That your —"

"Husband. Richard *is* my husband. Surely you're not suggesting that he's a suspect in those murders. If anything, Richard is as much a victim of events as are Herr Lantos and

Herr Grilling. One of his greatest and most important works is about to be given to the world and poor Richard is being torn apart!" As she uttered these last words, those grey-green eyes grew moist. "I cannot bear to see him like this, forgive me, Inspector." Tears were now forming and she dabbed her eyes with one of the carefully folded linen napkins that lay beside the tray. Experiencing now the depth of this woman's devotion to Wagner, I began to understand that even the most generous appraisals of that devotion offered by local gossips were grossly understated. However, I was not here to worship at Richard Wagner's shrine.

"Please, Madam Wagner, try to regard what is happening from *my* perspective. I'm confronted with not one but *two* challenges. One deals with the threat made to the Maestro. In my opinion, it is not a hoax. Despite your allegiance —"

"My *allegiance*? You call my feelings for Richard 'allegiance'? Richard Wagner, Inspector, is not some object of patriotism. He is the man I *love*."

"Very well, then. Despite your love for Maestro Wagner, you must be aware that he has many enemies. For example, your own father, Madam, has turned against him because of this ménage you and Wagner have established … not to mention political enemies, enemies in the artistic community, and, yes, a host of unpaid creditors. Were it not for the enthusiastic support of King Ludwig, this elegant tea set might well be in the custody of the bailiff."

Cosima Wagner put down her cup. "Inspector Preiss, it is one thing to be frank, quite another to be brutal."

"I make no apology, Madam. I do not earn my pay for being gentle. In a perfect world, truth would always be beautiful. Alas, we humans do not live in a perfect world, do we?

I repeat, Madam: in my opinion there is every reason to believe that the threatening note the Maestro received must be taken seriously. That said, my second challenge must be given priority at the moment. I refer, of course, to the murders of Sandor Lantos and Wolfgang Grilling. No, I do not believe Maestro Wagner is implicated, not even remotely. But someone is engaged in a plot to undermine him and the new production, someone who is prepared to stop at nothing to achieve his goal, not even murder."

I kept to myself the third challenge, namely the orders handed me by Commissioner von Mannstein and Mayor von Braunschweig under which I was commanded to excavate, as it were, the very earth under Wagner's feet and, like a worker in a gold mine, rise to the surface with some solid nugget of information that would warrant Wagner's exile from Munich.

"And you have no idea at the moment who such a person might be?" Madam Wagner wanted to know.

"Absolutely none," I replied. "My worst fear, of course, is that the killer may have a list. Lantos and Grilling may be only two, the first two. There may be others."

"Meaning Richard himself may be on the murderer's agenda?"

"Again I must be brutally frank. Even you, Madam, may be vulnerable."

"Better me, then. After all, Richard has so much to offer. But that's the way of the world, isn't it, Inspector? A man invents fire and gives it to the people as a gift, and they use it to burn him alive." She said this not with bitterness but with sadness and, I thought, resignation, as though Richard Wagner was doomed, like Christ, to die for the sins of mankind.

I thought about this last remark of hers for a moment, then said, "If you will pardon my frankness again, Madam Wagner, I find it amazing … indeed nothing less than amazing … that any woman would place any man on such a pedestal."

"Then you do *not* know Richard Wagner, Inspector. There is as much angel in him as devil, despite what you may have heard." Her eyes were clear again and a kind of tranquility returned to her expression. "One *can* fall in love with another's imperfections, you know. Take for instance your cellist friend … I believe her name is Helena Becker? … the beautiful young woman from Düsseldorf, and very talented too. Just performed here in Munich, did she not?" This last question she asked with another wise smile, as though she had managed to peek behind the veil I like to think I've erected between my public and private lives.

"I fail to see the relevance —" I began to say.

"Oh, but there's a great deal of relevance," she cut in. "You, too, Inspector Preiss, are not above being the object of gossip not only here in Munich but in other places as well. It's said that Fräulein Becker is in love with you despite *your* imperfections."

"*My* imperfections?" I pretended to be taken aback while, at the same time, dealing with my growing unease. "I wasn't aware that I had any."

"Dare I mention your past career in Düsseldorf?" Her manner was teasing now. "Your involvement with the Schumanns, Robert and Clara?" Her voice fell to a whisper as she added, "Especially with Clara. I mustn't speak her name too loudly. The very mention of her name brings out the worst in Richard. Word has it that one of the Schumanns, or possibly both of them, got away with murder literally, thanks to your infatuation with that woman. We all live lives of lights and shadows, don't we, Inspector?"

Carefully I put down my teacup. "Thank you so much for the refreshments," I said quietly but firmly, "and for refreshing memories I've chosen to tuck away for some years now." I glanced at my watch. "If you would be kind enough to fetch Maestro Wagner I would be most grateful. I *do* have some urgent business to attend to."

She gave me a steady look. "Then we understand one another, Inspector, I trust."

"Understand one another —?"

"I mean about Richard. What has happened to Lantos and Grilling is regrettable, to be sure, but the threat to Richard is what concerns me most and should concern *you* most."

"With all due respect, Madam Wagner," I replied, "my concerns are to a great extent determined by orders from my superiors, and to some extent by the degree of latitude which normally goes with my office." I rose from my chair to signal that, as far as I was concerned, this part of my visit was at an end. Then, speaking in as casual a tone as I could, I said, "By the way, Madam Wagner, does the name Judith Mendès have any special significance to you? Or Augusta Holmès? What about Cornelia Vanderhoute?"

I watched Cosima Wagner turn instantly into an ice sculpture. "You're absolutely right, Inspector. I should not delay for another moment your appointment with Richard."

With that, she rose, strode to the door of the sitting room and called out, "Richard, you are keeping Inspector Preiss waiting!"

CHAPTER SIXTEEN

Not surprisingly, Maestro Wagner did not bother to rise from where he was seated when I entered his study, nor did he apologize for keeping me waiting a half-hour. "Come look at this, Preiss," he said, his cerulean gaze fixed on an object the likes of which I'd never before seen. "It's a gift from the King, King Ludwig himself! A belated birthday present he calls it."

"Does it work, Maestro? I mean, to me it looks like a toy," I said.

"Does it work! Listen to this." Resolutely, almost fiercely, Wagner played what I took to be a fanfare, perhaps four or five bars of music. "The prelude to Act Three of my new opera," he said with evident satisfaction.

The king's birthday present to Wagner was a Bechstein piano with a full keyboard, but designed to sit on top of a desk. I guessed that two people could easily move the instrument from place to place. "The world's first portable piano," Wagner said, "and it is mine, Preiss, mine alone." He said this quietly, as though King Ludwig and he were the inhabitants of some deeply secret and exclusive society of gods.

Our young monarch's proclivities, despite the fact he had ascended the Bavarian throne only four years earlier, in 1864, were by now famous throughout Germany. Tall and lanky, with flashes of eccentric behavior that matched his extraordinary height, he had come in his short span of rulership to be known as the Mad King, understandable given that he was the descendent of the Wittelsbach family, a long line of royals whose chief contribution to German culture was to demonstrate down through the ages that even men and women wearing crowns and coronets could be utter fools. (One claimed to have swallowed a glass piano; another embarrassed the clan by loudly proclaiming abominable sins of the flesh before a crowded cathedral.) As for Ludwig himself, his sins of the flesh and other moral lapses were widely spoken of in whispers by his subjects, sometimes with envy but more often with disgust.

Ludwig's one redeeming quality was his patronage of the arts in general, and the art of Richard Wagner in particular. Indeed, it was said he worshipped the composer first and second, and God third. He must have been blind to Wagner's professed contempt for royalty, for Ludwig favoured the Maestro with a degree of largesse other musical geniuses could only dream about. Hence this latest gift.

"Can you imagine, Preiss, what this must have cost?" Wagner asked, shaking his head with awe. "Of course," he went on, "poor Mozart would have forfeited something like this in payment of a gambling debt; poor Beethoven would have pounded on it without being able to hear a single note; and poor Schubert would have pawned it to buy food for a week. I must count my blessings, Preiss, mustn't I?"

"Speaking of which, Maestro, I had the pleasure of Madam Wagner's company over tea while you were occupied counting your blessings."

"Ah, Inspector," Wagner said, his smile almost beatific, "no man on this planet has ever loved a woman as much as I love

Cosima. Of course, I would not expect you to fathom the depth of our love, Cosima's and mine. After all, you are in a profession not noted for the poetry of love. Besides, I'm told you are a bachelor, so what could you know of such things, eh?"

Stifling the urge to strike his precious new Bechstein with my fist, I responded, with an evenness that surprised me, "True, policemen are not given to flights of poetry as a rule, but I *do* enjoy the odd nursery rhyme. As for bachelorhood, it does have its moral advantages, you know."

Wagner looked dubious. "What moral advantages?"

"Well, take the matter of infidelity, for instance," I said. "As a bachelor, one can be unfaithful without leaving the trail of damage and destruction that an adulterous spouse leaves. Wouldn't you agree?"

Wagner frowned. "You'll have to pardon me, Preiss, if I'm not in a mood to be agreeable. I have more important things on my mind at the moment."

"Such as the unfortunate murders of your man Lantos and Wolfgang Grilling, you mean. Yes, of course, let us talk about that."

"Let us *not* talk about that!" Wagner said with some vehemence. "Their deaths are now *your* business, Inspector Preiss. As for me, whole days have gone by since I received that threatening note, and I've heard nothing but a deafening silence from our wonderful police force."

"Very well, let's deal with the question of the threat made against you. Until he was found dead today, I considered your tenor — I'm referring to Grilling, not Schramm, of course — as a suspect. I know for a fact that he was extremely resentful that you chose Henryk Schramm over him for the lead role in your new opera. Actually that is a gross understatement, judging from his reaction at the audition, and later from the bitter complaints he made to Sandor Lantos."

"I have nothing — absolutely nothing — to apologize for," said Wagner, his sharp facial features made sharper by a tone of defiance in his voice. "Grilling as a singer was competent; as an operatic performer, however, the man had no presence, Preiss; no profile, no personality. He occupied the stage like a rug!"

"According to Lantos, Grilling's anger was exacerbated by the designs you insisted upon for his costume and facial makeup. He said they made him look like a Jew."

Wagner suddenly sat bolt upright and let out a raucous laugh. "He did, did he? Well now, Preiss, I didn't think our late friend Grilling was so astute!" Just as suddenly Wagner's expression turned serious. "Of course the costume and makeup would make him look like a Jew. That is exactly what I had in mind, don't you see? The character of Beckmesser in *Die Meistersinger* represents the one poisonous element in German society today. The Jews, Preiss … *the Jews!* I take it you have not had the benefit of reading my article 'Judaism in Music.' It was published several years ago but it's still highly regarded among people of culture, people who care about the future of our great race."

I was aware of that particular tome but preferred for reasons of my own to confess otherwise, a confession that, as expected, brought a look of disbelief to Wagner's face. "My God, Preiss, are you deaf and blind?" he shouted. "Our 'friends' the Jews are professional plaintiffs. They keep up a constant cry in public and in the courts about how the Christian world oppresses them, even while they manage to sweep the wealth of the nation into their private hiding places."

"Maestro, I hate to argue with such a recognized authority on this subject," I said, "but it's common knowledge that Jewish bankers, especially the ones in Frankfurt, have helped to finance plans for German unity —"

"Yes, Preiss but with whose money? Ours, Preiss, ours ... yours and mine!"

"And their contribution to the arts and culture —"

"I suppose you're going to mention Felix Mendelssohn, eh? Spare me, Preiss. First of all, the Mendelssohn family didn't even have the courage to adhere to their origins and faith, so they converted to Christianity to enhance their personal fortunes. Secondly, despite his conversion, Mendelssohn's music reeks of Jewishness. Tunes to dance to, parlour ditties, a violin concerto that opens with a melody they chant in a synagogue!"

"Dare I mention Heinrich Heine then? No poet ever expressed his love for Germany as passionately as Heine."

Wagner looked away in disgust. "Preiss, you are so naïve, so pitifully naïve. I suppose during your earlier days in Düsseldorf Heine's poetry had an impact on people who didn't know better. But face it, Heine was another one of those converts of convenience who never understood the true German spirit. Do you know what he wrote once about us? Listen to this, Preiss: Heine is visiting in Italy, comes across a parade of soldiers, and notices that their officers are issuing commands to them in German. In *German*, do you hear? So what does our famous Jewish poet conclude from this? That German is the natural language of commandment? No! Instead he writes that we Germans are so accustomed to being ordered about that our beloved tongue is nothing more than the language of obedience. Do you know what I say about your wonderful Heinrich Heine, Preiss? He's been dead now a dozen years, and good riddance."

This line of discussion was proving totally fruitless from my perspective. "Maestro, I'm not here to debate what's good and what's bad for our country. I was hoping you might provide me with some valuable insights … clues, if you will … to help me solve the murders of Grilling and Lantos."

"And *I* was hoping you would arrive with news about the threat made against me. It seems, Preiss, we are both going to be disappointed today. In my case, I might add, bitterly disappointed."

As he said these words, Wagner half rose from his place at his desk, signalling that as far as he was concerned the interview was ended. Firmly I said, "One moment, Maestro. We are not quite finished." I made a gesture demanding that he sit, which, to my surprise, he obeyed. (It occurred to me in that split second that sometimes a *gesture* in German was more effective than a verbal command.)

"You're not here to announce that I'm a suspect, or something equally preposterous, Preiss?" Wagner asked this with a smirk, as though he were toying with me.

"I'm aware," I replied, "that you were furious with Lantos, and openly contemptuous of Grilling, but no, Maestro, in my eyes you are not a suspect."

"In *your* eyes?" Wagner looked at me suspiciously. "Are you saying that in somebody else's eyes I *am*?"

I lied without hesitation. "Not at all, Maestro. In police work we learn to rule nothing out, of course, but I like to think that I avoid the preposterous. I *do* need to encroach upon your valuable time to ask some questions concerning the threatening note you received."

With some enthusiasm now, Wagner nodded in agreement. "By all means, Preiss."

Sitting back in my chair, my fingers forming a loose tent over my chest, I said, "Augusta Holmès, Judith Mendès … those names seem to crop up in certain social circles in the same breath as your own name."

"For shame, Preiss! I thought you were a detective, not some idle snoop," Wagner regarded me stiffly, aiming that sharp nose, those steely eyes, at me.

Maintaining my relaxed composure, I went on. "Fortunately, Maestro, philandering has not made its way into our criminal code, at least not yet; otherwise many of us might be occupying prison cells."

The Maestro's lips formed a tight clamp.

I leaned forward. "The cliché about the wrath of a scorned woman … you've had enough experience in your time to become thoroughly acquainted with that particular phenomenon, haven't you?"

"Minor dalliances, that's all they were, Preiss. Here today, gone tomorrow," Wagner said. "Yesterday's laundry. Nothing more."

"And Madam Cosima, was she content with that explanation?"

"Our love, Preiss, is unshakeable."

"Well, thank goodness for that," I said, and added, "I assume your response would be the same in connection with another woman —"

"*What* other woman? There *is* no other woman, Preiss."

"I'm referring to one Cornelia Vanderhoute," I said quietly, studying Wagner's face for the slightest sign of recognition. None appeared. His expression became blank, and he shrugged as though the woman's name meant nothing to him. Softly I asked, not taking my eyes from him, "Are you quite sure, Maestro?" Slowly I repeated the name: Cor-ne-lia Van der —"

Before I could finish Wagner snapped: "I'm not an idiot, Preiss. I heard you the first time. Come to think of it, yes, the name's vaguely familiar. From Amsterdam or Rotterdam, some place like that in Holland. Soprano. Not solo material, but good enough to sing in the chorus. Last worked here in a production of *The Flying Dutchman*. I believe she chose to return to her homeland for some reason or other." Wagner paused, and I had the feeling now that he was studying *my* face to determine whether or not his off-hand reply satisfied my curiosity. "In any event, Preiss," he said, with another devil-may-care shrug, "I've lost track of her."

"Well, Maestro," I said, "it seems the lady has not lost track of *you*."

A blank look returned to Wagner's face. "Oh? That's strange. I don't recall receiving any communication from her. I must ask Mecklenberg. Perhaps she wishes to become engaged here in Munich again and has been in touch with him."

"I doubt that is the case," I said. "You see, the reason this young woman 'chose' — as you put it — to return to Holland was that she was pregnant."

"Really? Well now, Preiss, that's not unusual is it?" Wagner said. "Women *have* been known to become pregnant, you know."

"Indeed they have," I agreed, "but not all of them claim that you, sir, are the father, do they?"

Another surprise: Wagner leaned back in his chair, looked up at the ceiling and smiled. "My dear Inspector," he said with remarkable serenity, "if I had a thaler for every woman who has made such a claim against me, I would at this moment be ensconced in a proverbial castle in Spain surrounded by Moorish slaves feeding me grapes and pomegranates, instead of sitting here in Munich being a slave myself ... a slave to music, that is."

I said, "Fräulein Vanderhoute, with all due respect Maestro, is not your run-of-the-mill claimant. She alleges that she confronted you and that you cruelly rebuffed her, although you *did*, according to her, offer to put her in touch with an abortionist ... which, of course, is against the law."

Maintaining coolness under fire, Wagner calmly said, "Utter rubbish, Preiss. Wherever did you stumble across such a trash pile?"

"It may not surprise you that a rather thick dossier exists at the Constabulary containing records of your activities which extend far back, in fact long before I arrived to take a post here in Munich. The item concerning your relationship with this Vanderhoute woman found its way into that dossier. She had consulted an officer in our department with a view to bringing charges against you. I assume, however, that the resulting scandal would have tarnished her own reputation and she decided — or was persuaded — not to proceed. The matter *was* duly recorded, but the record itself was buried deep in the official file as though someone in the department for some peculiar reason hoped it would be overlooked."

With a touch of sarcasm Wagner said, "But you, naturally, went out of your way to unearth it, I suppose."

"Let's just say I was meandering through the dossier on a dull evening when I had nothing better to do. Tell me,

Maestro, would you by some miracle possess a sketch, or better still a photograph, of this woman?"

Wagner thought for a moment. "Yes, I believe —" he said slowly, "but why do you ask? Do you seriously think the threatening note ... no, Preiss, Cornelia would never be capable of such an act. The only thing is —"

Wagner abruptly silenced himself.

"Yes, the only thing? Please Maestro Wagner, I need you to be absolutely open about this."

"The only thing she did ... later, after the initial confrontation ... she met with me and demanded money. 'Pay up,' she said, or she would inform everyone in Europe that she and I ... well, I needn't go into details. Without admitting anything, simply to be rid of her, I offered her a sum of money. No trifling amount, I tell you, Preiss. She said it was not enough. I offered a bit more. Still insufficient. I refused a further increase, told her to go to hell. She cursed me and swore vengeance. But I'd been through this kind of experience before, and when she stormed out of that second meeting I put the whole ugly business out of my mind. As far as I was concerned Cornelia Vanderhoute was nothing but a blackmailer ... and not a very good one at that."

"And these confrontations took place where?"

"At an out-of-the-way tavern, the kind of establishment people like you and me seldom if ever frequent, Preiss."

"The picture ... may I see it?"

With a weary sigh, Wagner rose and bade me follow him across the room to a wall covered almost from floor to ceiling with framed drawings and photographs of himself, some alone, others in company with persons I took to be associated with him in his musical enterprises and productions. "Look here, Preiss," he said, directing my attention to a large photograph of what appeared to be the entire cast of an opera, all in costume. "This was taken the closing night of *The Flying Dutchman*. The young woman in the front row —" Wagner pointed her out with his finger "— is Cornelia Vanderhoute."

I peered closely at the subject, so closely in fact that my nose almost touched the glass. Wagner said, as though he were appraising a prize farm animal at an auction, "She's certainly well-endowed, isn't she?"

I looked closely again. "I didn't know you were given to understatement," I said. "Speaking of blessings, I would say she's *doubly* blessed."

"Well, Inspector, there have been no repercussions since she departed for Holland. If I were you, sir, I would waste no further time and effort in this regard. And now, Inspector Preiss, you must excuse me. I have Schramm and Fräulein Steilmann due here any moment for what will doubtless be an intense session."

As though on cue, the door to Wagner's study opened and Cosima announced, "Richard, Herr Schramm —"

"Ah, Schramm, right on time," Wagner responded, his approving manner reminding me of a stern schoolmaster. "But where is Steilmann? I thought you would be coming together as usual."

"Maestro, she apparently preferred to come on her own today," Schramm said. I thought he looked a bit embarrassed, but then I remembered that Schramm's instant rapport with Helena Becker at our dinner party the other night had not sat well with Karla Steilmann. Possibly a lovers' tiff had ensued as a result of Schramm's attentions to Helena. No matter, I thought. As far as I was concerned, Helena had done her work well on that occasion. Besides, my beloved cellist was now safely out of range, having returned to Düsseldorf, thus avoiding further entanglement with Schramm and, I was certain, staunching the flow of Steilmann's resentment.

Frowning, Wagner said, "Ach, these sopranos are all alike. Temperamental, arrogant, conceited. I should have written the part for a contralto. Next time I'll know better."

Turning to me, Schramm said, "Inspector Preiss, how nice to see you! Thank you once again for a splendid evening. Your friend Bolliger … I must say I've never seen a restaurateur strive so hard to please a patron. What did you do, Inspector, to merit such service? Save him from the hangman's noose or a firing squad?"

"Nothing quite so dramatic," I replied. "I simply saved him from his own base instincts."

"How so?"

"When I first encountered Ziggy Bolliger some years ago he was an excellent chef. Alas, he also had a penchant for stealing expensive ingredients … you know, items like rare truffles, Beluga caviar, and such. One of his victims, an importer of such foodstuffs, came after him with a pistol. I happened to come on the scene, persuaded the would-be assailant to put down his gun, convinced Ziggy to mend his ways, and the rest is culinary history, Schramm."

"Well, sir," Schramm said, ignoring Wagner's increasingly impatient look, "you must allow me to reciprocate. May I suggest dinner tomorrow evening, if you are free, of course?"

I answered with an exaggerated bow.

Wagner cleared his throat noisily. "And now, Inspector —"

"Of course, Maestro. Sorry to hold you up," I said. "However, before I go, might I have one more quick look at that photograph —"

I returned to the Constabulary by carriage, instructing the driver to cover the distance slowly. I wanted the time to think. The picture of Cornelia Vanderhoute ... I had seen her before. Of this I was certain. But *where? When? And with whom?*

And then it came to me. Came to me just as the cab pulled up before the main entrance to the Constabulary. Oktoberfest ... last Oktoberfest ... the woman dancing with Brunner, she with the impressively full bosom and a complexion as pure and fresh as farmer's cream.

Cornelia Vanderhoute. Who else?

CHAPTER SEVENTEEN

I wasted no time summoning Detective Franz Brunner to my office. Entering, he had a wide-eyed look of expectation, as though he were anticipating good news. "So, Preiss, I assume your little tête-à-tête with The Great Man himself yielded some real results. What have we got that will make the Commissioner a happy man?"

"What have *we* got? Well now, Brunner, I'm not certain what *we've* got, but *I* have come across something of more than passing interest. Does the name Cornelia Vanderhoute resonate with you?"

"Resonate? What do you mean 'resonate'?"

"Let me put it more plainly, then. Do the words 'Cornelia Vanderhoute' sound familiar?"

Brunner's brow furrowed, his eyes closed tightly, he pursed his lips, signs of a man searching earnestly, deeply, into a distant dark past. Finally he shook his head. "The name means nothing to me, Preiss. Why do you want to know?" As he asked this, his eyes, open again, fell on a sheet of paper which I had deliberately positioned on my desk exactly midway between us. The paper contained the report of Cornelia Vanderhoute's complaint against Wagner. I slid the report closer to Brunner's side so that it was now easily readable. He nodded. "Cornelia Vanderhoute ... ah yes, I see the woman's name," he said. "There's her signature, there at the bottom of the page." Brunner looked up at me. "What about her? What has she got to do with anything at the moment?"

"I have the distinct feeling," I said, "that you can answer that question better than I. For some reason, Brunner, your name doesn't appear as the complaints officer, but I recognize the handwriting. I'm sure you recognize it, too. The report is dated August 11, 1867. You happened to be on duty on that date." I paused, figuring Brunner was at least entitled to a sporting chance to offer some acknowledgement. When none was forthcoming, I asked, "Now, Brunner, is any of this beginning to 'resonate' with you?" Brunner shook his head and I thought I heard "No."

"Then I will continue. Bear with me, Brunner. When you recorded her complaint it was in August and she alleged that she was pregnant and spoke of the prospect of abortion. It's right here, in black and white. So is the name of Richard Wagner. I repeat: that was in August. Several months later, in October, at an Oktoberfest outdoor event, there you were, Brunner, dancing with the same lady, a woman of exquisite roundness in many parts but with a belly as flat as a veal cutlet. And energy? I confess I've not made a career studying the ways of pregnant women, but I have yet to witness a woman 'with child,' as they say, kick up her heels with such spirit!"

Brunner's face turned to stone. "What are you getting at, Preiss?"

"Whether or not Fräulein Vanderhoute was telling the truth about Wagner being the father of the child she was bearing I cannot say. Nor, I suppose, can you. But one thing seems clear: between the time you took her story and the time the two of you were dancing at Oktoberfest, her pregnancy must have been aborted."

"But she *was* close to Wagner," Brunner protested, though not as defensively as I expected. "Not just close, Preiss; intimate is more like it. But how —?"

I knew what Brunner's next question would be and proceeded to answer before he could speak it. "At Wagner's house I was shown a cast picture taken at the final performance of one of his operas. And there, in the front row, was a young female singer. And I knew I'd seen her somewhere before. And then it dawned on me. The woman Wagner identified as Cornelia Vanderhoute in the photograph is the same woman I saw dancing with you."

Brunner, who'd been sitting up to this point on the edge of his chair, leaned back, crossed his legs, and looked at me with hooded eyes, as though bored and indifferent to what he had just been told. "And your point is —?"

"My point is this," I said. "There are three possibilities here: one is that Fräulein Vanderhoute wanted directions to the nearest abortionist, and who better than a senior detective would possess that kind of information?"

"Oh come now, Preiss," Brunner huffed, "you know as well as I that abortions are against the law. What policeman would sacrifice his career —"

"Let me finish, Brunner. The second possibility is that the lady was lying, that, in fact, she was pregnant by someone *other* than Wagner but did some fine calculating and concluded that implicating the Maestro would not only give a boost to her singing career … you know, innocent ambitious little Dutch girl succumbs to celebrated but notorious German lecher … but might line her pockets with a thaler or two."

"And the third possibility?"

"Ah, now here's the most intriguing of all, Brunner. The third possibility is that Cornelia Vanderhoute wasn't pregnant at all, that her womb was, shall we say, *un*occupied at the moment she presented herself at the Constabulary. After all, Brunner, there's not a shred of medical evidence to support her tale, no doctor's report, not even a prescription from an apothecary, which is strange considering she professed to be suffering pains and nausea. Did she *look* pregnant, Brunner?"

"*Look* pregnant? Now, how the devil would I know that?"

"You *are* married," I said. "You have children, four if I'm not mistaken. I assume you're familiar with what happens to a woman's body —"

"Don't be ridiculous, Preiss," Brunner said. He was still leaning back in his chair, his posture affecting casualness but a distinct note of irritation in his voice now. "Of course I know what happens to a woman's body."

"Well, then, let me ask you again. Did Cornelia Vanderhoute appear to be expectant? Were there any outer signs?"

"She was wearing a coat of some sort. I really couldn't tell."

"A coat? In August? What kind of coat?"

"I'm not an expert in female fashion, Preiss. It was a *coat* … you know, with a collar and sleeves and buttons and pockets."

"Buttons you say? So, was her coat buttoned or open, that is, when she met with you to file her complaint?"

"It was buttoned. I suppose that's why I couldn't tell whether or not she was showing signs of being pregnant. Yes, of course, that's the reason, Preiss."

"So here we have presumably a warm day in August and this young woman shows up not only wearing a coat but one that is buttoned."

"I did not say it was a warm day," Brunner said, beginning to shift forward in his seat.

"August of 1867 was one of the warmest Augusts in years. The local press referred to it as a heat wave. How soon we forget!"

Angry now, Brunner shouted, "Damn it, Preiss, what do you think you're doing, playing some sort of game with me? What kind of coat? Was it buttoned or unbuttoned? Was it a warm day? I suppose the next thing you'll want to know is whether I personally conducted a physical examination to determine if the woman was in heat!"

"How clever you are, Brunner!" I said. "Yes, that is exactly the next question I was going to ask!"

"You may think this is all a joke," Brunner said, rising from his chair, his voice quivering with righteous indignation, "but I'm afraid I don't share your precious sense of humour." He pointed to the sheet of paper. "It's all in the report. Maybe you need to read it again ... more carefully this time."

"Oh, but I *have* read it, Brunner. Several times. And word for word."

"Then that's all there is, and to hell with you, Preiss."

It was my turn now to rise from my chair and put on a show of righteous indignation. "I'll thank you to remember, Detective Brunner, that I am chief of this branch; therefore, like it or not, you are answerable to me. And by answerable I mean a responsibility to fill in what I believe to be a gaping hole in this report of yours. I don't make it a practice to repeat your bon mots, Brunner, but I'm about to make an exception to the general rule. I believe you *did* personally conduct a physical examination to determine if the woman was in heat. Oh, not then and there, in your office, but in some private quarters in the course of a tête-à-tête — there's another bon mot of yours — the kind of get-together romantics like to refer to as a secret rendezvous. I prefer to regard it as mixing business with pleasure. Mind you, Brunner, I can't say I blame you. She certainly is a curvaceous young specimen and, I take it, a woman who is attracted to men of authority, be they famous composers or senior officers of the law."

Brunner's stance, all aggression when he rose from his chair, suddenly altered; his shoulders sagged, his long arms hung limp at his sides, the fingers of his hands loose, his head drooping. "I'm only human, Preiss," he said, his voice just above a whisper. "We may be officers of the law, but we're still flesh and blood, aren't we?" He looked up at me, inviting me to accept the notion that he and I were members of an exclusive male fraternity.

It was a notion I was not prepared to entertain. "Brunner, I might be inclined to go along with your 'flesh and blood' outlook on life but I'm beginning to believe your affair with Vanderhoute was more than a simple adulterous fling. Much more, in fact."

"Very well, Preiss, I'll admit it. I fell in love with her ... the moment I laid eyes on her. She was everything I wanted. We're both men of the world, Preiss, you and I, so you would understand. The difference between us is that I have a wife and four children that I must go home to every day of my life and —" Brunner shrugged, then gave a long sigh. "And there are times when going home to a wife and four children after a long day on duty ... well, you stand on the threshold, and you say to yourself, 'Do I really want to enter, or would I rather disappear?' Cornelia was my escape from reality, you might say."

"You've left out one other aspect of your burdensome domestic life," I said, making a point of keeping my tone sympathetic, figuring this approach would best draw some further truths from the man now looking rather helpless and pathetic. "Supporting a wife and four children on the salary of a detective — even a senior detective — must be stressful to say the least."

Brunner was quick to agree. "Oh yes, stressful, and then some. The wolf is never far from the door. You don't know how lucky you are, Preiss, with only your own mouth to feed."

"Speaking of luck, Brunner, let's consider for a moment how you sought to change yours."

Brunner's eyes narrowed. "But I've already explained —"

"Explained half. Now I want the other half."

"What other half?"

"The half which concerns money … money and the making thereof."

"Again you're playing some sort of game with me."

"On the contrary, Brunner this is no game, I assure you. See here —" I waved the report in the air, then replaced it on my desktop within easy reach of Brunner. "There is nothing — not one word — about Vanderhoute having gone to Wagner for financial assistance, is there?"

"But she *did* go to him," Brunner protested.

"And demanded money. Wagner offered a sum which she refused. Then, hoping to get rid of her, Wagner offered her a larger sum which she turned down as well."

Brunner suddenly brightened. "Ah, I see where this is leading," he said. "We would have grounds to charge Wagner with bribery. Yes, of course, that's it! I take it Wagner has already confessed to you, Preiss. A criminal conviction would be an absolute certainty in such a case. I have to congratulate you, Inspector!"

I held up my hands to restrain my effusive colleague. "I thank you for your kind felicitation, Brunner, but before you continue singing my praises let me come back to what I referred to a moment ago as the other half of this sorry business. I draw your attention to the fact that you neglected to sign the report as a complaints officer on duty would routinely do. Moreover, there is no mention whatsoever of the incident involving money which you now characterize as a bribe. I would have expected such details to be meticulously set out. But look, not a word; not even a measly punctuation mark!" Again I waved the report in Brunner's face.

"As I told you," Brunner pleaded, extending his arms in a gesture of helplessness, the palms of his hands open as though expecting a deposit of alms, "I was instantly and completely taken in by this woman ... her beauty, her innocence, her plight, her despair —"

"You left out something, Brunner," I said. "Namely, her ability to raise some ready cash. I was going to use the term 'easy money' but then you and I, being the seasoned policemen we are, well know that blackmail is not an idle pursuit. It requires planning, audacity, shrewdness, a perverse kind of courage I suppose. Throw in a pinch or two of greed. Put all of these into a stomach rumbling with a hunger for money. Then look for a collaborator ... preferably one who is thoroughly acquainted with the ins and outs of crime in all its varieties."

"You are actually accusing me of conspiring with that woman!" Brunner blurted out. "I cannot believe my ears!"

"Well, I could be euphemistic, I suppose, and designate your role 'Technical Consultant' to Cornelia Vanderhoute.

Would that suit you better? Let's cease this tedious circling around the topic and go directly to the epicenter. I need to know the woman's whereabouts, and I need to know *now*. Not tomorrow, not the day after tomorrow, but *now*."

Bluntly Brunner replied, "She returned to the Netherlands. Gone and forgotten."

"No, Brunner, that's not true. Every instinct in my being tells me she is here. Very much here, in Munich."

Brunner brushed this aside. "But she had no reason to remain in Munich."

"So you may think, Brunner. She shows up empty-handed after her failed effort to extract money from Wagner. As far as you are concerned, she is therefore of no further interest or use to you, so let her vanish to the ends of the earth. But vanish she did not. According to Wagner, Cornelia swore to get revenge for the way he treated her. In fairness, knowing the Maestro's ways with women, she probably had good reason."

"Even if your so-called instincts are correct," Brunner said, "what could a young woman like her possibly do in a case like this? Throw sticks and stones? Call him nasty names? Slip sinister notes under his door? You know how women act, Preiss. At most they bite and scratch."

"Wrong, Brunner. At most they go completely out of control and sometimes they even commit murder. Perhaps several murders. You know as well as I, Brunner, that when it comes to murder suspects, nothing — nothing — can be ruled out."

Brunner stared at me, a half smile on his face, shaking his head slowly from side to side. Quietly he said, "This is insane, Preiss."

I came around my desk and stood close to Brunner. "Detective, I could have you cashiered within the hour based on your little escapade with Cornelia Vanderhoute. But I'm going to give you an opportunity to redeem yourself. Find this woman and bring her in for questioning. I don't give a damn where you have to go or what you have to do. I want her in this office within the next twenty-four hours."

"Twenty-four hours! You can't be serious, Preiss. Munich is not a village. There are at least a hundred and one —"

Before Brunner could finish his protest there was a loud knock on my office door, and one of my junior constables opened it without waiting for permission.

"I beg your pardon, Inspector," the young officer said, "but there's a gentleman here —"

I recognized Henryk Schramm.

"Thank God you're here, Inspector," Schramm called out, rushing in. "You must come at once!" His chest was heaving and he was gasping for breath.

"Come where, Schramm? Calm down, man. Come where?"

"It's Karla Steilmann —"

"What about her?"

"She's dead. My God, Preiss —" Schramm burst into tears and seemed on the verge of collapsing. "Someone murdered her."

CHAPTER EIGHTEEN

"Outrageous! Intolerable! Unacceptable!"

Commissioner von Mannstein was reacting to the news of Karla Steilmann's murder, sputtering adjectives of anger in my direction as though it was I, Chief Inspector Hermann Preiss, who had done the terrible deed. I knew my superior to be a man of limited vocabulary and assumed that "outrageous, intolerable, and unacceptable" would pretty much exhaust his ability to express official displeasure. I was wrong. Out of his trembling lips poured "dastardly" followed by "despicable," then "deplorable," (indicating a modest gift for alliteration). I made as if to agree with him but his upraised hand silenced me. "I regret to say this, Preiss," von Mannstein said, his high tenor descending to a gravelly baritone, "but both the mayor and I are deeply deeply disappointed in you. Three murders in a row! All of them connected with Richard Wagner one way or another. It seems that wherever Wagner's shadow falls, evil lurks —"

"Nicely put, sir," I interjected.

"Never mind that," von Mannstein snapped. "I'm not looking for compliments from you, Preiss; I'm looking for results. Your report is as empty as ... as empty as —"

"A whore's conscience —?"

"Do me the honour, sir, of not interrupting! The plain fact, Preiss, is that our fair city of Munich, which should be known as Germany's centre of culture, is fast becoming known as Germany's centre of *homicide*! Tell me, Inspector: you have some knowledge of the ways of people in the arts; it has always been my impression that they die in more dramatic circumstances ... you know ... pistols at ten paces at dawn in some pasture, swordfights, maybe poisonings with strange potions concocted by hags and witches. But what have we here, eh? Two men and one woman, all slain with a piercing instrument aimed at the throat. Damned unfashionable, don't you think?"

"With all due respect, Commissioner," I replied, striving to be appropriately grave, "I have never come across a *fashionable* murder. As for people in the arts perishing dramatically, I'm afraid that is confined to people in the *literary* arts: novelists, poets, historians of questionable honesty, biographers who wallow in the sludge of scandal."

"You mean musicians are above that kind of thing, Preiss?"

"Above murder? No, not at all, sir. But their means are usually more subtle. They kill one another with sound. One man's music is another man's poison, so to speak."

"Then there's hope, after all," the commissioner said. "I've only heard one piece of music written by Wagner — thank God! — but surely there exists another composer who will come along and, as you say, Preiss, rid Germany of this villain. In the meantime, back to your report. It's rather sketchy."

"Fräulein Steilmann's murder was only brought to my attention late yesterday. I have not had time to complete even a cursory investigation. But I assure you that her apartment has been sealed and is guarded, and I expect to return there within the hour to conduct a thorough examination of everything in the place."

"Who discovered her?"

"A fellow artist. A tenor by the name of Henryk Schramm. She and Schramm were scheduled to attend a rehearsal session at Wagner's residence last evening. They are ... perhaps I should say *were* ... preparing for their leading roles in Maestro Wagner's new opera due to open in June. Schramm showed up for the session, but Fräulein Steilmann failed to appear. Singers are often rather fragile and unpredictable ... you know, sir, so much depends upon their physical state —"

This brought an unexpected chuckle from Commissioner von Mannstein. "So there's truth after all to the old wives' tale, eh, Preiss?"

"Which old wives' tale?"

"That opera singers never engage in sexual activity on the night before a performance. Supposed to be bad for their voices, makes them coarse, or some such nonsense."

For the first time since I'd joined the Munich Constabulary, I heard the commissioner giggle. Quickly he excused himself. "Sorry, Preiss, but I *do* have trouble taking these people as seriously as they take themselves. Please carry on."

"The rehearsal, much to Wagner's annoyance, had to be cancelled, and Schramm immediately went round to Fräulein Steilmann's lodgings."

"Why? Were the three of them romantically involved?" The commissioner cocked one eye, a familiar expression of his whenever he was suspicious. "This fellow Schramm, what about him? Were he and Wagner in some sort of tangle over this woman, is that it? Not tangle; triangle is more like it."

"No, sir, nothing that simple."

"Damn, Preiss! I was hoping it was that simple. Go on, then."

"According to Schramm, he arrived at Steilmann's apartment, which is on the ground floor of a building not far from the opera house. He knocked. There was no answer. He tried the door, found it was unlocked, entered, and found the young woman lying in a pool of blood, much of which seemed to have come from the area of her throat. A long hatpin had been left beside her body."

"A hatpin? A *hatpin*? What kind of man uses a hatpin as a murder weapon?"

"A man posing as a woman," I replied. "Or a woman, for that matter. More likely the latter, sir."

"I don't agree, Preiss," von Mannstein said, full of self-confidence. "Women are biters and scratchers, not murderers. You're a bachelor, of course, so I'm not surprised that you're unaware of that fact."

Where had I heard this insight expressed before? Ah yes, from Detective Franz Brunner no less. The wisdom of idiots, I told myself. But this was not the moment to challenge a higher authority. "I will certainly bear in mind your thoughts on the matter," I said.

"Not *thoughts*, Preiss," the commissioner corrected. "Accept the advice of someone who's had years of experience not only in the field of crime per se but in a more general field of crime known as women. Whoever wrote the story of the Garden of Eden got his facts wrong. It was *Eve* who was the serpent, Preiss. Still, women are not killers by nature, only tormentors. Carry on."

"The fact that Steilmann's door was unlocked and her rooms appeared undisturbed suggests that her assailant was invited to enter rather than making a forced entry. Perhaps the assailant was even known to the victim, but this remains to be seen."

"But what about this fellow Schramm? Isn't he a possible suspect? Come to think of it, Preiss, what about Wagner himself?"

The expression on the commissioner's face was so hopeful I hated to dampen it. "I never rule *any*one out, Commissioner, when it comes to murder. So I will certainly pursue every possibility and probability. But I have to say that on any list of suspects, Schramm and Wagner — at least for the time being — would be at the very bottom."

Impatiently von Mannstein demanded, "Then who the devil is at the very top?"

I paused. *Tell the truth, Preiss, commit yourself, and then if it turns out you're wrong, your career will never recover. Better to lie, be vague, suffer the commissioner's wrath, but at least leave a door open for yourself.*

"To be honest about it, sir," I said slowly, "I have not yet come to any conclusion about a prime suspect."

"Not even a *hint*?"

"No sir, not even a hint."

"Outrageous! Intolerable! Unacceptable!" von Mannstein repeated.

I held my tongue, expecting "dastardly, despicable, deplorable" to follow in quick succession. Instead, Commissioner von Mannstein called out to me as though he were God speaking to Noah moments before The Flood: "Preiss, our very civilization here in Munich is threatened. I want the perpetrator of these crimes in our hands before a fourth victim turns up. Until this ugly business is done, I expect that you will neither sleep nor slumber. Do I make myself perfectly clear?"

The only thing perfectly clear — much to my amazement — was that Commissioner von Mannstein apparently had once read something by William Shakespeare!

Stifling an urge to congratulate him, I replied, "Perfectly clear, sir," amazed at how obedient I sounded.

CHAPTER NINETEEN

In the immediate aftermath of Karla Steilmann's gruesome demise, a lighthearted evening spent as Henryk Schramm's guest over dinner at Ziggy Bolliger's was understandably out of the question. Instead, Schramm proposed a simple repast at his lodgings where we would share a fresh baguette, a wedge of Roquefort, fruit, and a red wine bottled at some château in France I'd never heard of, all of which Schramm had picked up at the only French pâtissèrie in Munich, located conveniently steps from his living quarters.

Perceiving that I partook of only modest amounts of the food and wine, Schramm said, "Forgive me, Inspector. I see that you are not an enthusiast when it comes to the products of France."

"No need to apologize, Schramm," I said. "As a matter of fact, *I* happen to be a product of France ... or so I've been led to believe." Schramm looked puzzled. "You see," I said, "some years ago when Napoleon's army invaded our part of the country, a number of French soldiers went on a rampage in my home town, Zwicken, raping and pillaging. My mother was one of their victims, and my father was convinced that I was the result ... the 'outcome' as he called me. I bear not the slightest resemblance to my father, which made him all the more certain that his seed was preoccupied elsewhere at the moment of my conception."

"That must have been quite a burden throughout your childhood."

"On the contrary, Schramm. The only burden through-out my childhood was my *father*."

"Still, he *was* the head of the household?" Schramm said.

"We — that is, my mother, sister, and I — preferred to think of him as the *tail* of the household. The happiest day of my life was the day I said goodbye to him. That was the day I left Zwicken to attend the police academy in Hamburg. Never saw the old man again. With a little luck, perhaps I'll manage to avoid him some day in heaven or hell."

"Well, at least now I don't feel guilty about your lack of appetite. Besides, with three murders —"

I did not wait for Schramm to finish his thought. "It's not the three murders that are weighing heavily at this precise moment, Schramm."

Topping up my wine glass, then his own, Schramm asked, "Oh? And what *is*, then? I would have thought that, as Chief Inspector, you would find yourself under enormous pressure to solve these cases, especially with all the criticism in today's press about police efficiency."

I couldn't help chuckling. "Press criticism? Schramm, the one good thing about being a policeman is that after a hard night's work you don't have to wake up to next morning's reviews in the newspapers."

"Is that the reason you didn't become a singer, Inspector?"

"It's the *second* reason. The *first* is that I didn't have a voice to speak of. No, Schramm what's troubling me chiefly at the moment is — of all people — you."

Carefully, Schramm put down his wine glass. His mouth and eyes collaborated to form a quizzical but cautious smile.

For a second or two he remained silent, like someone deciding whether to advance into or retreat from the topic. Then, that smile still present, he said, "*Me*? I'm afraid I don't understand."

"Ah, Schramm, that makes two of us. I'm afraid *I* don't understand either, and there's nothing I detest more than finding myself in a state of uncertainty like this. But since you're my host, and a gracious one at that, I feel that I owe you the courtesy of frankness, even though what I'm about to disclose is not unlike venturing into an uncharted swamp."

Schramm's eyebrows shot up but he still appeared amused. "An uncharted swamp! My goodness, Inspector, even in moments when I was being an incorrigible child my mother never referred to me as an uncharted swamp!"

I sat back, twirling the ruby contents of my wine glass with seeming idleness, but not taking my eyes from Schramm's. If he had any inkling of what I was about to dredge up — and I was now sure he did — then the young man meeting my gaze with a look of such complete self-assurance, even a flicker of mirth, without a shred of doubt had to be someone very much other than "Henryk Schramm." For a second or two I was tempted to come right out and tell him this. Then I thought: *No, a frontal assault may not work with this fellow Schramm, or whoever he is. Better to attack from what may turn out to be a vulnerable flank and reduce the odds of a blunt denial or counter-attack.*

Setting down my glass, I withdrew from an inner pocket of my jacket my notebook, its black leather covers faded into a shade resembling gunmetal, reflecting months of hard use and very soon needing to be replaced. Schramm did not fail to notice the notebook's condition. Still maintaining that look of amusement, he said, "Ah, the little black book! I've heard about that phenomenon in the work of policing but I've actually never seen one. So it *does* exist after all! Oh, if only the pages could speak, eh!"

"The pages needn't speak, Schramm," I said smiling back. "*I* speak for them." Then, from the centre of the notebook I extracted two fragments of an envelope and laid them on the table before Schramm with great care, as though they were precious jewels being offered for sale. "Do you recognize these, Schramm?" I asked.

Schramm responded slowly, his smile gone now. "No ... no, not at all."

"Would you care to examine them more closely then?" I nodded, encouraging him to pick up the two items, which he did, taking his time, turning the pieces this way and that, bringing them close to his eyes, holding them at a distance, examining the reverse sides.

"I have a magnifying glass —" I offered.

"Thank you, no. I'm gifted with keen sight."

"Splendid. Then you must indeed recognize that these are two parts of an envelope that contained a letter mailed to you from Russia ... from the City of Minsk to be precise. Am I correct, Schramm?"

I held my breath, waiting for ... waiting for what? A blunt denial? A startling admission? Or something in between, say, some form of obfuscation?

Schramm's smile returned, filled every bit with self-assurance as before. With almost a lilt in his voice he asked, "Is this your roundabout way of accusing me of some crime or other, Inspector Preiss?"

"I'm going to copy your custom, Schramm," I said, "by answering your question with a question."

"Ask away, by all means, Inspector."

"What is your connection with the City of Minsk? Have you lived there? Or are you related to people who live there? Perhaps you've performed there? Or is it possible that some part of your vocal training took place in that city?"

Schramm laughed good-naturedly. "Now hold on, Inspector! Those were *five* questions; I counted them. That's hardly fair."

"Schramm, my friend, one does not achieve the office of Chief Inspector because of a reputation for fairness. Please believe me, there's not so much as a milligram of fairness in all the blood that courses though my veins." I made this revelation about myself not with sharpness but rather in a tone of geniality, wanting to keep the atmosphere between us free of hostility. I followed this quickly with "You can also believe, Schramm, that I am not accusing you of any crime —"

"At least, not *yet*? Is that what you mean?"

"Let us return to the matter of the envelope, shall we?"

"Now *that* was *not* a question, was it? Very well, Inspector, back to the envelope. Yes, putting the two portions together, it is clearly addressed to me, and it is clearly from Minsk. Fairness or no fairness, I'm entitled to know how you came to be in possession of these. But first, another drop or two?"

I took up my wine glass, and extended it to my host. "In vino veritas, eh?"

CHAPTER TWENTY

Late that evening, following what Schramm jokingly referred to as "our petite picnic," I returned to my apartment thoroughly disgusted with myself. In part I blamed the menu my host served. I have long associated wine and cheese with the decline and fall of the French empire, the sort of dainty cuisine effete noblemen and their powdered courtesans thought of longingly en route to the guillotine. My own appetite demanded heartier fare ... well-garlicked sausage, potatoes, pickled cabbage, washed down with a reliable Munich lager, sustenance that fortifies warm-blooded Germans to defend hearth and home with sword and shield. Not wanting to insult Schramm, I bravely sampled the food, but only a nibble of this, a nibble of that, leaving my stomach largely hollow.

In part I blamed myself. I had every intention, when I presented the envelope fragments for Schramm's inspection, and after he acknowledged that the envelope was indeed addressed to him, to pursue burning questions concerning his identity and background. I hoped, of course, that faced with the evidence I'd laid before him, he would voluntarily open the vault in which, I was certain, he had locked away his true self ... *Very well Inspector, the truth about myself is* ... Instead, Schramm, very deftly I must say, turned the tables, and before I could drain what I vaguely recall as my

third glass of wine, I found myself in the uncomfortable role
of a suspect, Schramm playing the role of persistent grand
inquisitor, pressing me to explain how and where I came
upon the pieces of the envelope, while I, cursing myself
inwardly for having over-imbibed on an empty stomach,
managed to remain just sober enough to insist that this was
highly classified police information.

The result was a stand-off. Schramm told me virtually
nothing. I told Schramm virtually nothing. In the end, the
truth — or rather a number of truths — lay hidden still, to
be probed some other time.

Depressed over what I saw as failure largely of my own
making, I was about to seek comfort in a bottle of brandy
when my eyes caught an envelope the concierge must have
slipped under my door and which I'd overlooked when entering. And a welcome sight it was, for the handwriting was that
of Helena Becker. Even more welcome was the familiar scent
that greeted my nostrils when I held the paper to my nose, a
perfumed reminder of the times our faces touched, Helena's
hair loosened and spread across my eyes like a blindfold, our
fingers exploring each other's lips as though, sightless, we
were discovering them for the first time.

More welcome still was the news her letter contained.

Hermann dearest:

*As luck would have it, I shall be returning to
Munich this coming Friday. The Bavarian
Quartet has scheduled a performance of
Schubert's "Two Cellos" Quintet as part of
its Sunday afternoon program and it turns*

out that the cellist engaged to play the second cello part has had to cancel due to problems with her pregnancy. (I cannot imagine how one could possibly play such an instrument on a full stomach, Hermann. Can you?)

Knowing that I'm familiar with this music, they have summoned me to fill in. It's a magnificent piece, Hermann, one of Schubert's finest! I don't care, my dear, if you are investigating the mass murder of thousands of Munich's good citizens, I've reserved a front-row seat for you and expect you to lead the cheering.

And after the concert, Hermann, if you play your cards right, well, you may find yourself holding a winning hand ... mine! (Perhaps there'll be an encore or two as well!)

I do love you, Hermann ... as always without having the slightest idea why.

Helena

P.S. On hearing that I'm to play once again in Munich, Madam Vronsky, to my delight, and I hope yours, insists upon travelling with me. Her excuse is that Munich is so much more fascinating these days than Düsseldorf. What do I think? I think that despite her age (a secret she guards these days with less and less success) her loins throb with thoughts of you, Inspector Preiss! Again I wonder why.

CHAPTER TWENTY-ONE

The prospect of Helena's return to Munich and her presence throughout the coming weekend brought a smile to my face which was in place when I fell asleep that night, and still in place when I awoke next morning. In fact, it lasted all the way to the Constabulary. So evident was my buoyant mood that several of my junior officers, knowing my reputation for early morning irascibility, dared to wish me a good day, a risk they would never have taken most days.

And then Detective Franz Brunner showed up.

The look on Brunner's face — not unlike the look of a hound that had lost the scent of the prey — made words unnecessary. In a flash, my good mood was over.

"Don't tell me, Brunner. Your expression says it all."

"I swear to God, Preiss," Brunner said. "There isn't a nook, there isn't a cranny —"

"Yes yes, Brunner, spare me the clichés. Fräulein Vanderhoute remains at large, yes? What more is there to say?"

"At large, yes," Brunner said, "but there *is* more to say. I visited her last-known address … the one last-known to me, at least … in a rooming house not far, naturally, from the opera house. Fortunately, the landlady was forthcoming, by which I mean that she was a copious container of gossip. It seems Vanderhoute suffered no shortage of male attendants, the chief being one Thilo Rotfogel, who was a regular caller.

Of course, the landlady, being as she put it a God-fearing Christian, made it clear that the pair could not carry on their affair on *her* premises. Presumably they did so at Rotfogel's premises, which also happens to be in the vicinity of the opera house. How convenient, eh!"

"You looked up this fellow Rotfogel, then?"

"Yes. Thilo Rotfogel is a French horn player, Preiss. As a matter of fact, until recently he played French horn in the opera house orchestra."

"Until recently, you say?"

"According to him, there was an incident which resulted in his dismissal. It occurred during a rehearsal when the conductor — Richard Wagner, who else? — became enraged over Rotfogel's playing of a particularly crucial passage, so enraged in fact, that Wagner flung his baton clear across the heads of the other players and straight at poor Rotfogel. Luckily the missile struck Rotfogel's instrument. It was then that Rotfogel made his second mistake. He rose and protested that he had played the passage exactly as Wagner had written it. That protest resulted in Rotfogel's immediate expulsion. *Excommunication* is more like it, Preiss, because he claims Wagner shouted at him as he left the orchestra pit 'Rotfogel, you will never play in this city again!' Needless to say, Thilo Rotfogel is a very bitter man these days. In this respect, he and Vanderhoute are soulmates, you might say. Tell me something, Preiss: You seem to have a fair knowledge of music. Is there some peculiar quality about French horn players that makes them vulnerable to the sort of treatment Wagner meted out?"

Impatient to get on, I replied, "Look, Brunner, we don't have time for a lengthy discourse on the subject. I will tell you this: of all the instruments in an orchestra, the French horn

is the one untamed animal. Back in the sixteen and seven-
teen hundreds it was simply a coiled pipe with a mouthpiece
at one end used as a hunting horn. These days it has innards
that resemble human intestines, plus valves which suppos-
edly produce notes more accurately. But it's still a treacherous thing, treacherous for the hornist, treacherous for the
listener. So what occurred with this fellow Thilo Rotfogel is
the rule, not the exception. Now then, can he lead us to this
Vanderhoute woman, or not?"

"Well, that depends, Preiss," Brunner answered.

"Depends on what?"

"Let me explain," Brunner said. "Of course, he was curious to learn why I'm seeking Vanderhoute's whereabouts. I
couldn't come right out and inform him that she is a suspect
in one or more murder cases, could I? I mean, tell him that
and — who knows? — he might become as sealed as an oys-
ter. So I took an approach that I assumed would appeal to
him. I told him that we — the police, that is — are building
a case against Wagner in connection with his alleged abuses
of a number of women who have worked under him, including, of course, Cornelia Vanderhoute."

"Good thinking, Brunner. That loosened Rotfogel's lips?"

"Not quite. He knows where she can be located, but
there's a price for this information which he insists we
must pay."

"You mean he's looking for a *bribe*? That's totally out of
the question, Brunner! I'm surprised you would even entertain such an idea!"

I'm afraid my colleague saw through me as though I were
made of transparent glass. Smirking, he said, "This is hardly
the time, and you, Preiss, are hardly the person, to become

sanctimonious. Call it a bribe. Call it anything you want. The plain fact is, Thilo Rotfogel is prepared to co-operate, but first we must pay the piper."

"Pay the French hornist is more like it," I said, continuing to feign my disgust. "Very well, Brunner, what does the man want?"

"He wants us to see to it that he is reinstated as a member of the opera orchestra."

"He wants *what*? Is Rotfogel mad? Are *you* mad, Brunner? There's only one individual who can arrange to reinstate him and that individual is Richard Wagner. It would be like a dog chasing its tail. No, no, Brunner, totally out of the question!"

"No so fast, Inspector," Brunner said. "Rotfogel has a card up his sleeve, one that could trump our friend Wagner, maybe once and for all. Like it or not, the Great Man might have no choice but to put Rotfogel back in the orchestra pit."

"Please, Brunner, don't waste my time with another blackmail scheme. It didn't work when your friend Vanderhoute tried it. She achieved absolutely nothing with Wagner. The man has the ability to brazen his way through an avalanche of scandal if need be, as he has already clearly demonstrated."

"Ah yes," Brunner said, "but he will not brazen his way through the kind of avalanche Herr Rotfogel can stir up. Trust me."

Trust Detective Franz Brunner? Now *there* was a challenge! But beggars can't be choosers. Even if Brunner were grossly exaggerating the usefulness of this man Rotfogel, all for the sake of ingratiating himself with me, the plain fact was that I was desperately in need of whatever scraps of information I could possibly patch together, no matter whom they came from. I was a curator, not of a collection of tangible evidence, but of a collection of people — living curiosities, flesh and blood to the eye yet unfathomable, untrustworthy, conniving, everyone seemingly filing onto my stage carrying his or her own bundle of plots and lies, and at the centre of the stage, Richard Wagner himself, principal plotter and liar. Under the circumstances I had no choice but to go along with Brunner.

"Very well, Brunner," I said with a pessimistic sigh, "fetch this man Rotfogel. I want to see him before he, too, somehow ends up a statistic in this whole affair."

"No fear of that," Brunner responded, suddenly looking pleased with himself. "Thilo Rotfogel is here, waiting outside in the hall. As you can see, Preiss, I am leaving no stone unturned. But a word of caution: Don't be put off by Rotfogel's appearance. He is not what you might expect."

CHAPTER TWENTY-TWO

At first glance, Thilo Rofogle brought to mind an admonition delivered by my mother whenever, as a child, I expressed repulsion over someone's physical appearance. "Remember, Hermann," she would say, "we are creatures of God. He loves us all, each and every one. Therefore we too must love each and every one."

My father, on the other hand, adhered unswervingly to a set of self-made rules that governed his reaction to people's physical characteristics. "Remember, Hermann," he would say, in tones as solemn as my mother's, but grimacing as though he had just swallowed vinegar, "small eyes are a sign of a sneaky personality; warts are a sign of an evil mind; and beware of men who are underweight because they will cut your throat for a crust of bread!"

I will swear on the Bible that I made an earnest attempt to look at Thilo Rotfogel through my mother's charitable eyes. But it was no use. Rotfogel's features met my father's criteria one by one and to perfection. To regard this fellow as a creature of God would have taxed even the most willing believer. Two things were beyond imagination: that Rotfogel could manufacture sufficient wind to bring alive the most fickle musical instrument ever invented; and that Rotfogel could manufacture sufficient charm that Cornelia Vanderhoute would agree to share a bed with him not just once, apparently, but several times. Like Shakespeare's Cassius, Rotfogel had a lean and hungry look made more pitiable by ill-fitting clothes. Indeed, had he extended a hat, or perhaps a tin cup, I would have made a donation without a second thought. Instead, he extended a bony hand, and as I shook it I realized what Cornelia Vanderhoute saw in Thilo Rotfogel. Two gold rings adorned the fingers of his right hand, mounted on one of them a diamond which I estimated to be at least two carats. My attention was then drawn to his left hand, similarly graced with two gold rings, each bearing a precious stone, one a ruby, the other a sapphire. His jacket was open, revealing across his vest an expanse of gold chain anchored at one end by a gold pocket watch. His neckwear, though a simple unstylish black silk cravat, was nevertheless fixed into place by a diamond stickpin.

What could be more obvious? What Fräulein Cornelia Vanderhoute saw in French hornist Thilo Rotfogel was money!

Shunning perfunctory words of welcome, I came swiftly to the point. "Allow me to compliment you, Herr Rotfogel, on your choice of accessories. I see that you are a connoisseur of fine jewelry."

This brought an appreciative smile to Rotfogel's face. "Look here, Inspector," he said, proudly displaying a handsome set of cufflinks. "Genuine black opals no less!"

"Very impressive, sir," I said. "In my next life I intend to take up the French horn. It's clearly a much more lucrative career than mine."

Rotfogel quickly demonstrated that he was no fool. "You don't believe a word of what you've just said, Inspector. What you're really wondering is how I, a humble musician, can possibly afford what you call my 'choice of accessories.' So let me clear the air at once. I have lived all my fifty years as a bachelor, and a content one at that. Fortunately, I have only myself upon whom to shower my largesse, you see. Until a recent lamentable experience with a certain bastard conductor, I was much in demand and earned a steady living because French horn players do not grow on trees. At the risk of boasting, I'm one of the few who can play the *early* version of the instrument, which is no simple trick. Playing Vivaldi concertos on an early instrument, for instance, takes a certain genius because one must master the art of handstopping."

"I'm familiar with Vivaldi's music," I said, "most of which sounds to me as though it was composed on one very long sheet of paper, then cut into sections and sold by the metre. But what is 'handstopping'?"

"Ah, Inspector, it involves inserting a hand in the bell of the French horn, by which means one can flatten the pitch to produce chromatic notes. Believe me, sir, not every Fritz, Heinz, and Jürgen can do this! And bear in mind, too, that even a tiny bit of condensation from a player's breath can cause cracked notes. This does not happen with Thilo Rotfogel, sir. Not on a modern horn nor on an original horn. Never!"

"I'm beginning to understand something, Herr Rotfogel," I said. "Despite your age, and your apparent contentment with bachelorhood, women must be drawn to you because of this unique power of yours. Do you give private performances on your French horn for them?"

"Of course you are jesting," Rotfogel responded with a knowing grin. "No, I do not give private performances … at least, not on my French horn, if you take my meaning."

"You mean your prowess is not restricted to what you call handstopping?"

"Don't be misled by my physique, Inspector," Rotfogel said. "Despite my age and bachelorhood, as you put it, I know how to give pleasure to a woman."

"I'm pleased for your sake, sir," I said, "but does giving pleasure involve showering them with your largesse ... that is, when you're not too busy showering your*self*?"

"Ah, you are referring specifically to Fräulein Vanderhoute, are you not? Very well, yes, in her case it was more of a *flood* than a shower. And why not? It was she who opened my eyes, you might say."

"Opened your eyes to what —?"

"How can I put it delicately —?"

"Please, Rotfogel, I'm as much a man of the world as you. Let's dispense with delicacy. To what did Cornelia Vanderhoute open your eyes?

"Let me put it this way," Rotfogel replied, after taking a moment to think about his answer. "We Germans can learn a few things from Hollanders about what goes on in our bedrooms. Our Dutch friends display a certain fervency, a certain inventiveness, which we lack in this regard. I think it's because their country, lying so low and under constant threat from the sea, encourages in the inhabitants a sense of urgency, a sense of devil-may-care that frees them from puritan constraints."

"And so there was an ideal reciprocal arrangement," I said. "You were generous when it came to money. Fräulein was generous when it came to the boudoir."

"Ideal? No not quite," Rotfogel said. "Other men were attracted to her, which is not surprising. As for me, Inspector ... well, look at me. Do I look like the kind of man who could have claims to exclusivity with a woman like Cornelia

Vanderhoute? Of course not. But I'm enough of a man to be jealous of the attention others paid her."

"Were you aware that 'others' included Richard Wagner?"

"No, I was not," Rotfogel said, "not until your colleague Detective Brunner informed me."

"Then you must feel especially betrayed ... by her, I mean."

"Believe it or not," Rotfogel replied, "I feel nothing but *pity* for her. It's Wagner who is the villain here, not Cornelia. You see, she confessed to me that she was pregnant. She declined, however, to say by whom. I knew it could not be by me. The kind of 'relations' we engaged in ruled out the possibility of pregnancy. More of this I need not mention in detail. You say you are a man of the world, Preiss, so you will no doubt understand. But when Brunner explained to me that you are amassing evidence of Wagner's abuses against a number of women with whom he's been involved, and knowing Cornelia could well be one of such women ... after all, she had sung for several years in the opera chorus and even a totally blind man would have been keenly aware of her voluptuousness ... well, sir, I feel a moral obligation to do whatever I can."

"Splendid!" I said. "Then tell us where we may locate Fräulein Vanderhoute. Detective Brunner and I are eager to obtain a statement from her. There are rumours that she returned to Holland but we have reason to believe she is still here in Munich. Needless to say, she could be a very valuable witness."

Rotfogel shook his head. "She realizes that she has been living — shall we say — a somewhat overactive life and prefers to remain in seclusion for the time being. I feel bound to honour her wishes. You understand, Inspector, that she has a right to privacy which we must respect."

"But you said a moment ago that you feel a moral obligation to do whatever you can —" I was aware that unconsciously I had clenched my fists and that I was straining to remain civil with this man. The rules of my office prohibited physical assault but the temptation to circle Thilo Rotfogel's scrawny neck with my bare hands was almost overwhelming. "I take it, Rotfogel, that your 'moral obligation' comes with a price tag. You want us to intercede on your behalf with the Maestro so that you can return to your post with the opera orchestra. But aren't you being selfish? Aren't you placing your personal interests above those of the woman for whom you profess to feel pity?"

"The way I see the situation," Rotfogel said calmly, as though analyzing a financial statement or the results of a laboratory test, "the gods have handed me a golden opportunity. You see, Inspector Preiss, the humiliation I suffered when Wagner ordered me out that day weeks ago, and without a speck of justification, was enough to crush any man's spirit once and for all. But now ... now, at last! I can, and I *will*, bring Richard Wagner to his knees ... with the weight of Munich's Chief Inspector of Police, no less, behind me."

"Be sensible, Rotfogel," I said. "Fräulein Vanderhoute has nothing to fear from speaking to me. It is Wagner, as you yourself say, who is the villain." I hoped this lie would be convincing. "Tell us where we may find her. It is for her own good."

Again Rotfogel shook his head. "No no, Inspector Preiss," he said. "First give me Wagner. Then I will give you Vanderhoute."

CHAPTER TWENTY-THREE

Helena Becker's return to Munich on the Friday train from Düsseldorf turned out to be a frenzied affair. An engine breakdown halfway along the route resulted in a three-hour delay in her arrival. Met at the station by the frantic leader of the Bavarian Quartet, Helena had time only to blow me a kiss and wave an elegantly gloved hand before being whisked away for her first rehearsal with the group, leaving me to escort Madam Vronsky to the Eugénie Palace and see to it that she was comfortably settled in her room.

"Thank you for being so gracious," Madam Vronsky said, giving me a sympathetic smile. "I'm sure you'd rather have Helena's company instead of wasting your time with mine."

"Not so," I said. "In fact, things couldn't have worked out better for me. You see, Madam Vronsky, I have a little job for you ..."

"So, Inspector, a second piece of the Russian puzzle —"

Madam Vronsky was holding both fragments of the envelope addressed to Henryk Schramm up to the light streaming through the windows of her room at the Eugénie Palace, as though the paper were translucent and, thus exposed, might reveal some secret code. "I'm sorry to disappoint you," she said, pouting, "but the second piece contains nothing more than the name of the sender and his address in Minsk. And here I thought you and I were about to share a moment of high drama. The least you can do is tell me what this is all about. After all, I *am* appointed your official translator. Which brings up a question: Surely there are others in a cosmopolitan city like Munich who could have translated this for you?"

"I don't trust 'others,'" I replied. "True, Munich is cosmopolitan, but whisper a secret at one end of Munich at eleven in the morning and by noon everyone at the other end will be chattering about it. It's one of the lessons a policeman learns his first day on the job."

"Oh, I see. So you're worried that if you tell me more about Schramm and this mysterious business with the envelope, an hour from now I'll be mounted on a makeshift pedestal at Marienplatz shouting the news to thousands of passersby."

"You're pouting again," I said. "Mind you, you do have a particularly fetching way about you when you're like this."

"Shame on you, flirting with an old woman!"

She pretended to scold me. I pretended to be contrite. "You've always been able to see through me, haven't you, Madam Vronsky."

"If you're referring to your ambitions back in Düsseldorf … your dream of playing Beethoven's sonatas as they should be played … yes, I did see through your … shall we be charitable and say your digital deficiencies. And I told you so honestly, did I not?"

"And that is exactly why I trust you," I said.

"But not enough to tell me the details behind these envelope fragments —"

I threw up my hands in a gesture of helplessness. The fact was that, up to this point, I had chosen not to tell a soul about my discovery of the second fragment. Larger than the first, its torn edges closely matched those of the other fragment. Whoever had possession to begin with must have disposed of the letter the envelope contained, for try as I might I failed to find even the most minute portion. What was especially confounding was that the first fragment had shown up in the lodgings of Wolfgang Grilling, while the second was located — of all places — in the bedroom of Karla Steilmann, tucked away under a neatly bundled stack of letters in the drawer of her night table. I had not the slightest notion who initially would have had access to this piece of mail. Nor had I the slightest notion as to why both Grilling and Steilmann would have had an interest in it.

Purloined letters were the stuff of playwrights and novelists, an all-too-convenient and rather tawdry literary device I had long regarded with derision. In real life, I told myself, this kind of thing simply didn't happen.

Until now, that is.

"I apologize, Madam Vronsky, I sincerely do," I said. "Here you are, once more about to do me a great favour, in return for which I'm compelled to stand before you tight-lipped and seemingly ungrateful."

She gave me a forgiving smile. "Apology accepted," she said, adding quickly, "though now I understand what Helena means when she speaks of you. She says what you demand most from a woman is a bottomless well of patience. Those are her exact words, not mine, my dear Preiss … a bottomless well of patience. A word of advice, if I may: even a bottomless well may run dry. Ah, but I see that your eyes are fixed once again on these —"

She held the envelope fragments in the open palm of her hand, the two pieces, when joined, forming an almost perfect whole. "To business, then. The return address reads: Professor M.J. Klayman, care of Imperial Conservatory of Music, Minsk. The penmanship is that of an educated person, done with a certain flourish and meticulous punctuation."

"Does the name 'Professor Klayman' sound familiar to you?"

"Again I'm sorry to disappoint you. No it does not. But two things immediately come to mind: Klayman is a fairly common Jewish surname. And any Jew holding a professorship in a Russian institute of higher learning must be a man of remarkable accomplishment. There's an old saying, Inspector Preiss: *In the heart of every Russian there's a cold spot for a Jew.* Of course, it's possible that this Professor Klayman has converted to Christianity in order to secure his position. After all, here in Germany some Jews have resorted to conversion to advance their careers."

"Would a conservatory in Minsk typically have an opera department?"

"Most definitely. Opera is very popular in Russia among the upper class. Attending the opera is a kind of status symbol in high society. The women sit fanning themselves, imprisoned in their tight corsets; the men sit perspiring in their evening clothes and military tunics; everyone, having overeaten beforehand, tries desperately not to belch or let wind; and during intermissions they pretend they're French and fawn all over one another. Why, even your Richard Wagner has had his works performed in Russia, although his experience as a conductor of an opera orchestra there has gone down in the annals as the greatest upset caused by any foreigner since Napoleon's invasion! It's one of the choicer bits of gossip to come out of my humdrum homeland in at least a generation, believe me. Oh, but you've undoubtedly got too many urgent concerns and too little time on your hands for gossip, so we'll leave it for another time."

"No, Madam Vronsky," I said hastily, "please ... gossip is to a policeman what —" I paused, struggling for a suitable comparison.

"What mother's milk is to a baby?" Madam Vronsky offered, coming to my rescue. "Very well, to gossip, then. Maestro Wagner toured a couple of Russia's major cities several years ago ... I think it was during the year 1862 ... and tales were circulating throughout the musical world that he was in every kind of trouble imaginable. He had separated from his wife Minna; he was drowning in debt; he'd had some colossal failures in Paris and Vienna, and performances of his operas had ground to a halt. He was desperately in need of a patron but none was then even distantly on the horizon. The journeys by train to Moscow and St. Petersburg were exhausting, what with sleepless nights and unbearable food. His ability to communicate to Russian musicians was limited, some German here, some French there, an occasional bit of Italian, all delivered at the top of Wagner's lungs on the supposition that the best way to speak to people who don't understand a word you're saying is to shout at them. And shout he did, so much so that at one point in Wagner's first rehearsal with the orchestra in St. Petersburg the concertmaster, a violinist who happened to be fluent in German, shouted back at Wagner. "We're not deaf, Maestro Wagner," he said, "and what's more, we are accustomed to beginning a piece not on the *up*beat but on the *down*beat. In fact, we are having difficulty following your beat altogether."

"Was this fellow — this violin player — insane?" I asked. "Nobody ... not even The Holy Trinity ... would dare speak that way to Richard Wagner."

"Wait, Inspector, that's not all. A few minutes into the first selection, Wagner's *Overture to Rienzi*, the Maestro yelled at the musicians to stop. He ordered the first violin section to replay the passage they had just played, which they did, then demanded they play it again, glaring at them the whole time, watching every move they made as though through a microscope. Signalling the concertmaster to rise from his chair and come forward to the podium, Wagner shouted to the members of the orchestra, 'You see, this is what happens to a violin section when there is total absence of discipline, of leadership, all the bows going in different directions like bulrushes in a windstorm instead of in unison.' Pointing accusingly at the concertmaster, Wagner went on: 'And *this* one should be in charge of a band of gypsies on a street corner, not sitting at the first desk in a concert hall in St. Petersburg. But then, what else would one expect from a man with a name like Simon Socransky, eh?'

"With that, Wagner summoned the orchestra manager, declared that he would not proceed so long as 'that Jew Socransky' was present, whereupon the unfortunate Simon Socransky was dismissed on the spot."

I was shocked that an orchestral player could be sacked in such a summary fashion, but Madam Vronsky explained that musicians were regularly hired and fired at will, even the most senior of them. "It's a precarious way to earn a living," she said, "especially when your fortunes on any given day depend upon which side of the bed the conductor arose that morning."

"Tell me, Madam Vronsky, how did you come to hear of this incident? You seem to know all the gory details as though you were actually there."

"In the world of music and musicians, bad news travels faster than an off-key entrance," she replied.

"But if I understand you correctly, hirings and firings are not all that unusual or remarkable," I said.

"Ah, but this was both unusual *and* remarkable, Inspector. And tragic, too. Horribly tragic. You see, Simon Socransky was distraught; after all, he'd slaved for years to achieve the high position of concertmaster, had been obliged to spend much of each year away from home and family in order to hold the post in St. Petersburg, suffered such appalling humiliation right there in front of the entire orchestra, then found himself suddenly and cruelly unemployed. And so he returned to his native city … but in a coffin."

"You mean he took his own life?"

"Suicide. Yes."

"Where was he from? Where did his family live?"

Madam Vronsky paused, rubbing her forehead, a slight frown showing between her beautifully manicured fingers. Slowly she replied, "Well now, Inspector Preiss, that's an odd coincidence, isn't it?"

"What's an odd coincidence, Madam?"

"Come to think of it, Simon Socransky was from Minsk."

CHAPTER TWENTY-FOUR

"The strangest thing happened today, Hermann. You will never guess in a million years who showed up at our rehearsal!" Helena Becker had a peculiar look in her eyes and I knew instinctively that even if I were to guess correctly, I would not be pleased with the answer.

"You know how I despise guessing games," I said.

"Oh, don't be so petulant!" she said, giving my shoulder a not-too-gentle poke. "Go on, guess."

"Very well. Schubert. Old Franz himself."

"That's ridiculous, Hermann. Schubert died exactly forty years ago."

I pretended to be surprised. "He did? Funny, there's not a word about it in his police record."

"What police record? I never knew Franz Schubert had a police record."

"Ahah! So the great Helena Becker still has a thing or two to learn about life in the musical world. Your turn to guess."

Fascination was written all over Helena's face now. "Stop being coy, Hermann. What police record?"

"Tit for tat," I said. "You tell me who was the mystery guest at your rehearsal, and I'll reveal the secret about Schubert."

"Henryk Schramm, that's who. Now what about Schubert?"

Of course there was no police record concerning the late composer, so hastily I fabricated one. "When he was nine years old Schubert stole a tune from Josef Haydn. Now then, what was Henryk Schramm up to?" The expression on my face made it clear that I was indeed not pleased with Helena's news.

"Henryk Schramm wasn't 'up to' anything," she shot back defensively. "In fact, I thought it was rather sweet of him, sneaking in and sitting all by himself in the back row of the hall."

"I take it Schramm just happened to find himself in the neighbourhood and dropped in to say hello, eh?"

"Actually, Hermann, he stayed right from beginning to end," Helena replied, relishing the feeling of annoyance mixed with jealousy which I tried, but failed, to conceal.

"And afterward —?"

"Afterward I was famished. After all, I'd gone straight to the rehearsal from the train without so much as a morsel of food. So Henryk treated me to a light supper at a nearby coffeehouse, a delightful little place that served —"

"Spare me the menu, Helena," I interrupted. "I've already had the dubious pleasure of being exposed to Schramm's taste in light suppers. Let's get to the point, shall we."

"The point? What point?"

"Now who's being coy, Helena? The last time I saw Schramm was when he burst into my office to inform me that Karla Steilmann had been murdered. He looked like a man who had just seen the sky falling. It was as though a piece of his *own* life had just been hacked away. And now you're telling me that it's *goodbye Karla, hello Helena*? Simple as that?"

"Poor Henryk —"

"Oh, so it's 'poor Henryk' now, is it? Go on, what about poor Henryk?"

"You are being beastly, Hermann. Really, you are!"

"I don't have time to be nice!" I yelled. Then, ashamed of my ill-temper, I said in a calmer voice, "Helena, please try to understand: Am I jealous when a handsome talented fellow like Henryk Schramm shows interest in you? Yes, yes, and yes. There, you can put that admission on record. But if I'm impatient, angry … *beastly*, as you put it … it's because the sky seems to be falling for *me*. I'm besieged from every possible quarter. I have a monster-genius who is under threat of ruination from an unknown source; a tenor who we *think* is Jewish willing for some strange and possibly perverse reason to play a leading role in an opera by a notorious anti-Semite; a soprano on the loose somewhere out there who may be wreaking havoc on a path of extreme revenge; three murders to date and, God knows, more to come; a mayor and police commissioner who have dumped the future of Munich on my doorstep; a wily French horn player whom I would gladly strangle except that I need his co-operation to locate the aforementioned soprano; and, lo and behold, a corrupt detective for a partner who would love nothing more than to see me burning on a funeral pyre. There you have it, Helena."

I expected — or at least hoped — that this spewed recital of my troubles would elicit some decent show of sympathy on Helena's part. What I received instead was an incredulous stare. "Why, Hermann," Helena said, "in all the years we've known each other I have never seen you wallow in self-pity."

At this I flew into a carefully manufactured rage. "Self-pity! Self-pity! Is that all you have to say to me? It's not self-pity I'm wallowing in; it's a sea of evil I'm drowning in! The one person I hoped would throw me a lifeline was you, Helena. Instead, what do I get? Sympathy? No. Support? No.

Understanding? Not even a smidgen." I paused, looked away, and added in a low voice, "Not even a measly offer of help."

By now a dark cloud hung over our conversation but something told me a silver lining was about to show itself. And it did. Reaching out and taking my hand in hers, Helena said, "I apologize if I offended you, Hermann. How can I help?"

How quickly I managed to make it to shore from my "sea of evil"!

"Schramm," I said. "A moment ago, I asked you what he was up to and you rushed to reply that he wasn't up to anything. I believe otherwise, Helena. You see, I have a theory about Schramm. I suspect his real name is Socransky and that he's related in some fashion to a family by that name that lives in Russia, in the city of Minsk to be exact. What *is* questionable is why on earth *this* man would go to great lengths — as he has obviously done — to win a role, not an ordinary role, but *the* major role, in a Wagner production. There is something undefinable about Henryk Schramm ... a fog I've thus far failed to lift, a shell I've failed to pierce. At the moment facts are in short supply, so I have to rely on my instincts, and they tell me our friend Schramm is here in Munich on some mission, that he has an agenda which involves Richard Wagner, but not in a good way."

"It sounds preposterous, Hermann," Helena said. She gazed at me as though she were attempting to diagnose an illness. "Perhaps you've been overworking and need a rest and a change. I'm completely free this evening. Why don't we —"

"Thank you, Helena, but that's not the sort of help I have in mind."

Unaccustomed to this kind of rejection, Helena eyed me coldly. "Then what *do* you have in mind?" At the same time she removed her hand from mine. Suddenly it was as if the distance between us could be measured in kilometres. "You're not suggesting —"

"Believe me, Helena, nothing is more painful for me than the thought of you and Schramm ..."

"You can't even bring yourself to finish, can you?"

"You *did* offer to help —"

"I have my limits, Hermann, in case you hadn't noticed."

"I need you to do what I cannot do, Helena. I *need* this!"

Helena looked away, as though she couldn't bear the sight of me. There was a long minute of silence.

Finally she spoke. "Damn you, Hermann Preiss!" she said.

CHAPTER TWENTY-FIVE

If there is one skill my years of training and experience did not impart it was the skill — or to give it its due — the *art* of diplomacy. Whether dealing with authorities or dealing with the underworld, I have always found it difficult to substitute euphemisms for blunt truths, or to circle around a potentially dangerous problem in hopes of overcoming it by attacking it from the rear. Not that I am above a little obfuscation now and then, mind you, whenever it suits me. How then, I asked myself, was I going to deal with Richard Wagner and the matter of reinstating Thilo Rotfogel as principal French hornist in the opera orchestra?

I thought of various approaches:

"Maestro, remember Cornelia Vanderhoute? Well, I have reason to suspect that she is out to ruin you ... no, to kill *you ... and the only person who can lead me to wherever she is in hiding is —"*

"Maestro, there's this French horn player with whom you've had some differences, but it seems there is *one thing you and he have in common —"*

"Maestro Wagner, I must tell you that allowing Thilo Rotfogel to return to his post in the orchestra could possibly save several lives, including your own —"

Any one of these, or similar, openings would leave Wagner staring at me as though I were delusional. Of that I had no doubt. But having neither the time nor the temperament nor the talent for subtlety, I made an urgent appointment to meet with Wagner and determined that I would come directly to the point: like it or not, Thilo Rotfogel would have to be given back his position. My job was to find Cornelia Vanderhoute and find her without delay, and if the great man was forced to swallow his pride, well, to hell with him. There would be the usual thunder and lightning. But I was fully prepared.

I was not prepared, however, for the scene that greeted me when I arrived at the Wagner residence. Ushered into the drawing room by the housekeeper, I found Wagner and Cosima huddled on a settee, he with his arms tightly around her shoulders, she appearing to have collapsed, her head resting against his, her eyes closed as though she were desperately attempting to erase some terrible sight. She was wearing a coat. A bonnet, gloves, and silk scarf lay carelessly at her feet.

Wagner looked up at me with watery eyes. His complexion was ashen. His lips were parted but something unseen behind them was preventing words from emerging. A man accustomed to making others tremble, Richard Wagner was himself trembling!

Not knowing what to say, I began with an apology. "I'm sorry ... I seem to have intruded on a private family matter —" I took a step back, intending to withdraw.

Wagner freed one of his arms and motioned vigorously for me to remain, which I did, standing awkwardly and hoping I hadn't blundered into the midst of a Wagnerian domestic crisis. I wouldn't have put it past him to have committed yet another act of infidelity, while she, having just found out, was now engaging in yet another act of forgiveness.

At last Wagner spoke up, his voice unsteady. "You couldn't have come at a more fitting time, Preiss. My wife has suffered a horrible fright ... horrible!" There was a pause, and the two of them seemed to cling to each other more closely, as though they were alone and abandoned in a hostile world. Gently, Wagner said to his wife, "Cosima, do you wish me to tell the Inspector, or would it be better if —"

Cosima Wagner's head was pressed still against Wagner's and her answer was muffled. "Give me a moment, Richard. I need to compose myself —"

A moment later she looked up. For the first time I saw her face. Tears had smudged her rouge, the hair over her brow was unruly, the corners of her mouth drooped. Her expression was one of utter exhaustion. "You'll have to bear with me Inspector —" was all she could say. A full minute went by, then she gathered herself up, sitting erect now. Once again she was the Cosima Wagner I'd met a few days earlier, fully in charge of herself, despite whatever had occurred that had so unnerved her prior to my arrival.

"I was on a shopping expedition," she began, quietly, slowly, "at Reichmann & Company, near Leopoldstrasse. I assume you are familiar with that establishment, Inspector?"

Before I could answer Wagner interjected, "They are Jews, Preiss, but one can't avoid shopping there. The plain fact is, they have the finest upholstery fabrics in Munich and, believe it or not, they don't overcharge."

"Richard, please," Cosima said sharply, "do *not* interrupt. Let me finish what I have to say." As if to soften this rebuke she gave Wagner a pat on the cheek, then went on: "I was browsing

on the main floor of the store, looking at window coverings —
curtains, drapes, those sorts of things — and then at an assort-
ment of lace antimacassars —"

"Antimacassars?" I said, smiling curiously. "I thought
they went out of fashion a century ago, Madam Wagner."

"Not at all, Inspector. You would be surprised at the
number of guests, men mostly, who stain our chairs and
sofas with their abominable hair oil and pomades. It offends
my standards of housekeeping, I tell you. But we are digress-
ing, are we not? I had completed my inspection of materials
on the main floor where, incidentally, there were a number
of customers, and had moved to the second storey to look
at furniture coverings. There was only one other person on
that floor, a woman who had followed me up the stairs. She
was dressed in black, head to toe, wore a large black hat, and
her face was heavily veiled, as though she were in mourn-
ing. I thought it strange that a woman in such funereal attire
would be shopping at a store like Reichmann & Company
but, as the French say, *chacun à son goût*. So I paid no further
attention to her at first. But then it occurred to me that wherever I moved on that floor she followed … followed closely,
almost tracing my steps. I began to feel a bit uncomfortable,
as you can perhaps imagine, Inspector. After all, there were
just the two of us; none of the store staff were present at the
moment. So I turned abruptly and made as if to take the
stairs back to the main floor but this woman blocked my
way, not accidentally but very deliberately. I said, 'Excuse
me,' but she stood rooted in such a way that I could not possibly get by. The stairway is narrow and she was forming a
complete barrier. I repeated, 'Excuse me.' Still she did not
budge. Then, without a word she pressed an envelope into

my hand, turned swiftly, and practically fled down the stairs. I did not see her again."

"Give the envelope to Inspector Preiss, Cosima," Wagner said, again displaying a gentleness I had not imagined him capable of.

Cosima Wagner reached for a small leather handbag and extracted a plain white envelope, the kind one used to enclose a calling card. As she handed it to me her composure melted somewhat and she sank back on the settee, once again allowing Wagner to cradle her.

I opened the envelope, took out a card, and read its message, the first time silently, the second time aloud. "Richard and Cosima … like Tristan and Isolde you will both very soon enter the realm of the Night."

"Did you manage to get at least a glimpse of the woman's features?" I asked.

"Not really, Inspector, I'm sorry to say. As I mentioned, she was all in black, and rather thickly clothed. The only thing that strikes me, now that I think of it, is that she was rather tall. And despite her apparel, it was evident that she possessed a rather imposing figure. Somewhat bosomy, one might say. The way she moved … I mean she *flew* down the stairs … I would judge her to be a young woman, perhaps in her twenties." With a shudder, Cosima Wagner added, her voice trailing into a sob, "I hope to God I never see her again."

"Would this note have anything to do … any connection at all … with the note that was slipped under our door … the warning about June twenty-first?" Wagner wanted to know. The answer to that question was clear to me but I preferred to furnish it in Cosima Wagner's absence. "Madam Wagner must be exhausted after such a frightening experience," I said, addressing Wagner. "May I suggest she retire. There will be time for me to take a more detailed statement of this affair from her tomorrow, I assure you."

I was relieved that Cosima did not resist my suggestion. Holding her tenderly, Wagner assisted her as she made her way out of the drawing room. I heard him call to the housekeeper to escort her to their bedroom. On his return he wanted again to know if the two messages were related in some way.

"Yes, I believe they are," I replied. "I recognize the printing ... the same crude block letters."

"And the writer is —?"

"My guess is ... Fräulein Cornelia Vanderhoute."

"Your *guess*? Is that the best you can offer at a time like this?"

"Maestro Wagner, let me make one thing clear, if I have not already done so. I will not tell you how to write music. You will not tell me how to investigate crime."

"But if you suspect this Vanderhoute woman, why are you not arresting her? Good God, man, what more do you need?"

I took a deep breath. "I need you to hire a certain French horn player by the name of Thilo Rotfogel. And not tomorrow or the day after tomorrow. I mean today!"

Wagner gave me a look of utter disbelief. "In a crisis like this you make jokes, Preiss?"

"This is not a joke," I said. "In fact, my reason for wanting to see you so urgently today is that you must agree to reinstate this man Rotfogel. Let me explain —"

CHAPTER TWENTY-SIX

I left the Wagner residence with the realization that a miracle of sorts had occurred, though one not entirely of my own making. In the face of tangible evidence that the life of his beloved Cosima was at serious risk, the Maestro agreed to allow Thilo Rotfogel to return to his post as principal French hornist in the opera orchestra, this concession nevertheless accompanied with a stern directive: "Tell that insolent bastard to behave himself or I swear I'll throw him out again!" I promised to convey the warning word for word, though in truth I hadn't the slightest intention of doing so. There is a time for everything, and this was *not* a time to ruffle Thilo Rotfogel's feathers.

In fairness to Brunner — after all, it was he who had produced the Rotfogel piece of the puzzle — I invited him to accompany me to the hornist's lodgings to break the good news, following which Brunner and I would proceed as planned to apprehend the elusive Fräulein Vanderhoute with all due haste.

Rotfogel occupied rooms in a quite respectable apartment building in the Old Town just off Marienplatz, close enough to the town hall that Brunner and I were able to check our pocket watches as the glockenspiel in the hall tower above the main entrance chimed six o'clock.

"He may be dining out somewhere," Brunner said. "Being a bachelor he probably takes all of his meals in restaurants."

I thought I detected more than a hint of envy in Brunner's voice. (I guessed mealtimes in the Brunner household — what with a wife and four young children — were regularly the same kind of stomach-churning occasions as mealtimes in the household of Wolfgang Preiss during my childhood back in Zwicken.)

According to the concierge, our man *was* at home. "Second floor, east end, last door down the hall. Name's just above the door knocker. Oh, and don't be surprised if it takes him a while to open up. He's got more locks and chains on his door than the Bavarian State Prison."

We found Rotfogel's door without difficulty, but several stout raps with the brass doorknocker brought no response. Annoyed, I said to Brunner, "Try the damned door. We don't have all night —"

"But you heard the concierge —"

"Try it anyway, Brunner."

A single twist of the doorknob, as it turned out, was all that was required. No locks. No chains. "Well, that was easy!" Brunner said. He took the first step inside, I followed. "Herr Rotfogel?" Brunner called out. There was no reply. Again: "Herr Rotfogel?" Silence.

"Rotfogel," I called out, quite sharply. "It's us — Inspector Preiss and Detective Brunner —"

We were past a small entrance hall and into the sitting room now. Not a thing was out of place. Obviously Thilo Rotfogel was as much a perfectionist when it came to house-keeping as he was when it came to playing the French horn. Every piece of wooden furniture was polished almost to a mirror finish. Down-filled cushions and pillows on the sofa and side chairs had been puffed to fullness, as though they had never been sat upon. There was even a white vase at the centre of a small round dining table filled with fresh flowers, a rarity at this time of year in Munich and not cheaply purchased. Only one minimal sign of neglect appeared: an open bottle of plum brandy on a silver tray next to the flower vase, the bottle half empty, cork next to it, and next to the cork two fine crystal snifters both seemingly abandoned while still containing small amounts of the liquor.

I pointed in the direction of a closed door at the far side of the sitting room. "Something tells me," I said to Brunner, speaking just above a whisper, "that our friend has company and they're both asleep there." I moved across the room, placed my hand on the doorknob, looked back at Brunner, and said, again in a low voice, "I hate to do this but duty calls —"

I opened the door. "Brunner," I called back, "come here ... take a look at this —" Now I understood why our "host" had failed to respond. When a man's throat has apparently been crudely pierced by some long sharp object it is entirely excusable if he fails to greet his "guests" in a hospitable manner.

It is one thing for a person to die before his or her time, but quite another thing for a person to die without dignity. Rotfogel died without dignity. He lay sprawled across his bed, on his back, naked, the sheet in the immediate area of his neck blood-soaked. His clothing — trousers, jacket, shirt, neckwear, footwear — was neatly arranged on a nearby chair, suggesting that the shedding of his garments was not all that spontaneous an act, that perhaps this was all part of an established ritual: first a copious amount of brandy, then a few minutes of amorous talk, arousal, followed by a trip to the bedroom.

Whoever was admitted and participated in this ritual with Rotfogel — and I was certain it was none other than Cornelia

Vanderhoute — left not a trace in the bedroom, not so much as a hair or a thread as far as Brunner and I could see after a quick survey. Similarly the sitting room afforded no clues.

"If you're right and it was Vanderhoute," Brunner said, "she certainly did a meticulous job of tidying up after herself."

"I think she had nothing to tidy up," I said. "I think Rotfogel let her in, she saw to it that he had plenty to drink, lured him to the bedroom where, it appears, he very methodically undressed despite the effects of the brandy, and while he lay on the bed anticipating the joy to come, she finished him off more or less the same way she finished off the others … all without so much as removing her hat!"

"But why? She couldn't have known Rotfogel was going to lead us to her," Brunner said. "What reason would she have to kill him?"

We were back in the bedroom. "There's the reason," I replied, indicating a heavy polished mahogany jewellery case, which sat atop a matching chiffonier. The case had been thrown open and, except for a handful of inexpensive shirt studs and what looked like a child's ring, its contents had been removed, tray by tray. "She was meticulous all right," I said.

Brunner looked crestfallen. "So with Rotfogel dead, how do we find her?"

"Simple," I said. Then, in a rare moment of biblical inspiration, I added, "Whither Rotfogel's jewellery goeth, there also goeth Cornelia Vanderhoute."

CHAPTER TWENTY-SEVEN

"So, Helena," I said, "what have you got for me?" It was the morning after her evening with Henryk Schramm.

"What have I got for you, Hermann?" Helena pretended to be searching for a thoughtful answer. "Well now, let me think. What *have* I got for you? A great deal of contempt? Yes, I would say that sums it up quite nicely."

"Look, Helena, I apologize if my question wasn't subtle —"

"*Wasn't subtle,* you say? It was the kind of question you'd put to a whore! You ask a favour of me, I comply, and then you don't even have the decency to inquire where we went, what we ate, what we did afterward, was it pleasant or unpleasant, how I felt playing the role of your sneaky little helper."

"There will be time for me to show my appreciation, Helena," I said, reaching out to grasp her hand, and having my hand thrust aside.

"Oh, yes, that empty promise of yours about a holiday in Lucerne. In June was it? Should I begin packing my bags, Hermann? No point waiting to the last minute."

With every word Helena's voice was rising, her temperature too. We had been seated across from each other at a small table in a fashionable coffee house a few doors from the Eugénie Palace and by now Helena's vociferous indignation was beginning to attract the attention of nearby patrons.

I rose and took up my coat and hat. "You're tired, my dear. Let's continue this later when —"

"Sit down, Hermann!" So loud was Helena's command that several of our neighbouring coffee drinkers, witnessing what they took to be a lovers' quarrel, smirked. Embarrassed, I met their smirks with a shrug, as if to say, "Women — what do you expect?" Nevertheless, I obeyed, laid aside my coat and hat, and settled into my chair again.

"I have something to tell you, Hermann —"

"Please, Helena, lower your voice —"

"I have something to tell you —" To my relief, she repeated this in a half-whisper. "His real name isn't Schramm."

"Ahah! So my suspicion was not misguided after all. I *knew* there was something behind that façade of his."

"If you're not too busy congratulating yourself," Helena said, "would it interest you to know how I found this out?"

"I'm not sure I want to hear the details," I said.

"There are no 'details,' Hermann," Helena said, speaking quietly but eyeing me coldly. "But I will tell you this: I would not have resisted — not for one moment — if it had come to 'details.' He is everything you are *not*, Hermann … kind, considerate, charming, not to mention incredibly handsome."

"You've forgotten to mention one other thing," I said. "The man is very likely a fraud, an imposter of some sort. I'm not sure exactly what he's up to but I wouldn't trust him from one side of this table to the other. So, how *did* you learn that he's living under a false name?"

Helena looked away. "I'm so ashamed —"

I reached out, took Helena's face in my hands as gently as I could given that I was quickly losing patience, and said, "Helena, look at me. I have no time for shame, yours, mine, *any*body's. I am a policeman. I do what I have to do."

Helena pulled my hands away. "But I am *not*, and I hate what I did."

"Which was —?"

"Which was to spy, to violate the man's privacy, to do something to him which I would never want anyone to do to me, Hermann. Never!" Helena paused, as though preparing to make some dark confession, then said, "We were in his sitting room, and he left and went into this tiny kitchenette to open a bottle of wine to go along with a small cake he'd bought. And while he was busy there, I used the time to look about the sitting room. There was a small writing table in one corner. And that is where I saw it."

"Saw *what* —?"

"A letter. Just a single page. Written in Yiddish."

"Yiddish? How could you tell, Helena?"

"Yiddish was my parents' first language. Mine too, until my mother decided it wasn't fashionable. Don't look so surprised, Hermann. Chayla Bekarsky may be Helena Becker today, but she still remembers how to speak and read Yiddish. There was not time to read the entire letter but it began 'My dear Hershel' and ended 'Your loving mother.' The handwriting was beautiful, as though the writer might have been an expert at calligraphy. And the stationery looked quite elegant, even though there were numerous rips and creases, as though it had been stuffed away, perhaps in somebody's pocket. Oh yes, one other thing, Hermann: the writer's name was embossed in Hebrew letters at the top of the page, which is a bit unusual. The name was Professor Miriam Socransky."

"Socransky? Are you certain it was Socransky?"

"You look as though it has a familiar ring, Hermann."

I repeated the name several times. Then it came to me, Madam Vronsky's tale about the concertmaster of the St. Petersburg orchestra whom Richard Wagner had dismissed and who, in despair, had committed suicide.

Helena leaned across the small table and looked searchingly into my eyes. "Hermann Preiss," she said, "whenever your face takes on that faraway expression it tells me that I'm no longer in the same room with you, that I've ceased to exist, gone up in smoke. I might as well leave —"

She drew a shawl snugly about her shoulders, and made as if to rise from her chair. Quickly I reached out and held her in place. "Helena, don't leave. Hear me out. Our 'friend' Schramm ... I wondered who he was, and what he was up to. Now I know!"

CHAPTER TWENTY-EIGHT

"The officer who delivered your summons said it concerned a matter of extreme urgency. I don't understand, Inspector Preiss. Am I a suspect?"

The man asking this question had just been escorted to the Constabulary by one of my officers. Visibly nervous, he glanced around the small room as though searching for some means of escape, a perfectly understandable reaction given the uninviting interior of the Constabulary and the likelihood that it was his first ever visit to this, or any, police establishment.

I moved quickly to put him at ease. "No, sir, you are *not* a suspect, not at all. Indeed, Sandor Lantos —"

"You mean the *late* Sandor Lantos —"

"Yes, of course … described you as a gentle and decent man. We were speaking, he and I, of an incident involving Wolfgang Grilling —"

"Regrettably, the *late* Wolfgang Grilling —"

"Alas, yes. For the record, sir, your full name is Friedrich Otto —"

"Friedrich Karl Heinz von Zwillings Otto, to be precise. I am a professional manager of musical artists. But I assume you already know this. I was Wolfgang Grilling's manager, which you must also know. But I know nothing, absolutely nothing, about how those two came to be murder victims."

By now Otto was sitting on the edge of his chair, his hands gripping the brim of his hat, almost crushing it.

A dossier lay open before me. I took several moments to review one document in particular, then looked up at Otto. "I see that you were also the manager of Karla Steilmann … the *late* —"

"Please, Inspector Preiss, what is this all about? Why am I here?"

"I will be candid with you, Herr Otto," I said. "You are here because of a game of darts. I see that you are not amused, and I apologize if my answer sounded flippant. But the truth is that there are times — many times, in fact — when a detective stumbles across a sense of direction in a baffling case in much the same manner as one throws darts at a dartboard. Hear me out: Let's say Maestro Wagner is at the centre, the bull's eye so to speak. Here and there, in the surrounding area, are numerous names that spring to mind: Grilling, Lantos, Steilmann, Mecklenberg, von Bülow, Liszt, an eccentric French hornist by the name of Rotfogel, a soprano by the name of Vanderhoute. And then, Herr Otto, your name shows up and my mental dart lands on it … and here you are!"

"You forgot to mention another name," Otto said.

"Did I? How careless of me." I pretended to be impatient with myself, hoping at the same time that the name he seemed about to supply was the one I had deliberately omitted to mention. "And that name would be —?"

"Henryk Schramm."

"You're referring to the fellow who won the leading role in Wagner's new opera … the role your man Grilling coveted?"

Suddenly Friedrich Otto's demeanor changed. He relaxed his grip on the brim of his hat. The furrows on his brow disappeared. I detected a cautious smile. "You put this to me in the form of a question, Inspector, but it's obvious to me that you already know the facts. Yes, Grilling lost the role. Yes he was jealous, upset, not merely upset but enraged. And with good reason. After all, Inspector, this Schramm … or whatever his name is —"

"Whatever his name is? Pardon me for interrupting you, Herr Otto, but are you suggesting Henryk Schramm is *not* Henryk Schramm?"

"Suggesting? No, sir, not suggesting. *Informing* is what I'm doing."

"Informing? Informing to a policeman means information, not just rumour or supposition but concrete evidence. Your reputation as a decent man precedes you, Herr Otto; a man like you would not capriciously float some idle gossip about Schramm merely because of Grilling's resentment or your own pique. What makes you so certain that you are right about Henryk Schramm?"

"Let's just say, Inspector, that many years of experience managing these artists has brought me in contact with just about every kind of personality conceivable. In my field one does not play dart games. One deals intimately with every range of ability from talent to genius; with every range of aspiration from naïvety and blind faith to ruthless ambition." Otto pointed a finger sharply at his forehead. "I have all the 'concrete evidence' right here, you see."

"And nothing else?"

Otto looked at me cautiously. "I don't know what you're alluding to," he said.

I turned a page of the dossier and removed the two fragments of the envelope addressed to Schramm. I explained how and where I had found them and how I had concluded that they were addressed to Schramm from a correspondent in Minsk. "Do you not find it curious, to say the least, Herr Otto, that one fragment was located in Grilling's apartment, the other in Karla Steilmann's? Let's get back to suggestion, shall we. I suggest that somehow a letter was — I was going to say purloined, but 'purloined' sounds too genteel. The letter was *stolen* … stolen by someone who harbored a deep grievance against this man Schramm. Or perhaps by someone in the *employ* of someone with a deep grievance. All of which points to two people: Wolfgang Grilling, and his manager Friedrich Karl Heinz von Zwillings Otto." I paused, expecting Otto to react with a vehement protest of innocence, the predictable show we policemen find so terribly tiresome.

Instead, Friedrich Karl Heinz von Zwillings Otto caught me completely off-guard. "You know, I trust," he said, "that he's a Jew. His real name is Hershel Socransky, your man Henryk Schramm." Otto's pronunciation of "your man Henryk Schramm" — the tone slightly sneering, the look on Otto's face one of certainty, even of superiority — left me feeling as though it was I, and not Otto, who was on the defensive; as though, whatever the cause, carelessness or stupidity or dereliction of duty, I was guilty of shielding not only a scoundrel, but a Jewish scoundrel!

Egged on by the sustained expression on Otto's face — an expression of self-satisfaction, of a point scored — and wanting to regain the offensive even if it meant being reckless, I said, "Whether Schramm is or is not Jewish is not the issue. Let me tell you what I now believe really happened, Herr Otto. What really happened is this: Wolfgang Grilling was furious on three counts: first, the loss of the role he thought he deserved; second, losing to a stranger whose origin and operatic background were a total blank; and third, facing the prospect of performing in Wagner's new opera in makeup and costume he despised. Determined to uncover the mystery of Henryk Schramm's background, he went to Schramm's lodgings, spied a letter addressed to Schramm on the concierge's desk, and made off with it. He showed the letter to you. He, or perhaps you, had it translated at least to the extent that it became apparent Schramm's name is Socransky."

"Ridiculous! Your imagination has run away with you, Preiss!" Otto scoffed.

"I'm not finished, Herr Otto. There's much more to the story. Armed with what he regarded as damning evidence against Schramm, Grilling immediately dashed to Karla Steilmann, expecting to enlist her as an ally, the plan being that the two of them would present the letter to Wagner. And that would put a speedy end to the career of Hershel Socransky alias Henryk Schramm, Jewish tenor from Minsk. Karla retained the letter, perhaps on the pretext of wanting to study it further, but the fact is that Fräulein Steilmann was very much taken with Schramm. Indeed, Herr Otto, you saw the man, you heard him sing. What female wouldn't be attracted to him?"

Again Otto interrupted. "Really, Inspector, one moment you speak of hard evidence, the next moment you throw imaginary darts at imaginary targets. As a citizen I would hate to think that this is how law enforcement is conducted in a civilized city like Munich. Perhaps in some rural backwater —"

"In a civilized city like Munich people do not steal private mail in order to sully someone's reputation —"

"Damn it, Preiss, the man's a Jew!" Otto shot back. "What's a Jew doing in an opera by Richard Wagner? Steilmann was wrong, I tell you. She flatly refused —"

"Flatly refused what?"

"To co-operate. The woman was a fool. She took the letter to Socransky. I suppose she did so because she was in love with him, or *thought* she was. With his true identity exposed, what would you expect the man to do? It's obvious, isn't it? Socransky confronted Grilling, then killed him. Then, in an act of betrayal, he did away with Karla Steilmann. That would account for those torn bits of the envelope. As for the letter itself, God knows where it's ended up. Probably Schramm burned it or tore it to pieces and tossed them down a sewer. What motivated him to murder poor Sandor Lantos is beyond my understanding, Preiss. You'll probably have to throw your precious darts into the air once again and pray that you hit upon the answer. Now then, I trust I am free to leave." Without awaiting my response, Otto stood and put on his hat.

"For the moment," I said, "you are free to leave. I must tell you, however, that you remain subject to further investigation, Herr Otto, as an accomplice."

"An accomplice! To what crime?"

"Theft of private property. I'm referring to the letter, of course. By your own admission, Herr Otto, you participated to some degree in that rather shoddy business."

"And this … *this* is how you demonstrate your gratitude? This is my reward for helping you find your way through this maze? It's this fellow Socransky you should be subjecting to further investigation. *He's* your culprit. Who knows what further disasters he's out to create!"

Seizing his coat, Otto threw it roughly over his arm, as though the garment somehow were as guilty of offending him as I was. Barely in control of his anger, he said, "It's the Socranskys of this world who pollute the divine, Preiss ... the *divine*, do you hear? Opera, sir, is purity. An opera is proof that God exists!"

"Perhaps," I said. "But the more I see of it, the more I'm persuaded that the stage manager is the Devil. Good day, Herr Otto."

CHAPTER TWENTY-NINE

"What news, Brunner?"

"Some good, some bad," Detective Franz Brunner replied. "Which do you want first?"

The session with Friedrich Otto had left me morose. I had wanted so much to believe that whoever Hershel Socransky was, acts of violence couldn't possibly be committed by a man possessing such copious gifts of talent and charm. Nevertheless I said to Brunner, "The bad first."

"Very well, then," Brunner said. "A few minutes ago I was spotted by Commissioner von Mannstein on his way to a meeting with Mayor von Braunschweig. Pulling me aside, he demanded to know what progress has been made with regard to what he terms 'the case against Wagner.' I suggested that the proper protocol was for an up-to-date report to come from the officer in charge, namely yourself, Preiss. 'To hell with protocol!' the commissioner shouted in my ear, practically splitting my eardrum. The commissioner was *not* happy when I told him that we are still gathering evidence, that nothing at this precise moment is conclusive. 'Inform Chief Inspector Preiss that I want a full report by this hour tomorrow ... and it had better be one that I can proudly present to the mayor!'"

"What about the good?"

Brunner removed from his coat and placed on my desk a small black velvet box. "Take a look inside, Preiss," he said.

I opened the box. "Well well, where have I seen *these* before, eh?" I turned the box upside down. Out fell a pair of cufflinks, the stones black opals. "Rotfogel's cufflinks. Pawned, I suppose." Brunner nodded. "And the person who pawned them? Let me guess: Cornelia Vanderhoute."

"Well, she gave a false name. No surprise there, of course. But the pawnbroker's description leaves no doubt. I confiscated these, but there are numerous other items still at that shop, pawned by the same woman. There's for instance a sterling silver cigarette case with the initials TR, and a pocket-size brandy flask with the same initials engraved on the silver cap. I checked on the address she gave. False as well. A rooming house. They had never heard of her."

I said, "A professional thief would have tried to sell these things outright to an underground dealer rather than deal with a legitimate pawnbroker. Obviously Fräulein Vanderhoute is not a professional thief, only clever enough to provide false identification. So the problem still exists: where to find her."

"That may not be too difficult. Here's why, Preiss: When I entered the shop and showed him my badge, the pawn-broker became very uneasy. Probably thought I was there to charge him with some impropriety and revoke his licence. When I spotted the cigarette case and flask I swear the old man openly began to perspire. He said to me, 'Of all the pawnshops in all the world, why did she have to walk into mine ... and not just once but twice!' The fact that she made *two* trips to that particular shop, the most recent only yes-terday ... and remember, Preiss, there are at least a dozen pawnshops scattered throughout Munich ... well, odds are she must live somewhere in the neighbourhood of Simon

Regner. That's the owner of the shop in question. Trouble is, there'll be ice storms in hell before Vanderhoute returns to Regner's to redeem these items. Whatever money she managed to get from the pawnbroker she has probably already used to buy passage out of Munich bound for God-knows-where. She would have to travel by train. Riverboats are few and far between this time of year. We can set up surveillance at the railroad station immediately."

"You may be right, Brunner," I said, "but something tells me this woman is on a mission and that she has unfinished business which she means to attend to here in Munich."

I related to Brunner what I'd heard in the course of interrogating Friedrich Otto and my doubts about Otto's version of events leading to the deaths of Grilling and Steilmann. "That there is something profoundly suspicious about the man I now know as Hershel Socransky, I am certain," I told Brunner. "That he is capable of murder, however, I cannot imagine."

"Surely you're not saying Jews are incapable of murder!" Brunner said.

I knew Brunner was baiting me. There was still enough spite in him that by tomorrow the word would have spread throughout the police force that Chief Inspector Hermann Preiss was a lover and defender of Jews. "I'm sorry to disappoint you, Brunner," I said, "but I am *not* saying anything of the sort. I am simply saying that this particular Jew, Hershel Socransky, in my opinion does not have the makings of a killer."

"Then what *does* make you suspicious of him?" Brunner asked.

"The threat that was delivered to Wagner —" I reached into a cabinet and produced the note from my file on Wagner.

I read the message aloud: "JUNE 21 WILL BE THE DAY OF YOUR RUINATION." I slid the note across my desk. "Here, Brunner, you read it aloud."

Brunner obliged, then shrugged. "Cornelia Vanderhoute," he said, as though the matter were beyond question.

"No, Brunner," I said, "it makes no sense whatsoever that she would mark time until June twenty-first before carrying out whatever plan she had in mind."

Brunner reread the note, this time silently. He looked across the desk at me, a faint smile turning up one corner of his mouth, nodding as though a sudden revelation had struck him.

"Yes, Brunner," I said, reaching for the note and tucking it away in the file. "Only one person would write that note … Hershel Socransky, alias Henryk Schramm … the man I now call the Mastersinger from Minsk."

CHAPTER THIRTY

In the pale gaze of Commissioner von Mannstein I thought I caught a flicker of longing, in his voice a wisp of heartbreak. His grey eyes seemed to be straining for a vision of some unexplored horizon beyond the horizon immediately visible from the windows of his office. "You know, Preiss," he said, "other nations are blessed. The British have penal colonies in Australia, the French have Devil's Island, the Russians have Siberia. But what have we Germans got? Switzerland! A place of magnificent mountains, shining lakes, fine chocolate, and spotless chalets. What Germany needs, Preiss ... needs desperately, is some lonely, out-of-the-way pile of rock set in the midst of a vast ocean so treacherous no captain worth his papers would sail a ship there more than once. And there ... *there* ... is where Richard Wagner should be deposited for the rest of his natural life. Correction: the rest of his *un*natural life. Now then, Preiss, how close are we to realizing our dream?"

"Our dream?" I said. "You mean Germany's dream about possessing a more suitable location for exiles?" Of course I knew exactly what "our dream" referred to, but every moment of delay was precious to me, given that the report I was about to deliver was *not* one that the commissioner would be able to present "proudly" (as he put it to Brunner earlier) to Mayor von Braunschweig.

"No no!" the commissioner said testily. "I'm asking you about Wagner."

"*Richard* Wagner —?"

"Good heavens, Preiss, how many *Wagners* are there?"

"Well, sir, as a matter of fact, I have been looking into that very question. Genealogically speaking, it seems the name can be traced back to the invention of the wheel, which of course led to the invention of *wagons*. Hence the name Wagoner, or Wagner. It is especially interesting to note —"

"Damn it, Preiss, I didn't summon you here to deliver a lecture."

"Pardon me, Commissioner, I was only about to add that, in the course of peeling back the layers of history, I discovered that one Erich Langemann von Mannstein back in the late 1700s had married into a family of Wagners in the city of Essen, owners of the largest and most prosperous carriage business in that part of the country. Am I correct that Erich Langemann von Mannstein was your grandfather, sir?"

"I'll thank you to keep that information under your hat, Inspector," von Mannstein said. "The last thing I need is for word to spread to the effect that the name von Mannstein is tied to the name Wagner by even the thinnest thread of coincidence! Under your hat, Preiss!"

"Understood, sir. Under my hat. Absolutely!" I recalled that the commissioner had recently lauded me as a man of "exquisite discretion" after I had recognized him departing from Madam Rosina Waldheim's whorehouse. I was comforted, facing the unpleasant task ahead of me at the moment, knowing that I now possessed additional capital in my mental ledger, another asset to fall back on, a card to be played, so to speak, in the likely event that von Mannstein, hearing the report I was about to give, threatened demotion (at best) or outright dismissal (at worst).

"Once again then, Preiss, where do we stand with Richard Wagner?" The chill in the commissioner's grey eyes was palpable as he sat forward in his high-backed seat expectantly.

I began slowly. "Well, sir, perhaps the word 'stand' is not quite appropriate. I would have to say that … well, we are *leaning* rather than standing. In fact, it's probably more accurate to describe our present posture as sitting … yes, that's more like the reality of our situation regarding Maestro Wagner."

Glowering at me, von Mannstein brought both fists down hard on his side of the desk. "Leaning … sitting … what the devil are you talking about, Preiss? No, don't bother to answer. *I'll* answer my own question. What I am hearing is the sound of failure, miserable incompetent inexcusable failure! Look here, Preiss —" The commissioner drew a piece of stationery from a file that lay before him. I could see that the file bore the official gold seal of Mayor von Braunschweig. "This arrived this morning by special courier," von Mannstein said, "marked 'Urgent.'" Von Mannstein's hands shook as he read aloud:

"*It has come to the attention of the Government of Bavaria that the musician and revolutionary Richard Wagner is about to embark on a fresh course of attacks against the existing regime with ever more radical ideas about German unification that could lead to a loss of autonomy for our State as well as of our beloved traditions. It is therefore incumbent upon the City of Munich to deal with the Wagner crisis with utmost dispatch, failing which payment of certain appropriations set aside by the State, in particular to subsidize the completion of new waterworks and gasworks for the city, will regrettably be suspended for an indefinite period of time."*

"The letter," von Mannstein said, "is addressed to the mayor and signed by the governor of the state. So what we have here, Preiss, is an abundance of communication — from the governor to the mayor, from the mayor to the commissioner, from the commissioner to the chief inspector Hermann Preiss. Meanwhile, it is apparent, Preiss, that your report to me this morning is as devoid of content as a ... as a —"

"*Tabula rasa?*" I offered.

"Damn it, Preiss, I don't speak Italian —"

"Tabula rasa is Latin, sir —"

"I don't care if it's what Jesus Christ said to the Pope!" von Mannstein shouted. "Have you *nothing* you can report this morning?"

"I *can* report, sir, that we are getting closer to solving the question of who has committed the murders of Sandor Lantos, Karla Steilmann, and Wolfgang Grilling and may be out to do similar harm to the Wagners. You previously expressed doubt that such killings could be the work of a woman —"

"You're referring to that business about the hatpin —"

"Exactly, sir. But the fact is, the female in question is more and more a suspect and I have good reason to fear that either one or both of the Wagners may be on her list."

Suddenly the commissioner's expression changed. It was as though he had just witnessed his first sunshine after days of rain. "Wait a moment, Preiss! Hold on! You say this woman may be out to do away with Richard Wagner? Is this a serious possibility?"

"Yes," I replied hesitantly.

Von Mannstein was positively beaming now. His lips moved and he seemed to be talking to himself, seemed to be mulling over what I had just told him. In a quiet voice, his tone almost reverent, he said, "You see, Preiss, there *is* a God —"

"There is?"

"Yes, indeed. And He has just made his countenance to shine upon our fair city. Here are your orders, Preiss: You are *not* to arrest this woman, whoever she is. We'll call her Fräulein Hatpin. Heaven has sent her to do the work *we* are forbidden to do. Let it be so. Do you follow me, Preiss? *I* will give you the proper signal when the proper time comes to arrest her."

I was incredulous. "Those are *your* orders, Commissioner?"

"No, Preiss … that is God's will!"

CHAPTER THIRTY-ONE

I left Commissioner von Mannstein and made my way up three flights of stairs to my office, finding the climb more laborious than usual, shaking my head with disbelief all the way, pondering how bizarre it was to be handed an order so perverse as to be downright criminal while being assured at the same time by the commissioner that it was a manifestation of God's will! Many impressions about von Mannstein had crossed my mind over the years, but never had he struck me as a man skilled in divinity. As far as I could tell, his sole connection to the supernatural consisted of being born into a family of sufficient wealth and influence that, following a lackluster decade spent in the militia, he was awarded a senior post in Munich's civil service. There, thanks to his years in the army, he was delegated the onerous responsibility of overseeing the designs of dress uniforms for various municipal officials. It was soon said of him that he never met a brass button or a gold-encrusted epaulet he didn't love. His own wardrobe of tunics, trousers, riding breeches, and ceremonial helmets, once he was appointed commissioner, made King Ludwig's by comparison look like remnants from a royal rummage sale.

This was the officer who would have me stand aside, complaisant as a batman, while the life of Richard Wagner was conveniently snuffed out by a deranged creature now given the code name Fräulein Hatpin. The irony of it all stuck in my throat. *Cornelia Vanderhoute unintentionally does a favour of incalculable benefit for an eternally grateful realm, thus becoming in her own right an instrument of divine will!*

In the privacy of my office, behind a firmly closed door, I said aloud to myself over and over, "No, this cannot be!" Never imbued with an overwhelming curiosity about God (for a policeman steeped in the culture of solid evidence, there isn't all that much to go on, is there?) I nevertheless could not bring myself to believe that the fate which von Mannstein proposed for Richard Wagner was something upon which God would bestow a smile of approval.

Orders were orders, yes. But *this* was one order I hadn't the slightest desire to carry out. I had commanded Brunner to find Cornelia Vanderhoute and was not about to rescind that injunction. "To hell with von Mannstein," I whispered to myself. "And to hell with the mayor and the governor. I will *not* be a partner in this nefarious business. Never!"

This was how it would be: We — that is, Brunner and I — would continue to spare no effort to locate the Vanderhoute woman and put her out of commission. If my supervisor was displeased, well, then let *him* make his peace with God.

With a warming sense of satisfaction over my decision, I sat down at my desk intending to pen a memorandum of my conversation with the commissioner for my private file, a self-serving measure that might stand me in good stead should my conduct come into question later by some higher authority. Scarcely had I touched pen to paper when I heard a knock on my door, called out, "Enter," and was greeted by Franz Brunner shaking his head much the same way as I had shaken mine earlier.

"Don't tell me," I said, laying aside pen and paper. "I can see by your expression that you've just had another of your random encounters with the Commissioner. Well?"

"I've been instructed in no uncertain terms to halt the search for Vanderhoute," Brunner said. "No explanation, Preiss, not a word. Just like that, von Mannstein corners me upstairs in the lounge, no one else present, I'm just sitting there minding my own business ... well, with a mouthful of a leftover chicken leg, actually, and His High And Mighty gives me one of those looks, you know, where his eyebrows and mustache come together, and he says to me, 'Brunner, I've issued an order that Chief Inspector Preiss and you are to waste no further time on the alleged killer Vanderhoute.' He used the word 'alleged,' Preiss. What the devil is going on?"

I explained the commissioner's motivation for ordering a temporary cessation to the hunt for Vanderhoute.

"The search for the woman goes on unabated, Brunner," I said. "You and I took the same oath to uphold justice and neither of us needs the blood of Richard Wagner on our hands. Call off the search? Not for one moment, Brunner. In fact, we are going to *double* our efforts. It is the right thing to do. This is one of those times, Brunner, when conscience comes before obedience to orders."

From Detective Brunner I expected an instant pledge of support. After all, von Mannstein's directive should have been as repellent to him as it was to me. (Besides, if Brunner owed anything to anybody, his debt of gratitude to me for my earlier forbearance surely ranked ahead of all other debts.)

I should have known better.

Instead of a pledge of support, Brunner gave me a look of bemused skepticism. "Our oath to uphold justice ... the right thing to do ... conscience before obedience ..." Stroking his mustache, rubbing his chin, he seemed to be turning over these phrases in search of hidden meanings.

A bit impatiently, I asked: "Is there something you don't understand, Brunner? I thought I spoke plainly."

"Plainly?" Brunner said. "I would have thought a better description would be sanctimoniously. Yes, sanctimoniously is more like it. Oaths to uphold justice ... doing the right things ... putting conscience ahead of obedience. My God, Preiss, you sound more like an archbishop than a chief inspector. But I wasn't born yesterday, Preiss. I see what's behind that little homily of yours. You want *me* to ignore the commissioner's order, you want *me* to double *my* efforts, and then when I produce the woman ... ah, then you have the immense satisfaction of thinking you've 'done the right thing' while I, Franz Brunner, end up scrubbing the Constabulary latrines ... or worse. Well, Preiss, if this is how you are scheming to get rid of me, think again. And as for the future safety and welfare of this man Wagner, frankly I care more about the safety and welfare of the organ grinder's monkey!"

I rose from my chair behind the desk, strode purposefully to my office door, and threw it open. Quietly I said, "You'd better get out, Brunner, before I kill you."

Fortunately for both of us, Detective Brunner didn't need a second invitation.

CHAPTER THIRTY-TWO

There was only one thing to do now: warn Richard Wagner that he was at greater risk for his safety than before. But what if he should demand to know why? How could I explain truthfully? *Well, you see Maestro, it's like this: formerly you were an ordinary target for murder, but as of the latest orders from my superior you are now what might be termed a government-approved target for murder. What? You say you find this outrageous? Sorry, Maestro, but it's God's will ...*

I headed straight for the opera house assuming (correctly) that at this hour of the day Wagner could be found there keeping a watchful eye on rehearsals for the new opera. Unnoticed, I slipped into an aisle seat in the rearmost row of the main parterre.

The Maestro had stationed himself at the railing in front of the orchestra pit, his back to me, facing the conductor von Bülow, the orchestral musicians, and a company of singers on stage. Although the hall is renowned for its flawless acoustics (a hiccup in the fifth gallery, it is said, resounds like a cymbal-crash backstage), Wagner chose to bellow in the manner of a drill sergeant castigating cadets for sloppiness on parade.

"You ... members of the chorus ... you are failing to pay proper attention to the way I have placed words under the musical notes! Failing miserably! You are cutting short many of the words and destroying the flow of the text as well as the music! My score is quite clear and the words must be sung precisely as I have written them. If Beethoven would not stand for singers who took careless liberties in the choral movement of the Ninth Symphony, why should I have to tolerate second-rate work? *Third-rate*, in fact!"

Turning his attention to the orchestra and conductor, Wagner ranted on, "The overture … God in heaven! … I create an elaborate climax where the three main themes are interwoven … and what do I hear? *What*, I ask you?"

Wagner then began, in a high-pitched raspy voice, to imitate what he heard, his right hand pretending to saw wood, his other hand clutched to his left ear as though hoping to shut out his own noise. "This is music that conveys youthful passion. You are playing it as though it's dinner music." The Maestro then proceeded to demonstrate, this time in a baritone voice, how the opening fanfare, intended to symbolize the nobility of the Mastersingers, should be played. "Full-bodied, generous, proud!" he shouted. His hands punching the air, he sang out the first four notes. "This … *this* … is what I wrote. *This* is what I expect to hear!"

Dropping his shoulders, looking and sounding exhausted, Wagner said, addressing von Bülow quietly, "Tomorrow let me hear something far better."

It occurred to me, watching Wagner's tirade, that any one among the assembly both in the orchestra pit and on the stage could be regarded as a potential assassin of the man, and with good reason. I could even envision a fatal attack by the group collectively, like the slaying of Julius Caesar. Yet not a single person dared to speak up, express resentment, challenge, or even politely beg to differ.

Without another word to the cast and players, he turned and started up the aisle. Catching sight of me, his face darkened into a scowl. "Preiss, what are *you* doing here?" he demanded.

"Maestro, I must speak with you."

"Not now, Preiss. Thus far this has *not* been a productive day, as you could no doubt surmise if you were sitting here long enough. I need to get out, get some fresh air, enjoy a bit of a stroll."

"Then I'll join you," I said.

"I was hoping to go alone, Preiss."

"This cannot wait."

"In case you hadn't noticed, Preiss, I'm not accustomed to having my plans interfered with."

"Nor am I, Maestro Wagner. The English Garden is close by. Shall we?"

I hailed a carriage and we rode in silence along the short route to the expanse of greenery that lies on the west bank of the Isar River, Wagner looking disgruntled all the way. But once we came in sight of the place, a sudden smile lit up his face, and as we dismounted and readied ourselves for our stroll he pointed his walking stick at the lawns and shrubbery spread out before us. "You see, Preiss, *this* is what *Die Meistersinger* is really about ... the greatness of German culture, of German art. Look at the planting, the designs of the flowerbed. Why why *why* do so many Europeans try to emulate the French and English when we Germans have so much more to offer the world?" (I was tempted to remind him that the English Garden was modelled after a similar London park, but decided to hold my tongue.) Shaking his head with a mixture of frustration and disgust, he added, "And for saying this,

I'm told that I have no business engaging in political issues. But art and politics are inseparable, don't you see?"

Wagner shook his head again. "Ach! Let's walk. Enough aggravation."

It was at this point that my attention was drawn to the Maestro's walking stick. Made of ebonized wood, it was topped with a gold handle engraved with scrolling rococo foliage and Wagner's initials in elegant script. "Your stick, Maestro," I commented, "is another example of superior German craftsmanship, I presume."

Wagner halted and handed it to me to examine more closely. With a twinkle in his eyes, and smiling sardonically, he replied, "Don't breathe a word of this, Preiss. I purchased it in London at a shop just off Piccadilly called, of all things, 'Cane & Abel.' Like the French, the British take themselves and their role in the universe much too seriously. Still, the odd Englishman *does* have a sense of humour, eh?"

Our walk began at a leisurely pace, a kind of contemplative slow motion, and we soon found ourselves passing between two rows of tall trees standing at attention as though lined up for inspection, their early spring leaves leaving plenty of space for sunlight to speckle the walkway. A pair of hawks circled overhead complaining about another pair which had beaten them to the carcass of a tiny field mouse, bringing another sardonic smile to Wagner's lips. "Ah Nature! Now there's a death you should be investigating, Inspector Preiss."

I had waited for an opening. Nature, in the form of two ravenous hawks and a dead field mouse, came to my assistance. "Speaking of investigations, Maestro, something has come up ... something of a rather unusual ... perhaps I should say unconventional or unorthodox —"

But Wagner was paying no attention, none whatsoever. As though he hadn't heard a word I'd said, he chuckled. "I gather you are no stranger to music, Preiss. What do you think of Johannes Brahms's stuff?" Without waiting for my reply, he went on: "To judge by what I've heard, the man's possessed by a burning desire for anonymity, don't you agree?" Again not waiting for my answer, he said, "Cosima and I are off to a concert tonight. The orchestra is from Weimar. The program opens with a Brahms symphony and I am so excited, Preiss!"

"But Maestro, your aversion to Brahms is well-known. From what you've often said about his music, in five minutes you'll be fast asleep."

"Of course. That's why I'm so excited!"

We both stopped to laugh, Wagner beaming with pleasure over the wickedness of his own joke. And for the first time since our initial meeting, I detected beneath the sooty layers of his past misdeeds and his boundless self-centredness a few gratifying flickers of wit.

I waited for this rare moment to pass, then said, "Maestro, I regret having to change the subject, but —"

"Yes, yes, of course, Preiss. You did say we have something important to discuss. Well?"

"It concerns this woman Cornelia Vanderhoute —"

"You've found her?"

"I'm afraid not."

Wagner halted abruptly. "But I don't understand, Preiss. Rotfogel was supposed to lead you to her. You twisted my arm until I agreed to rehire him, but the bastard didn't have the decency to show up today for rehearsal after all the upheaval he created. How do you explain that, I'd like to know."

"Thilo Rotfogel is dead, Maestro. Murdered. I was going to add 'in cold blood' but actually it appears the circumstances were hot-blooded, if you take my meaning."

Wagner gave me a knowing smile. "You mean that poor excuse for a human male was done away with while trying to make love, don't you? Well, I'm not surprised. He was a brilliant hornist, Preiss. Brilliant! But I always suspected that his private life was a tunnel with no light at the end. And Cornelia … how does she fit into the picture?"

"I'm certain she killed him."

"But why?" Wagner asked. "He was a strange man in many ways, certainly not the easiest musician I ever worked with. In fact, he was annoying much of the time. But the woods aren't full of great French horn players, so I put up with him. If *any*one wanted to kill Rotfogel, it was I who had good reason, believe me. But Vanderhoute —?"

"She may have had several motives," I said, "robbery being one. We both know she wanted money, don't we, Maestro?" As I expected, Wagner made no comment. I continued: "Rotfogel's jewellery was missing and we have evidence she pawned some of it. But for the moment, Maestro, I'm more interested in another murder I'm certain she committed. I'm referring to the death of Karla Steilmann. Why would Cornelia Vanderhoute want to kill Karla Steilmann? And the answer that keeps flashing before my eyes is … jealousy. Now, why would Vanderhoute be jealous of Steilmann? Because Steilmann was a better singer, indeed your star soprano? From my conversation with your chorus master, she was aware of her limitations and quite content to be a member of the chorus. So what reason would she have to be jealous? Perhaps you have some idea, Maestro?"

Again Wagner remained silent, and looked away.

"Perhaps you have some idea?" I repeated, not pressing him, but not letting him stray from my question. "Well, Maestro?"

At last Wagner spoke up. "I need to walk a bit more, Preiss. The air and the exercise are good for these old bones of mine."

We began to walk at the same measured pace as before, which gave Wagner an opportunity to avoid my gaze. Staring straight ahead of him, he said, speaking in such a matter-of-fact way one would have thought he was reading from a police report, "September, the year before last … Dresden … the opera house there … we were performing *Tannhäuser*. One of the leading female roles, that of the Venus, was to have been sung by my favourite dramatic singer, Wilhelmine Schroeder-Devrient. Alas, being somewhat past her prime, she was not up to the task either vocally and physically. Venus must be youthful, sensuous, and have a voice to match. Steilmann auditioned for the role. Long story short: audience fell in love with Karla Steilmann in Dresden."

We walked on several more paces before Wagner added, in the same detached way, "I too fell in love with Karla Steilmann. The two of us spent a night together at our hotel in Dresden … one night only. Somehow — God knows how — Vanderhoute found out. When she — Vanderhoute, that is — tried to extract money from me, besides claiming to be carrying my child, she threatened to inform Cosima about Dresden."

"And has Madam Wagner any knowledge of this?" I asked.

"God forbid!" Wagner said. "Listen to me, Inspector. I *love* Cosima, love her so deeply I cannot express it enough in words. For her next birthday, I am going to surprise her with a piece of music composed especially for her. Her birthday is on Christmas day, you know. The piece is titled *Siegfried Idyll* and I'm arranging — very secretly, of course — to have a small chamber group play it on the landing outside our bedroom. She will wake up to the sound of it, and the *music* will say to her what mere words cannot say, Preiss. So, am I a rogue who misbehaves now and then? Yes. But when I speak of true love, I speak only of Cosima!"

Coming to a sudden halt, Wagner, sounding remorseful now, said, "So it seems, Preiss, that Karla, and not I, has paid the price for what was really nothing more than one night in a hotel room in Dresden. You must find Cornelia Vanderhoute, Preiss. I trust the entire police force of Munich, including the commissioner no less, is on a mission to put her behind bars."

How could I possibly inform Wagner that the very opposite was now true? "I assure you, Maestro," I said, "that this matter is receiving the fullest concern at all levels of authority."

"I take it, then," Wagner said, "that the note I received when all of this began … the one threatening my ruination on June twenty-first … this must have been written by Vanderhoute."

"We are still looking into that," I replied.

Stunned, Wagner blurted out, "But that's ridiculous, Preiss! What is there to look into? Who else on God's earth would have written such a note?"

"We … that is, I … have a suspect, someone other than Fräulein Vanderhoute. Police policy, however, prohibits me from revealing names of suspects for fear that, if word gets out, they will flee."

"But surely you can disclose this information to me, Preiss. I give you my word it will stay with me and no one else."

The word of Richard Wagner? Now *there* was a phenomenon worthy of hours and hours of scrutiny! The man had already left a trail of broken promises from one end of Europe to the other: promises to lovers, to creditors, to fellow artists, to publishers, politicians, and yes, even to his own wife, Cosima, whom he professed to love with a passion that defied description.

The word of Richard Wagner? I think not, I said to myself.

"I'm sorry, Maestro Wagner," I said, "but I cannot violate departmental policy. I can say only that I have ruled out Vanderhoute as the author of the note."

"Then what has been the point of this conversation?" Wagner angrily demanded.

"The point," I replied, "is to advise you, and Madam Wagner, too, of course, to be extra cautious."

"Well, Inspector Preiss, thank you," Wagner sneered, "thank you for *nothing*."

Despite the scarring tone of his sarcasm, Wagner stood before me a figure of abject despair, wilted with self-pity. I knew exactly what was going through his mind. How dared fate deal so callously with a man of such immense genius?

"If you don't mind, Preiss," Wagner said, "I prefer to finish my walk alone."

"I understand perfectly, Maestro. Bear in mind, however, that for the time being —"

Wagner shot me one of his steely eyed looks. "If anything happens to Cosima, Preiss, I will never forgive you. Never! As for me —" He waved his walking stick in the direction of the nearby river. "As for me, Inspector, don't take me for an idiot. I have no intention whatsoever of throwing myself into the Isar the way your friend Schumann threw himself into the Rhine. I'm like my music … inextinguishable!"

"Good. Then, if you will excuse me —"

I turned and started to leave, then turned back. "Oh, by the way, Maestro Wagner," I said, "purely as a matter of interest, I'm curious to know if the problem you had with Thilo Rotfogel ... the 'upheaval' as you called it ... does that sort of thing occur often in the musical world?"

"Preiss, discipline is every bit as important in my profession as it is in yours. Want to see a complete autocrat with a baton? Watch Hans von Bülow during a rehearsal when I'm not present! As for me, I've had my differences with musicians from time to time. French orchestras are havens for revolutionaries. British are worse; they are too moribund to have any thoughts about anything. My worst encounter, however, was with a Russian orchestra. St. Petersburg of all places. An unruly bunch of Cossacks with a Jew for a concertmaster! Can you imagine! Fired the Jew, whipped the Cossacks into shape. Napoleon didn't succeed in Russia. But Richard Wagner did. This satisfies your curiosity, Preiss?"

"You have satisfied more than my curiosity, Maestro," I said.

Without another word, Wagner turned away and resumed his stroll, each step accompanied by the tapping of his elegant cane on the stone walkway, each tap reminding me of a firm and steady downbeat as he receded.

"June 21 will be the day of your ruination ..."

The message kept repeating over and over again as I left the English Garden. How did Hershel Socransky, alias Henryk Schramm, plan to carry out his threat? And how soon could I prevent him from accomplishing whatever he'd planned?

CHAPTER THIRTY-THREE

Evening brought relief from the troubling questions of that day. The Bavarian Quartet outdid itself, a fact I attribute to the presence of Helena, who augmented it for the performance of the Schubert quintet. Let any red-blooded man challenge me to define what is arousing about Helena's way with a cello and I will challenge him to put into words what is arousing about a waft of a subtle French perfume, or a lock of silken dark hair that trespasses over a smooth brow, or the seductive line that curves its way magically from a woman's shoulder to her waist and hip. There occurs, seemingly without effort, a fusion of body and instrument with player and cello as with no other musical instrument. In Helena's case, that image remains long after the music ceases.

The audience surrounding me in the intimate hall reserved for chamber concerts burst into shouts of "Bravo!" and "Encore!" Even Erich Krauthammer, second only to the notorious Eduard Hanslick as Europe's most petrous music critic, allowed the granite slab of his face to crack into a narrow smile of satisfaction!

I made a dash for the reception lounge backstage hoping to be first to congratulate Helena, only to find more than two dozen eager members of the audience ahead of me, the men, as expected, lingering a bit longer than necessary when they came to Helena, gushing, kissing her outstretched hand;

the women enthusiastic but far less demonstrative, probably out of envy, or so I imagined. Last in line, I leaned forward intending to exercise my special privilege — a kiss on
the lips — only to find my lips buried somewhere deep in
Helena's coiffure. From previous experience, I knew immediately that this was not a good sign. Still, I was taken aback,
unable to recall any recent transgression on my part that
would warrant such a cold reception. I did not have to wait
long for an explanation.

"I suppose you, too, are about to desert me," Helena said,
rejecting my embrace.

"Desert you?"

"Leave me to spend the rest of this night alone in
Munich —"

"Whatever gave you that idea?" Fortunately we were now
alone in the room, the well-wishers and members of the
quartet having left, and I was able to speak freely. "All right,
Helena, let's have it. What have I done wrong now?"

"You are a *man*. That is what you have done wrong. And I
am sick of men! You are all alike, each and every damn one of
you!" Again, from previous experience, I knew enough not
to interrupt or protest. (How does one stop a cloudburst?)

Helena went on, "A few minutes before the program
began I received a note from Henryk Schramm —"

"*Alias* Henryk Schramm —"

"— informing me that he was in the audience and could
we have supper afterward at your friend's restaurant, Maison
Something. So what happens? Before you arrived, Hermann,
I see him waiting in line —"

"That's odd," I said. "Schramm was here? In the audience? I didn't see him."

"Perhaps he arrived late. What does it matter? So there he is, in line, and some woman approaches him, and they engage in a very animated exchange, the woman looking very pleased ... too pleased, if you ask me ... and next thing I know, he's gone ... vanished, without so much as hello and goodbye!"

"Face it," I said trying to make a joke of it, "perhaps she was younger, prettier, more talented —"

"Younger maybe. But prettier? Only if you think a bosom the size of a cow's udder, with a derrière to match, pretty. But then, that's what really attracts men, isn't it?"

I hung my head in pretended shame. "At last you've discovered our filthy little secret."

The joke not only failed, it proved to be inflammatory. Turning her back to me, Helena said, through tears, "Go to hell, Hermann!"

I've never been good at remorse and my next comment did nothing to improve that reputation. "I'm sorry, Helena, I had no idea you've become so infatuated with this man. But with all due respect, if all it takes to distract him is a bosom the size of a cow's udder —"

While I was in mid-sentence I spotted Madam Vronsky entering the lounge. She looked flushed with excitement. "I just saw that handsome tenor," she said, "in tow behind a very awesome specimen of womanhood, I must say." She gave a wistful sigh. "Oh, to be young again!" Then, observing that Helena was standing with her back to me, a handkerchief at her eyes, she said softly, "Oh dear, I'm afraid my timing is bad."

"Not at all," Helena said, making an effort to recover her composure. "In fact, your timing is perfect. You can accompany me back to the hotel."

Madam Vronsky looked crestfallen. "Oh? I thought we would ... how do the British say it ... paint the town red? You should be celebrating tonight, Helena."

"I'm in no mood to celebrate. I simply want to return to the hotel." Helena turned back to me. "You needn't come with us, Hermann. We can manage, thank you very much."

I stood by, speechless, feeling like a fifth leg on a sheep, while Helena, her cello case in one hand, her free arm linked with Madam Vronsky, prepared to take her leave.

They were halfway out of the lounge when a question bolted through my head. I called out, "Please ... a moment. Did you notice anything else about the woman ... the one that made off with Schramm?"

There was a pause.

Then Madam Vronsky called back, "Her hat. One of those enormous Paris creations. You know, wide brim, lots of floral stuff. God knows how they stay put on women's heads."

CHAPTER THIRTY-FOUR

Alone on the curb in front of the concert hall, I watched a cab bearing Helena and Madam Vronsky pull away, yet I could think of one thing only: the woman who lured Hershel Socransky away … her figure and costume all flash and flamboyance … the hat, especially the hat … *God knows how they stay put on women's heads …*

It had to be her. Cornelia Vanderhoute, of course!

If her plot consisted of the systematic assassination of people vital to Wagner beginning at the outer rim of his current circle and working her way, one by one, inexorably toward the centre point of that circle, namely the Maestro himself, then why not Hershel Socransky (or, as she would know him, Henryk Schramm)? Through her connection to Thilo Rotfogel, or through the normal buzz of gossip in Munich's musical hive, she would no doubt have heard about the handsome young tenor, the sketchiness of his background, unanswered questions about his career, the magnificence of his voice, his pivotal role in Wagner's new opera.

Henryk Schramm. What better target? Schramm … next on the list of Cornelia Vanderhoute.

I had to find them. But where? In typical police parlance I had designated her in my file as a person "of no fixed abode," all attempts thus far to pin down her precise dwelling place having produced merely the assumption that she was quartered in close proximity to a certain pawnshop. But given the proliferation of rooming houses and cheap hotels in that section of Munich — an area much favoured by young and impecunious artists — it would have been pointless at this late hour to roam the streets in search of a likely spot where the two might be ensconced, or, more to the point, where Hershel Socransky might be ensnared. It was unlikely, too, that they would be found at a restaurant, coffeehouse, tavern, or other public place. Murder, like prayer, or the performance of bodily functions, is an act best done privately, a rule Fräulein Vanderhoute had faithfully adhered to up to this point. I could not envision her wasting time over food and drink when there was urgent business on her agenda.

There was nothing sensible to do now but return to my own apartment, hoping by some miracle that something would occur to thwart Vanderhoute's mission, and hoping by another miracle to get a decent night's sleep. (And hoping, by a third miracle, that Helena Becker's heart would reopen to me in the morning.)

I hailed a cab, its driver and horse both looking drowsy, the former probably looking forward to his bed, the latter to its hay-strewn stall.

I started to call out my address.

Then I had a thought.

"Never mind," I said, and handed the driver more than the usual fare. "How fast can you get me to Wilhelmstrasse Number 17?"

CHAPTER THIRTY-FIVE

Within moments of my arrival at Number 17 Wilhelmstrasse I had slipped by the dozing night porter, bounded up three flights of stairs, and come, somewhat out of breath, to a door at the far end of a narrow dark hallway. A thin yellowish strip of light leaked under the doorway from within the apartment. *Good*, I said to myself, *he's home*. Not wanting to disturb adjacent residents, I knocked gently. No response. A second knock, a bit firmer. Still no response. A third; same result. *To Hell with it*, I murmured, and my knuckles came down hard on the thickly panelled door.

A muffled voice filtered through the door, the tone suspicious, unwelcoming. "Who's there? Who is it?"

"It's me, Hermann Preiss."

I heard a key working in the lock, followed by a door chain being unlatched, both steps seeming to take forever. Finally, slowly, the door opened.

Henryk Schramm stood aside by the open door. He was silent which I took as tacit consent to enter. The first thing that caught my eye was the yellowish glow throughout the place created by a half-dozen votive candles, an effect not unlike the chancel of a church, but more romantic. I thought I detected a hint of perfume which, despite the prevailing smell of burning candles, threaded its way through the thick air. I turned to Schramm. "I apologize for the intrusion," I said. "Fact is, I happened to find myself in the neighbour-hood and —" I pointed to a bottle of brandy and a collection of drinking glasses on Schramm's small dining table. "Ah, what luck! You must be a mind reader, Schramm. Mind if I sit? It's been a very long day."

"By all means, Inspector, make yourself at home," Schramm said, his voice flat. "Let me get you a chair." With little enthusiasm he dragged a wooden chair across the room to the table, all four legs screeching against the floor in protest. Seizing the bottle, he poured out a glassful of brandy. In his haste to hand it to me he spilled half the contents on the tabletop. "I *beg* your pardon, Inspector," he said, rushing to sop up the spill with his handkerchief.

"What's the old saying, Schramm? The glass isn't half empty, it's half full? Anyway, it is I who should be begging *your* pardon." I lowered myself into the chair and accepted the drink. "Will you join me?"

"Thank you, no. I find it has a tendency to keep me awake at this hour."

"Well, it's thoughtful of you to keep it on hand in case company drops in." I leaned forward and said in a low tone of confidentiality, "Liquor *is* quicker, *n'est ce pas?*"

Schramm pretended not to understand my little jest. "I'm sorry I can't offer you something more substantial, Inspector."

"At this hour? No need, really. A good cigar would go well with this brandy, though."

"I don't smoke, unfortunately."

"Fortunately, I happen to have a cigar on me. I hope you don't mind."

"Not at all. Make yourself at home, as I said before."

From a leather case I extracted a cigar and clipped the end. With perfect timing Schramm produced an ashtray, which he thrust in front of me. "Oh, so you *do* smoke?" I said. "You know, Schramm, I've always considered a good cigar to be the second greatest pleasure a man can experience." I gave him a wink. "I leave it to you to guess the first greatest pleasure." This jest, too, fell on deaf ears. "I take it you must have matches, then."

Schramm reached inside a chest, produced a box of matches, struck one, and held the flame to the tip of my cigar, his hand trembling. I edged forward and placed a reinforcing hand over Schramm's to steady the match, finally succeeding in drawing some fire into the tobacco.

I sat back, took a few long puffs, my arms and legs stretched comfortably, taking my time, but watching my increasingly uncomfortable host. I sensed that Schramm was counting the seconds until my departure. "You seem a little distracted," I said. "I suppose working with Wagner on one hand, and constantly bearing in mind this string of murders on the other, the strain must be overwhelming."

"Yes and no," Schramm said. "I'm managing to carry on."

"Very good. You've probably heard rumours ... I mean that we have a suspect?"

"Yes."

"What have you heard, Schramm?"

Schramm forced a smile. "Rumours, that's all. You know what rumours are worth, I'm sure."

"For instance?"

"Really, Inspector, I'd rather not say. You of all people must know how silly such talk can be. If idle hands are a source of evil, idle gossip is worse, don't you agree?"

"Oh, yes, absolutely. There's much wisdom in what you say, my friend. But let's put wisdom aside for one moment. Tell me, just one man to another, forgetting that I'm a police-man … what have you heard, Schramm? It's something about a woman, isn't it?"

Schramm gave an unconvincing laugh. "It's always about a woman, I suppose. Adam and Eve, and all that biblical non-sense. I couldn't take this business about a woman seriously."

"You *couldn't*? That makes it sound as though you may have changed your mind."

"I meant, I *can't* take it seriously."

I kept my eyes on Schramm, as he kept his eyes on me, while I finished off the brandy.

There was a pause. Then I stood and nodded in the direction of Schramm's bedroom.

"She's in there, isn't she?" I said.

"Who?"

Without replying, I walked with firm steps to the closed door of the bedroom and opened it.

A woman lay on the floor, her head resting against the wrought iron railing at the foot of Schramm's bed. A large hat with generous floral decoration lay on the floor beside her. Her eyes were open, but there was no need to kneel and search for a pulse. I had seen enough of death's postures to know Cornelia Vanderhoute was dead.

CHAPTER THIRTY-SIX

"Cornelia Vanderhoute? But she introduced herself to me as Celeste Vlanders. I don't understand, Preiss. Why would she lie about her name?"

I bent to shut the young woman's eyes. I was close enough to detect a whiff of a very heady perfume with which she must have doused herself, its fragrance as potent as a siren song. In death she resembled a lush flower that had suddenly lost its bloom, and yet I had not the slightest difficulty imagining what men like Franz Brunner, and others more discriminating, like Wagner and Rotfogel, saw in her. Schramm too, for that matter.

Schramm repeated his question. "Why would she deceive me by giving a false name?"

"It's despicable, isn't it?" I said. "Makes you feel as though you've been made a fool of. But the worst thing is, people who make a practice of veiling their true identity turn out almost invariably to be involved in some kind of nefarious activity. At least, that's been *my* experience, Schramm. Now tell me, how did this happen?"

"Must we stay here like this? Can we not discuss this in the other room? I can't bear to look —"

"I'm sorry" I replied, "but I need you to tell me the exact details of what took place on this very spot. Obviously she was quite persuasive because I understand you were originally planning to have a late supper with Helena Becker and somehow you were enticed away and ended up here. You produced the bottle of brandy and glasses, a drink or two followed, one thing led to another, then the two of you found yourselves in your bedroom. Am I correct thus far?"

Schramm nodded, his head hung like a truant schoolboy.

"So here you are, she and you, you in your partly unbuttoned shirt and shoeless — as you are at the moment, I see — and perhaps preparing to shed more. The woman has thrown her coat across the foot of your bed, but the bed is undisturbed indicating that matters hadn't progressed all that much. She too is shoeless and the buttons of her blouse are undone. There is a smudge of her rouge on your shirt collar, Schramm, and another on your left cheek. The overture before Act One Scene One, I suppose. Still correct, Schramm?"

"I swear to God, Preiss, I had no intention of killing her. None! You must believe me. The picture you've painted … it's all true. But for some reason I found strange, she insisted on wearing her hat into the bedroom, and kept it on even while —" Schramm hesitated, then looking sheepish went on, "even while we were beginning to … well, you've already observed how far we got, haven't you? I looked away for a moment. Actually, I was looking down at the floor. I'd dropped a shirt stud, you see. My back was turned to her. I stopped to pick up the stud, and as I rose and began to turn about … my God, Preiss, her right hand was plunging toward my neck with this enormous hatpin. I managed to seize her wrist and twist her arm back over her shoulder, pushing her at the same time with all my might. She fell back. Her head struck the bedpost. I was defending myself, Preiss, I swear!"

"The hatpin … where is it?"

"She dropped it as I was twisting her arm. It's probably there —" Schramm pointed to the woman's body "— somewhere under her."

Gently I raised the woman's right shoulder. The hatpin was there, on the carpet, a thin but sturdy-looking piece of steel the length of a crochet needle, with a tiny knob at one end.

I lifted the hatpin and held it up for both Schramm and me to examine closely. "Strange, isn't it?" I said. "One moment the servant of a woman's vanity, the next a potential murder weapon. The good and the bad, life and death … all in one, all at the same time."

Schramm said, not wanting to look further at what might have ended his life, nor at the person who brandished it, "I assume, by the way you're wrapping it in your handkerchief, that you're taking it to the Constabulary. Am I to be charged then?"

"Charged? Charged with what, Schramm?"

"Murder, of course."

"That depends," I said.

"On what?"

"On how truthful you are."

"But I've *told* you the truth, Inspector. I swear!"

"Yes yes, Schramm, so you've sworn, not just once but twice now. And I'm fully prepared to accept your account except — well, except for one rather important item."

"I don't know what you're referring to," Schramm said. "I've hidden nothing."

"That is not quite true," I said. "You have managed to hide your real identity up to this point. But as I said a moment ago,

I despise people who play that game. So, my friend, here is how the game ends: *I* will report this incident as a case of self-defence, pure and simple. But *you* must first admit that your true name is not Henryk Schramm but Hershel Socransky."

"My name is *what*? I don't know what you're talking about, Inspector. Whatever gave you —"

"Please, Socransky, don't waste my time and yours. Be straight with me, or I promise you I will make life very difficult for you over this incident with this woman. I repeat ... and I will tell you this once more only: admit who you really are, then I will file a report exonerating you from any criminal conduct. These are my terms."

The young tenor studied me for a full minute, his lips pursed as though deciding whether or not he could take me at my word. "How do I know I can trust you?" he said.

"You don't," I replied flatly. "But you have no choice, do you?"

"How did you find out ... about my name?"

"Ah, there you go again," I said, "answering my questions with questions of your own. How I found out is neither here nor there. The business of a detective is to *detect*."

"And to solve murder cases," Socransky put in. "So I assume Fräulein Vanderhoute's demise is a kind of blessing in disguise. I mean, it's obvious, is it not, that I was intended to be the next victim in her string of murders? You may recall I suggested this might happen the night we dined at your friend's restaurant, Preiss, and you didn't rule out the possibility. Come to think of it, Inspector, I've probably done you ... you and the entire city of Munich ... a great favour, even if it was inadvertent."

I felt myself at a crossroads. Socransky hadn't denied

the revelation of his real name. To that extent, and that extent only, the air had been cleared. But beyond that revelation lay deeper unanswered questions: What was Hershel Socransky's purpose — his *true* purpose — here in Munich? And what would happen if his identity became known to Richard Wagner? Should I press these questions here and now? Or should I pretend that, with the death of Cornelia Vanderhoute, an immense burden had been lifted from my shoulders giving me cause to celebrate, and leave it at that for the moment?

I decided on the latter course. Not for one second did I doubt that the man I no longer needed to call Henryk Schramm was on a mission to avenge the suicide to which the elder Socransky had been driven by Wagner. But a confrontation with Hershel Socransky at this point, without better evidence, would achieve nothing but denials and more denials.

And so I chose instead to lay a trap.

"Actually, Socransky, you've done me — or Munich, if you will — more of a favour than you think. The question of who wrote the note threatening Wagner is now put to rest. I had originally discarded the notion that Cornelia Vanderhoute wrote that note on the grounds that murderers don't customarily announce their plans in writing, and well ahead of time. Well, I've changed my mind. I'm convinced that this was an amateurish attempt on her part to terrify not only Wagner himself but everyone connected with him and his latest venture." I heaved a false sigh of relief. "We can write 'fini' to that ugly little chapter too."

"Yes, absolutely," Socransky said a little too agreeably, as though he'd known all along about the note.

But how could he have known? *I* had never mentioned

it to him. I was certain Brunner would have had no reason to mention it, nor old Mecklenberg who first brought it to my attention.

There was only one way Hershel Socransky could have known about the note threatening Wagner's ruination on June twenty-first. Hershel Socransky was the author of the note.

CHAPTER THIRTY-SEVEN

Commissioner von Mannstein received the news of Cornelia Vanderhoute's death with the look of a martyr whom God had forsaken. "Well, Preiss," he said in a sepulchral voice, "thus perishes the one slim hope I cherished." I was tempted to point out that Vanderhoute may have been a source of hope but that "slim" was not exactly an apt description — a quip that ordinarily would have elicited a comradely chuckle and wink, given his fondness for voluptuous females. But not this morning. Peering at me over his pince-nez, von Mannstein continued: "So now, the radical notions of this malcontent Wagner will go on fermenting. Richard Wagner ... the one brewer Munich can do without! Tell me, Preiss, how could you allow this to happen?"

"With all due respect," I said, "I believe my report makes clear —"

"Your report, Inspector Preiss, makes clear that you suffer from an apparently incurable attraction to these artist types. As a result, they seem to get away with everything from minor sins to major transgressions while you, sir, stand enchanted on the sidelines. I remind you, Preiss, that the whole point of assigning you to this Wagner business was that you were the one person on my staff intimately acquainted with the habits of these exotic hothouse flowers. Looking back at your record — I refer of course to the Schumann affair in Düsseldorf — I suppose I ought to have known better. And now you hand me a report which asks me to accept that a man possessing the physique of a gladiator overpowers a mere woman, kills her, and claims he did so in self-defence! Self-defence against what, I ask you? A heaving bosom? A suffocating embrace?"

I leaned forward and pointed to a section of the report. "There's the matter of the woman's hatpin —"

"You mean that 'Fräulein Hatpin' nonsense?"

"It was you, Commissioner, who coined that name. As I recall, you considered her skill with that rather unorthodox weapon not only entirely credible but conveniently useful … if you get my meaning."

"Well, Preiss, that's all beside the point now, isn't it? That I hoped and prayed Richard Wagner would become her next victim, I will admit. God fulfills Himself in many ways; regrettably, this was destined not to be one of those ways. And now, to make matters worse you rub salt in my wounds by asking me to believe this fellow Schramm is innocent. Which, by the way, brings up another troubling matter: I'm given to understand that the man's name is *not* Henryk Schramm, but Hershel Socransky. The man's a Jew, Preiss … a Jew, of all things! Two questions spring to mind. Earlier this morning, as I was reviewing your report with your colleague Brunner —"

"You reviewed *my* report with Brunner —?" I felt as though I had just swallowed an icicle.

"Don't look so astonished, Preiss. After all, Brunner *is* a senior man. I have to tell you, in all honesty, that Brunner on occasion is more assiduous when it comes to shedding light on the finer nuances of a case. It was he who informed me that Schramm's real name is Socransky and that he's a Jew. Why does this fact not appear in your report?"

"Because I did not regard the man's racial or religious origins to be germane in these circumstances, any more than if he were a Roman Catholic, a Lutheran, or a Druid for that matter. You said there were *two* questions, Commissioner. The second is —?"

"The second is: what the devil is a Jewish singer doing in an opera composed by the likes of Richard Wagner?" Suddenly von Mannstein, whose expressions up to this point had ranged from annoyed to profoundly annoyed, broke into a half smile. "D'you suppose, Preiss, that circumcision affects the voices of these people? Gives 'em some kind of advantage? Wagner is a menace, yes, but the man's no fool. Maybe he's learned their secret, eh?"

Just as suddenly, von Mannstein turned serious again. "Less than two hours from now I am going to find myself standing before Mayor von Braunschweig stumbling and mumbling through a string of pitiful excuses. There'll be damned little rejoicing when I announce that the one good thing to come out of this ... if one can call it a good thing ... is that a murderer is no longer loose among us. But I will not compound this unsatisfactory turn of events by fixing my stamp of approval on a report which labels this tenor of yours innocent. You forget, Preiss, that there is a moral dimension to what we do, you and I. If we yield to hypocrisy, to concealment, to favouritism, where are we, Preiss? *Where*, I ask you?"

A moment went by, and then I heard a voice uttering the following response to the commissioner's question: "You ask where are we, sir? We are in places and situations which we prefer not to be made public, such as a certain house in Friedensplatz operated by one Rosina Waldheim, or a certain relationship — albeit it distant — to a family by the name of Waggoner."

Much to my amazement, the voice that spoke those words was mine!

"Damn it, Preiss, I could have you sacked for such impertinence!" von Mannstein shot back through clenched teeth.

"Indeed you could, sir," I admitted, "but then this discussion would have to come to light, wouldn't it? Not a pleasant prospect for either of us ... with all due respect."

For the next minute or two I found myself participating with von Mannstein in a silent game I hadn't played since I was a child. The two of us sat staring uncompromisingly at one another, neither one of us daring to blink.

It was Commissioner von Mannstein who blinked first.

"Very well, Preiss," he said, eyeing me coldly, "we will consider the case of Fräulein Vanderhoute officially closed. We will attempt to put the best complexion on it that we can. 'A deranged murderer has fortunately met her just end' ... that's how my report to the mayor will read. For what it's worth, I shall also have to add, distasteful as it is, that with her death the threat to Wagner has died as well. As for your man Schramm, or Socransky, or whatever his name is, and as for all the rest of these artistic pests ... well, Preiss, enough is enough. Your orders are to return immediately to *real* police work. This Wagner business is over, Inspector. Understood?"

"Perfectly, sir," I replied.

Returning to my own office I set the Wagner file squarely before me on my desk. I leafed through numerous pages of notes, clippings from newspapers and magazines, official and unofficial reports, several state documents, until I came across a single sheet of inexpensive stationery upon which, written in a crude hand, was the message:

JUNE 21 WILL BE THE DAY OF YOUR RUINATION

I sat back, holding the paper at arm's length.

I read the message over and over, aloud but in a quiet voice.

Then I replaced the sheet of paper in the file. I locked the file in a private drawer of my desk.

This Wagner business may have been over for Commissioner von Mannstein, but it was far from over for me.

CHAPTER THIRTY-EIGHT

Every May, when the sun has finally ended its annual winter game of hide and seek and bursts from behind April's clouds as if to shout "Surprise!" Munich spreads itself bare under the warming rays so that by the time May has slipped effortlessly into June the city once more blooms with newborn gardens. There is a sense that every blade of grass, every leaf of every tree, every petal of every flower is out to prove that Nature, which has treated the city with callous indifference over the long winter months, possesses a softer side after all. Total strangers, having shed the constraints of cold weather along with their heavy coats and hats and boots, pass one another in the streets and smile. On the surface, Munich at this time of the year is a collection of sunbeams and greenery and charm and civility.

Crime, on the other hand, possesses no softer side. Indeed, this spring, which brought balmier-than-usual temperatures, inspired Munich's denizens of the underworld to burst forth from *their* hiding places with a kind of vigour and audacity not seen here in recent years. In the Old Town, almost within the shadows of the onion-shape domes of the ancient Frauenkirche Cathedral, petty thieves were stealing their daily bread regularly at the stalls of the Viktualienmarkt, helping themselves brazenly as well to expensive meats and vegetables, fruits and cheeses. Nothing but the best for these non-paying gourmands! Climb the high tower of nearby Peterskirche for a view of the area and, if you had sharp eyes, you would catch sight of pickpockets here and there following closely on the heels of affluent pedestrians like stray dogs, waiting for the right moment to capture a fat wallet or snatch a loosely held purse, their skills revived after months of inactivity due to the cold. As June's temperatures climbed, so did both the quantity and quality of lawlessness in the city. At the beer gardens frequented by ruffians, evenings of heavy drinking intended to afford relief from the heat erupted into quarrels, which in turn led to vicious beatings and stabbings, many with fatal results.

Once again a rapist was creating fear, this time in the vicinity of the Botanical Gardens adjacent to the Schloss Nymphenburg, a favourite spot of young couples for a romantic stroll after dusk. The method was the same in every one of a half-dozen cases: the rapist, described as having the build of a professional wrestler, would attack the male from the rear, dispatching him with a single blow to the head; the female would then be dragged off behind a hedgerow. If she were lucky she would lapse into unconsciousness before her assailant was finished.

In many of these crimes, one way or another I found myself involved, all as part of what Commissioner von Mannstein regarded as my rehabilitation — that is, my return to "real" police work. My reward for acquiescent behavior came in the form of ever more "real" police work thanks to von Mannstein's determination to "save" me from the temptations that had led me astray earlier in the year.

I'm forced to admit the odd moment of gratification. Remembering how a disguise worked to my advantage in the

Friedensplatz rape cases, I once again resorted to disguise, this time as a young student (no easy feat at my age) in the typical garb of university students — a small felt cap with the school insignia on the badge, a high-button jacket worn open with a collarless shirt, narrow striped trousers. The young "woman" with whom I strolled arm-in-arm was actually Constable Emil Gruber who, dressed in headscarf, flowing dirndl, a light shawl about the shoulders, made a remarkably appealing female companion. Sure enough, as Gruber and I ambled along, our arms interlocked, we heard footsteps behind us on the remote and deserted path we'd chosen at the Gardens. The expected blow to the back of my head was interrupted, however, by the swift swing of a truncheon Gruber produced from under his skirt. As a result it was the rapist's head, not mine, that ended up cracked. For the swiftness of his response, Gruber received a promotion to constable first class, along with my heartfelt thanks. *My* reward came in the form of a magisterial note from von Mannstein granting me a three-day leave of absence to — as he put it — "enjoy a respite and refresh yourself for the challenges to come."

Three days. Seventy-two hours. What can a weary worn-out, fed-up aging police inspector accomplish in such a short time span? I asked myself.

Düsseldorf … Helena Becker! That was the answer. I would send a telegram immediately. "Dearest Helena … a bit of luck …" I would pack quickly, make a dash for the late afternoon train. Seventy-two hours of heaven!

I began hastily to tidy up my office, humming a passage from Schubert's "Trout," the second movement, a happy little tune that reflected my mood perfectly. Finished, I looked about, saw that everything was in order, blew a kiss to my

modest workplace, whispered, "Auf Wiedersehen," and prepared to leave.

At which point the door was thrown open and in came
Gruber, his young face flushed with excitement. "Inspector
Preiss, you won't believe what's happened," he yelled, as
though I were stationed in some remote section of Bavaria
instead of a metre or two away. "You know Detective
Brunner, Detective *Franz* Brunner?"

"Of course. What about him?"

"He's been murdered."

CHAPTER THIRTY-NINE

If I were a wagering man I would have bet my last pfennig that the person who had just confessed to murdering Detective Franz Brunner was incapable of slaying a common house fly, let alone an overweight human being. She was at least a head shorter than her victim and her physique was anything but robust. Indeed, so thin was she that, had it been possible, I would have interrupted my interrogation and ordered up a square meal for the woman. Lines of exhaustion fanned out across her brow and her hollow cheeks were barely supported by a drooping mouth and weak chin. It was not difficult to understand the state of her appearance. I had only to look about me to realize that, despite the modesty of the place, and despite the burdens of raising four young children, there was not so much as a speck of dust or a crumb to be seen anywhere. If one needed evidence that fastidiousness has nothing to do with affluence, here was proof absolute! Throughout the small house, part of a row of similar small houses in Munich's working-class district, there were signs that this woman must have spent all her waking hours cleaning — when she wasn't busy cooking, that is. Even the children's rooms were as orderly as military barracks. I wondered where their playthings were stored until it occurred to me that there probably were *no* playthings. I wondered also who could have imposed such a pattern of tidiness, such a standard of perfection. (Even I, who admire good housekeeping, doubted that I could maintain this level of cleanliness and neatness in such confined quarters.)

"My husband was sloppy and clumsy but insisted his home be as spotless as a clinic. The only thing that interested him about children was the act of conceiving them, if you must know the truth, Inspector."

But this was not all Helga Brunner had to say about the man she had just slain. We were seated at a plain wooden dining table in the kitchen. Between us, at the centre of the table, lay a large butcher's knife. Not surprisingly, its blade and handle were spotless, Franz Brunner's blood having been typically scrubbed off. (Brunner's body had already been carted away for an autopsy, and the Brunner children dispatched to the nearby house of their grandmother.)

"He would routinely arrive home from work with his clothing rumpled and messy and stained," Helga Brunner went on, "and always with the same excuse. 'Ours is not a life of tea parties, Helga,' he would say. 'Be happy you're a housewife, Helga,' and he would hand me his shirt to wash and his suit to clean and press as best I could. I must say, Inspector Preiss, you don't seem to fit the picture my husband painted about police life."

"So that is how you happened upon this photograph and a note pinned to it?"

"I was going through the pockets of his jacket, you know, and came to the inner pocket where apparently you detectives normally carry your identity cards and badges. I always did this before starting to iron out the creases. And yes, the picture and note were there. Obviously he'd forgotten to remove them."

I asked, "Is it possible that he actually *intended* you to see these? That he deliberately —"

Before I could finish my question Helga Brunner tossed aside the suggestion with a harsh and bitter laugh. "Not a chance of that! He was too stupid. Anyway, a woman can always tell when her husband is unfaithful, especially when her job is to look after his clothes. This certainly was not the first time I came across signs — signs I would rather not have to describe to you in detail, Inspector, disgusting signs — signs that he was doing with other women what he'd stopped doing with me, may he rest in hell!"

"I take it," I said, holding up the photograph for both of us to see, "that this, and the woman's note, were the last straw —"

"I have no regrets, Inspector. I'll probably burn in the same hell that I've sent him to, but this ... this, as you say, was the last straw."

"Does the woman in the photograph mean anything to you?" I asked.

"No, nothing at all."

"Her name was Cornelia Vanderhoute," I said.

"Was?"

"She, too, is dead, though her death had nothing to do with your husband," I said. "Or so I thought, until now. It is clear to me now that your husband was much more involved with this Vanderhoute woman than I was led to believe, and for a much longer time."

"The note says something about the two of them working together and hoping ... how does she put it? ... hoping to make progress soon with H. S. Who or what is 'H.S.'?"

Once again a well-used excuse came to my aid. "I'm afraid that is a highly sensitive matter under police investigation which I am not at liberty to disclose."

Helga Brunner received this reply with an air of resigna-tion. "Then there's nothing left, I suppose, except for you to arrest me for murder. Does the law go easier if it's a crime of passion, Inspector?"

"I have to be honest with you," I said. "Crimes of pas-sion are a French phenomenon. We Germans go out of our way to avoid linking the two things … crime, and passion. I wouldn't count on too much leniency in our courts, but I *will* tell you this: I had the dubious honour of working with Franz Brunner, and I will do my very best to convince your judge that Detective Brunner was the kind of man that even a *saint* would have taken a knife to."

I watched Constable First Class Emil Gruber take Helga Brunner into custody and leave the Brunner house in a cab destined for the Constabulary. I myself had other plans. Hailing another cab, I ordered the driver to take me to the opera house. At this hour of the day — it was just short of noon — I knew it was most likely that "H.S." could be found there, participating in the last-minute frantic rehearsals that are part and parcel of an immense operatic undertaking like *Die Meistersinger*.

CHAPTER FORTY

At the stage door of the National Theater I was confronted by a security guard, posted there presumably at the behest of Maestro Wagner. A man of brutish demeanor with hands that could crush rocks, he demanded to know the purpose of my visit, his stance suggesting that nothing would have sweetened his day more than an excuse to send me — or *anyone*, for that matter — flying clear across Max-Joseph-Platz. So crestfallen was he when I presented my police identity card and badge that my heart bled a little for him.

Standing aside, he pointed with his thumb over his broad shoulder to the auditorium behind him. "Final dress rehearsal," he grunted. "It's holy hell in there!"

Hell it was, and then some.

Surrounded by principal singers and choristers, while below in the pit members of the orchestra and conductor Hans von Bülow sat with eyes fixed up at him, Richard Wagner, at centre stage, was breaking his own record for verbal fire and brimstone. "Must I once again remind all of you," he shouted, "that an octave contains twelve semitones ... twelve equal parts of what is known as the chromatic scale ... something with which I hoped you would be at least *vaguely* familiar, each and every one of you? Do you suppose I wrote certain notes in the score with the intention that singers and instrumentalists could ignore them at will? Listen to me:

There are *no* throwaway notes in my score, absolutely *none*! *Singers* are dispensable. *Players* are dispensable. Yes, even *conductors*. But not *one* single semiquaver I take the trouble to insert in my score is dispensable! Is that understood?"

Without waiting for responses, and totally indifferent to the expressions of exhaustion and sagging postures of the cast, Wagner barked, "Von Bülow, the singers will take a pause … ten minutes. Meanwhile I want to hear again the introduction to the third act. Woodwinds and horns, remember: this is what I call the Renunciation theme. It is supposed to reflect the sadness and frustration experienced by the hero Walther, and by his mentor Hans Sachs, because hidebound tradition at this point in the opera seems to be triumphing over freshness and creativity. The opening phrase must be played with subtlety, do you hear? It must convey at one and the same time a sense of obstruction *and* a sense of hope! You must play the phrase loudly but not too loudly, firmly but with a feeling of compassion. Life is full of difficulty, but life is not coming to an end. That is what I want to hear from you."

Turning to the singers, Wagner snapped his fingers. "All right, the rest of you … go … ten minutes and not a minute longer."

As the singers began their retreat from the stage, I managed to catch Hershel Socransky's eye and signalled that I would meet up with him backstage.

He was not happy to see me. "What's this all about? As you can see, we're in the midst —"

"We have to talk," I said firmly.

"Talk? About what? What is so important that —"

"Trust me, I would *not* be here if it weren't important."

"Then tell me —"

"Not here. Not now. I will wait until the rehearsal is over. I'll be sitting at the back of the auditorium. You will join me there. Then we'll go where we can talk privately."

"But the rehearsal will last at least another hour."

"I said I would wait until it's over."

"I'm very tired," the young tenor pleaded. "As you can see, all of us are ready to collapse. Can't this wait?"

"It cannot. And I am in no mood for any foolishness. I'll be in the back row of the house. Be there!"

CHAPTER FORTY-ONE

O ne hour, as it turned out, exploded into two hours, at the end of which mutiny hung in the air like a thundercloud, the cast on stage whispering conspiratorially among themselves, the players in the pit shooting hostile glances at von Bülow who in turn shot hostile glances at Wagner. The soprano engaged to replace Karla Steilmann had earlier stormed off the stage in tears. The tenor engaged to replace Wolfgang Grilling in the role of Beckmesser followed closely in her footsteps vowing not to return until a suitable apology was offered (Wagner's choice of "lifeless" to describe his rendition of a particularly key passage had not sat well with him). Only the man known to Wagner as Henryk Schramm seemed, by some act of God, to escape the Maestro's scathing criticism. Only he, "Schramm," despite evident fatigue, managed as he departed a courteous nod toward Wagner, then to the musicians below grumbling as they laid aside their instruments.

"I must say, Herr Schramm, you displayed extreme courage and coolness under fire. You possess amazing resolve." We were seated now opposite one another at a table in a small quiet café on Odeonsplatz, not far from the opera house. The customary supper crowd would not arrive for an hour or so.

I ordered coffee and two cream buns.

"Make it three, I'm famished, please."

"Good. One for me, two for my friend," I said to the waiter.

"Oh, so now we're friends? In that case, Inspector, let's drop the 'Schramm' business. You know my name is Hershel Socransky. You know my background. What more needs to be said?"

"Much much more," I replied. "Consider the facts, Socransky: Your father was an outstanding musician tragically driven to suicide, for which you blame Richard Wagner. You are a Jew in a world of opera not widely hospitable to Jews, especially the world of Wagnerian opera. You come all the way from Minsk, and gamble that you will be hired to sing the leading role in this new production. You manage to add a threatening note into the picture hoping, no doubt, to unsettle Wagner, though the man already lives such an unsettled existence one wonders how on earth he manages to get out of bed every morning and face himself in the mirror!"

I waited for Socransky to deny any of this but he sat silent, looking me straight in the eye. The waiter arrived, set down two cups of coffee and a plate with the cream buns. "Will that be all, gentlemen?"

"I'd like a cognac," Socransky piped up, as though catching his second wind. "A *large* cognac, please." Returning to me, he said, "Please, Inspector, don't let me interrupt your train of thought." I noted a slight smile on the young tenor's face, a mixture of patience and amusement. "Has the 'train' arrived at the station?" he asked.

"Not quite," I said. "There's one more stop on the route."

A snifter of cognac arrived, which Socransky finished off in a single draught.

"That's *not* how they do it in France," I said.

"That's how *we* do it in Russia," he responded, biting hungrily into a bun. "Pardon me for speaking with a mouthful. Please go on, Inspector. You were saying there is one more stop —"

"Yes indeed. This woman Vanderhoute ... remember her? Well, here's another fact, my friend. You knew her for some period of time before the night she died. She and my late colleague Detective Brunner had some prior contact with you. In fact, they were attempting to blackmail you ... for money of course. You resisted. Somehow you learned that she was on a mission of her own that might involve killing Wagner. That would interfere with your own mission — whatever it was, or is — and so you decided to dispose of her. You lured her to your rooms and did away with her, making it appear that you killed her in self-defence."

A smile returned to the tenor's face. "There's still one cream bun, Inspector. Care to share it with me?" I indicated my refusal with a shake of my head and waited while he ate it and finished the remains of his coffee as though we had all the time in the world. He used a snow-white linen napkin to dab the corners of his mouth and wipe his fingers clean of crumbs, then sat back with a sigh of satisfaction. "God bless Germany," he said, "land of canons and cream buns! Now then, Inspector, let us suppose ... just for the sake of argument, of course ... that your theory is correct. What then?"

"You have two choices," I replied. "One: Withdraw immediately from your role in *Die Meistersinger*. By immediately I mean today. There is a train which leaves tonight for Russia. Be on it. I will see to it that your necessary travel papers are in order. Two: Stay and face prosecution for the murder of

Cornelia Vanderhoute, as well as for threatening the life of Richard Wagner."

Socransky's eyes narrowed. "Something doesn't make sense, Preiss," he said at last. "If you have proof, why would you offer me an opportunity to leave the country? Why wouldn't you simply do your duty, arrest me, imprison me while I await trial for my *alleged* crime? I don't understand what is happening here ... I mean, what is *really* happening."

"I don't owe you an explanation," I said, "but I suppose it would be unfair that you be exiled to Minsk only to spend the rest of your days wondering why."

"Excuse the interruption," Socransky said politely, "but aren't you being a bit presumptuous? You *did* offer two choices —"

"Don't be a fool, Socransky. I have enough evidence to convince a court of law that you had a perfect motive and a perfect opportunity to do away with the woman, and that you have an equally perfect motive to take some drastic form of revenge against Wagner and need only a perfect opportunity ... which I am *not* about to hand you. No, my young friend, go east, and leave Richard Wagner's fate to others. Trust me, Socransky: the authorities to whom I answer have their priorities well set when it comes to Wagner. Trying one murderer for murdering another murderer doesn't rate so much as a single phrase on their agenda."

"In other words," Socransky said, without bitterness, "you can't wait to get rid of *me* —"

"Yes, I suppose that sums up my message pretty succinctly —"

"— while Richard Wagner remains at large, so to speak."

"For the time being, yes."

Socransky studied me for a few moments, then stared into his empty coffee cup, biting his lips, mulling over the choices. Then, looking up, he gave me a smile best described as a sign of subtle defiance. "One of the things I've learned about you, Inspector Preiss, is that you have a reputation for making allowances for people whom you regard as special ... geniuses like Robert Schumann, his wife Clara, and now Wagner. Why in God's name would you take it upon yourself to shield a villain like him?"

"A villain, yes," I replied, "but a rare villain, one who does *not* besmirch everything he touches. Even *you* must admit that."

"I admit no such thing. You cannot separate the man from his creation no matter how great his music. To me that is crystal clear, and if you will pardon my frankness, Inspector, I'm shocked that you show such ambivalence."

"When you have spent years and years dealing with every kind of human emotion imaginable, as I have, you learn — if you have any brains at all — that a healthy dose of ambivalence is like a tonic. Clarity, on the other hand, often comes back to haunt you and stop you in your tracks. Take my advice, Socransky. Whatever grievance you have, leave it to destiny. Destiny, if you let it be, eventually veers toward some kind of just resolution."

I signalled to the waiter for the cheque. "And now, enough talk," I said. "You need time to get your things in order, pack, and so on. I should let you go about your business."

"You *do* appreciate that today is June twentieth, Inspector," Socransky said. "Tomorrow night, seven o'clock —" He shrugged.

"The world will not come to an end," I said. "Besides, the

tenor hired to replace Grilling as Beckmesser is familiar with your role. *His* understudy can sing the part of Beckmesser."

"So you have it all neatly figured out, I see. You Germans are so efficient!"

"Efficiency is our religion," I said, "although that, too, often comes back to haunt us. Your train leaves for the east at ten. I will meet you a half-hour earlier at the *Ostbahnhof* and clear the way for you with the officials. By the way, I've arranged a first-class ticket for you, courtesy of the taxpayers of Munich. It's a long journey, but at least it will be a comfortable one." The Ostbahnhof is the second largest railway station in Munich and handles most of the railway travel towards the east. I hoped to see Socransky at one of those trains.

"And how do you propose to break the news of my sudden departure to the Maestro?"

"Ah yes," I replied with a rueful chuckle, "that little detail will be attended to the moment you and I wave our last goodbyes to each other." I gave the young tenor a playful jab on the arm. "You see, Socransky, whenever you ask me a question, unlike you I respond with an answer, not another question. Nine-thirty at the Ostbahnhof?"

Socransky returned the playful jab. "Why not?" he replied.

CHAPTER FORTY-TWO

At the Ostbahnhof I took a position in the rotunda directly under the ornate gold dome, a central spot that enabled me best to keep my eyes on the constant waves of humanity flooding in and out of the terminal. There is a clock mounted on the wall just above the main entrance, its face large and bright as the sun, its classic Roman numerals giving time an extraordinary measure of elegance. When it announces the hours and half-hours, the terrazzo floor underfoot trembles and one would swear God Himself had struck the chimes.

Tucked securely under my arm was a leather portfolio containing all the necessary paperwork hastily prepared to clear the way for Socransky's return to Russia, including a personal note from Commissioner von Mannstein addressed to the German border authorities certifying the young tenor to be a visitor of good reputation bound for his homeland with the blessing of the entire population of Munich. (Shaking his head as he handed me the note, von Mannstein muttered, "I'll never for the life of me understand why these Slavs love their country.")

As I had promised Socransky, I arrived precisely at nine-thirty, just in time to feel the ground beneath the Ostbahnhof quaking as the big clock did its job.

At precisely ten o'clock the train leaving Munich for the east departed, right on schedule. On the station platform now, I watched the last passenger car grow smaller and smaller, heard the train's whistle grow fainter and fainter, until there was nothing but darkness and silence at the end of the tunnel leading away from the terminal.

Everything was accomplished on schedule. Everything was in perfect order ... with only one exception: Hershel Socransky was not aboard the train. In fact, he failed to show up at all.

And so I was left standing on the platform, now nearly deserted, my arms limp at my sides, one hand still clutching a sheaf of crisp official documents I had gone to much trouble to procure, all in vain, all useless. I would have cursed every bone, every drop of blood in Hershel Socransky's body for betraying my trust in him, had I not been too busy cursing every bone and every drop of blood in my own body for having trusted him in the first place. Our parting words earlier in the day came back to me:

Nine-thirty at the Ostbahnhof?

Why not?

Always ... *always* ... a question answered with a question! Of course the man hadn't the slightest intention of leaving on that train. Even a fledgling police cadet would have seen through Socransky's vaporous response.

An unseen hand forcefully pushed me out of the Ostbahnhof. A voice belonging to someone ... was it mine? ... hailed a cab and ordered the driver to deliver me to the place where the young tenor had rented lodgings since his arrival in Munich. There I was met by the superintendent, at this hour already in his nightclothes and bathrobe.

"Oh, you mean that nice young man, Schramm is it? Well, I'm sorry, Inspector, but he checked out just before the supper hour. Paid his rent right up-to-date like a decent fellow. You know, Inspector, most of the time those itinerant types leave in the middle of —"

"Never mind that," I snapped. "I need to see his rooms."

Another disappointment. There was not so much as a speck of lint or a single strand of hair as evidence that Hershel Socransky had inhabited the place.

"Did he leave any forwarding address?"

"None," replied the superintendent. "All he said was, if any mail came for him, I was to put it away, and he would arrange to have it picked up, maybe in a week or two. As far as I can remember, he only received one or two letters the whole time he was here, so I guess there's not much chance of any mail showing up."

"Was he carrying anything … luggage, that kind of thing?"

"Only one bag, a large canvas one, looked quite heavy. I offered to fetch him a carriage but he said he didn't need one, that he could manage." The old man chuckled. "I was once young and strong like him, but I don't think *any*body could get far lugging a bag that size."

Clever bastard, Socransky. Even at this late hour of the night there are at least a hundred carriages for hire in Munich. No doubt he preferred to take one well out of the superintendent's sight. Take one where? There are at least a thousand destinations — hotels, rooming houses, hostels, taverns — where the man could find temporary refuge. What was the point, then, in commencing a search, even if I were to enlist a small army of police constables to hunt him down?

But what about the residence of his target, Richard Wagner?

It was almost midnight when a cabdriver deposited me on the curb outside Wagner's house. To my surprise, the place was aglow. Every window on the main floor was filled with light.

As I climbed the few steps leading to the door I could hear clearly sounds of merriment from within, as though a celebration were in progress. There was laughter and applause, and someone was playing a waltz, pounding out the rhythm in three-quarter time in an exaggerated fashion, on the Maestro's grand piano. I recognized the piece: it was Strauss the Younger's "Blue Danube Waltz," introduced a year earlier in Vienna and by this time a favourite in every dance hall in Europe. I knocked on the door and was admitted by Wagner's housekeeper who escorted me into the living room, where a throng of men and women holding glasses of Champagne were humming and swaying in time with the music. At the keyboard sat the Maestro, and next to him on the bench Cosima. Wagner, grinning, began to launch zestfully into a repeat of the waltz. (This was a sight I never expected to behold: Richard Wagner playing dance tunes written by a composer with Jewish blood in his veins!) After a slow introductory passage, he gave a cue to the young man standing in the curve of the piano. On cue, the singer began the lyric:

Oh Danube so blue ...

I recognized the singer at once.

CHAPTER FORTY-THREE

*E*ncore! *Encore! Bravo! Bravissimo!* Mass adoration … there is no other way to describe the audience's reaction to the handsome young tenor's rendition of the waltz. It didn't seem to matter that the lyrics to "The Blue Danube" (penned by some poet whose obscurity was well-deserved) were as banal as bratwurst, or that the music itself was a mere cut above a beer garden drinking tune. Sung by "Henryk Schramm" in a voice that was pitch perfect and surprisingly spirited given the late hour, this "Blue Danube" outdid the river for which it was named.

Hoisting their glasses of Champagne in a toast to the singer, the crowd persisted with cries of *Encore!* Wagner, however, rose from the piano bench and, smiling genially, waved his arms to signal that a second chorus was out of the question. Moving to Socransky, he placed a fatherly arm around the young man's shoulders. "We must let our *heldentenor* rest now," he declared. Then, addressing Socransky directly, Wagner intoned, "Tomorrow you will do yourself honour; you will do me honour; you will do all of Germany honour!"

Someone shouted "The 'Prize Song,' Maestro … let us hear the 'Prize Song,' just once, *please*! …"

Suddenly the room erupted with cries of "The 'Prize Song' … the 'Prize Song' …"

Socransky looked at Wagner and shrugged as if to say "Well, I'm willing if you are ..." But the Maestro was firm. "Sorry, dear friends," he said, waving his arms again. "For the 'Prize Song' you must wait until tomorrow night, but I promise you it will be worth the wait. I make no pretense to modesty. It is simply the greatest song I have ever composed. You will not be disappointed." Glancing down at Cosima, he said, "Am I not right, my darling?"

Cosima Wagner responded by springing up from the piano bench and wrapping the Maestro in a girlish embrace, her lips planted on his cheek, giving rise to warm applause. But then she turned to Socransky and repeated the gesture, her arms locked about his waist, her lips on his cheek. At this the crowd broke into cheers and loud whistles while the man known to them as Henryk Schramm stood motionless, as though stunned, the flush on his face a sign that this sudden and extraordinary attention paid him was overwhelming.

"And now," Wagner proclaimed, "more Champagne everyone. King Ludwig has graced our house with a case of his finest and issued a royal decree that the entire lot is to be consumed before this night is over!" Ever the person in command, he gave a curt nod to his servants who moved quickly to circulate among the guests with freshly uncorked bottles, filling slender crystal flutes held out by eager hands.

I had purposely stayed at the back of the room, preferring to remain as inconspicuous as possible, while hoping at the same time that I could lure Socransky away, perhaps with some discreet signal. But this was not to be, for by this time he was pinned against the grand piano by a bevy of women, some young, some middle-aged, one or two old, all of them worshipful. Meanwhile their male counterparts stood on the sidelines, some with smiles of approval, some with solemn nods of tolerance, all of them — I was certain — filled with envy. It seemed I had no choice but to venture into the crowd and somehow attach myself to the object of their admiration without disclosing the fact that I was about to place him under arrest. Before I could do so, however, a familiar voice called out from somewhere behind me. "Why, Inspector Preiss! What a pleasant surprise! But what brings you here?"

I turned about to find myself face to face with Cosima Wagner. "I happened to be in the neighbourhood," I said, adding quickly, "on an investigation. I assure you I had no intention to intrude. It's just that your house looked so inviting."

She pretended to be dismayed. "Don't tell me that villain Eduard Hanslick is on the loose again. I thought he was confined to a prison for the criminally insane for the rest of his life."

I pretended to be humble. Bowing my head as though in disgrace, I said, "I give you my word, Madam Wagner, we used every device in our torture chamber ... the ones especially reserved for unrepentant music critics ... but Herr Hanslick refused to recant. We had to let him go, however. It seems he kept whistling Brahms's *Hungarian Dances* day and night until the prison warden couldn't stand it any longer."

Cosima Wagner smiled knowingly. "Ah, yes, Hanslick, the bane of Richard's existence. I'll let you in on a little secret, Inspector. There's a character in Richard's new opera ... name's Beckmesser. A stodgy pretentious ridiculous hidebound fool. And a thief to boot! Guess who Beckmesser's modelled after? Need I say more? We have our ways of getting even. Now come, Inspector, have some Champagne before the bubbles disappear." She crooked her finger and instantly a servant appeared with a flute of Champagne, but before my lips could touch the rim of the glass there stood Hershel Socransky, smiling broadly, a welcoming hand outstretched. "Inspector Preiss! How flattering! I trust this is an unofficial visit?"

"On the contrary," I replied, smiling back, "I've come to arrest you, Herr Schramm."

"Oh? On what charge?"

"Hitting a wrong note." I tried to look grave.

"You must have keen ears, Inspector."

"Keener than you think, *Herr Schramm*. I'm also gifted with a keen sense of smell ... in case you hadn't noticed."

Cosima Wagner broke into a laugh. "You two obviously enjoy bantering. I wish more people had a talent these days for jocularity. I'll leave you to the pleasures of your own company."

Off she went, leaving the two of us alone. Making certain first that no one was within hearing range, I said, almost in a whisper, "Where the devil were you? *I* was at the station as agreed —"

"As agreed? I don't recall any *agreement.*"

We were smiling at one another, forced smiles. "Don't get technical with me. We had a firm understanding."

Our smiles were waning now.

"At the risk of sounding technical," Socransky said, "there *is* a distinction between an agreement and an understanding, is there not? I'm not a man of the law, Inspector, but the way I look at our last conversation is this: I understood *your* position, and you understood *my* position. That does not add up to an agreement."

"Don't take me for a simpleton, *Schramm*," I said, still keeping my voice just above a whisper. "I know exactly why you're here, here in the house of Richard Wagner. There's an ancient Chinese proverb: *Keep your friends close, and your enemies closer.*"

"Nothing wrong with that bit of wisdom," Socransky said, as though trumping me.

"But the Chinese have another saying you'd be wise to heed: *A person who sets out on a path of revenge should first dig two graves.*"

"You quite certain that wasn't said by a Russian?"

"Take my word for it," I said, "Confucius was definitely *not* Russian." I took hold of Socransky's arm and gave a rather forceful tug. "Now be a good fellow, *Schramm*, and bid goodnight to all these lovely people. You're spending the rest of this night where I can keep an eye on you."

"But that's out of the question, Preiss," Socransky said, shaking free. "You see, I was invited to be the Wagners' house guest. I'm sure you went to the rooms I occupied and found I'd checked out. Well, Inspector, here I am, and my belongings, and here is where I intend to spend the rest of the night."

"You must be out of your mind," I said, barely able now to keep my voice down, "to think I'd let you —"

Before I could finish my sentence I felt a firm clap on my back. "See here, Preiss, you're as welcome as the birds in spring, but you have no right to monopolize my *heldentenor* like this." Richard Wagner, still astonishingly genial, pushed the singer aside as though shielding him. "This man needs a good night's sleep. As Shakespeare said, 'tomorrow and tomorrow and tomorrow.' I forget the rest of the line but no matter." Wagner turned to Socransky. Gruffly, but affectionately, he ordered, "Off to bed with you now, Schramm."

"Maestro," I pleaded, "it's so rare that I have an opportunity to converse with a young artist with such talent and charm ... please spare him for a moment or two longer."

"Believe me, Preiss," Wagner replied, quietly, as though taking me into his confidence, "you will have countless opportunities to spend time with this man. After tomorrow night, the name 'Henryk Schramm' will be on everyone's lips for years to come. But now I must insist that he rest."

Wagner turned to Schramm. "The servants have made up the guest room for you, Henryk. It happens to be directly across the hall from our own bedroom." With mock severity, and wagging a warning finger, he added, "And I'm seeing to it that our doors are locked for the night ... ours *and* yours, Schramm. I've seen how Cosima looks at you!"

Socransky, extending Wagner's jest, gave me an apprehensive look. "Tell me, Inspector," he said, "what's the penalty for breaking and entering?"

I directed my answer to Wagner. "A word of advice, Maestro. There's an old Russian proverb: *Be friends with the wolf, but keep one hand on your axe.*" I punctuated this by giving Wagner a solemn wink.

Wagner looked at me for a moment as though wondering how I could possibly be serious. Then, with a slow smirk, he said, "You know what your trouble is, Preiss? You've lost your sense of humour. What a pity!"

CHAPTER FORTY-FOUR

Perhaps Wagner was right. Perhaps I had lost whatever knack is required to coax laughter out of life's ironies. And so the scene which next unfolded — a scene which under different circumstances would have inspired a playwrights to pen a comedy of errors — inspired in me instead a renewed and deeper sense of foreboding.

We are in the vestibule, Richard Wagner and I, standing almost shoulder to shoulder, a benign fatherly smile on the Maestro's face, looking on as "Henryk Schramm" dutifully marches off to bed. When he reaches the broad carpeted stairway that curves gracefully up to the second storey, one hand fingering the polished mahogany railing, he pauses at the first step, turns, and calls out "Bon soir, Monsieur Inspector, and pleasant dreams!" then energetically bounds up the stairs two at a time.

A thought crosses my mind: *out of sight but not out of mind* when suddenly those very words spill out of me, a purely involuntary utterance, barely whispered, but picked up nevertheless by the alert ears of the Maestro. With a quizzical look, Wagner asks, "Meaning what, Inspector?"

I grope for an explanation. "It's — uh — only an expression, Maestro. You know, 'out of sight, out of mind' —"

"But you said '*not* out of mind,' Preiss."

"Did I? Well, a slip of the tongue, I suppose. It's been a long day."

Wagner frowns; my hastily concocted excuse is less than convincing. In a tone of mild reproof, he says, "You know, Preiss, even a slip of the tongue can sound ominous, especially when it's from the tongue of a chief inspector." In a sudden change of mood, he gives me a good-natured poke in the ribs. "You're welcome to stay anyway, Preiss. Come join us. I trust your rules of conduct don't forbid the occasional glass of Champagne."

"A word first, if I may," I say. "I'm curious about your tenor. I was wondering about the reason for his giving up his lodgings and imposing himself —"

"Imposing himself? Nonsense, Preiss, it was at my insistence. We needed an hour or two of private time, just he and I, for some fine tuning, especially in the final scene of the opera. You must understand that *Die Meistersinger* is a totally new and different venture for me. It's serious one moment and comic the next, and the character played and sung by Schramm has to reflect the right balance throughout, which is a delicate feat, believe me. But when the throng on stage in the final scene is hushed and Schramm steps forth to sing the 'Prize Song', German art will ascend to glorious heights. I tell you, Preiss, this opera is not my work alone but part of the gods' master plan!"

In the time I've been exposed to Wagner, albeit short, I have never seen him so afire with hope, and I tell him so. He gives me an earnest look, his head inclined toward me revealing deep lines of stress carved into his face, connecting like rivulets just above that jutting defiant chin. "Let me tell you something in confidence, Preiss," he says quietly.

"*Die Meistersinger* is my miracle opera, miraculous because I have completed it during a period of my worst luck and my worst feelings of depression. The world has not been kind to me ... so much criticism, so much vilification, not just about my work but about me, even about my beloved Cosima. But I am back, Preiss, and stronger than ever. And soon not only Germans but people of culture everywhere will bless me for *Die Meistersinger*. Mark my words."

Wagner glances at his pocket watch. "Time to offer our friends one final round, then off to bed. I've a very full day ahead. I trust I have satisfied whatever it was you were curious about ... I mean about Schramm?"

"To be honest, Maestro, yes, and no —"

"Then it will have to wait, I'm afraid. You really must excuse me now."

I attempt to restrain him, my hand on his arm. "Another minute of your time —"

"Not *now*, Preiss."

"But there is a matter of some urgency —"

"If you're referring to that stupid note threatening my ruination, I've decided to ignore it, Preiss. I've come this far unscathed, have I not? And Cosima, too, thank heaven. So to hell with anyone who tries to stop us now!" Wagner's eyes are cold steel.

I begin to protest. "But Maestro —"

"Please, Preiss, no buts. Now come along before there's not a drop left in the house."

Abruptly he turns away and heads for the living room. I watch him melt into the golden glow of that chamber, his re-entry hailed with cheers and whistles, the sounds of men and women gaily tossing sobriety to the winds.

Above me, in the second-storey guest room, "Henryk Schramm" is surely smiling with satisfaction. How well it is all working out! he says to himself. There he is, going through the motions of bedding down for the night just steps from where his unsuspecting host will himself presently settle for the night.

What could possibly be more opportune!

I have no choice now but to intercept him. I start toward the stairway intending to confront him when suddenly I am stopped in my tracks by a firm hand on my shoulder. "You're travelling in the wrong direction," Cosima Wagner says. "Come, Inspector Preiss, join the party."

"Thank you, Madam Wagner, but —"

"You have the look of a man who's desperate for the company of law abiding citizens. I refuse to take 'no' for an answer, Inspector."

Though I am a head taller than her, and perhaps twice her weight, I find myself in the unyielding tow of this woman and moments later I too have melted in the golden glow.

CHAPTER FORTY-FIVE

June 21st.

I awoke with a start, my eyes stabbed by pointed rays of the sun, and the thought sprung to mind that, among Nature's myriad cruelties — earthquakes, famine, disease, pestilence, to list but a few — none is more cruel than the first light of day when one has drunk too much the night before. Nor was there much comfort in the discovery that, with the exception of my boots which must have magically removed themselves from my feet, I had fallen asleep fully clothed. I dropped my head back on my pillows and lay for a time lifeless, overwhelmed by a wave of self-disgust, and cursing myself for having allowed my persuasive hosts Richard and Cosima Wagner to ply me not just with one but three brimming flutes of Champagne. (I made a silent vow that, given a next life, I would be born into aristocracy, for only aristocrats wallow in intemperance without shame.)

It required a Herculean effort to pull myself together, make myself as presentable as possible, find a carriage and head straightaway for the Wagner residence, all the while dreading what I might find on my arrival there. The night before, I had attempted several times discreetly to draw Wagner aside and warn him about his guest in the second-storey bedroom, only to be rebuffed each time. Wagner simply would not be brought down to earth. The final rehearsal earlier that day had gone better than expected, news I was astonished to learn recalling his unrelenting displays of ill temper back at the opera house. This was a different Wagner now, a man aloft in some starry domain with his beloved gods, wrapped in a mist of euphoria. Sixteen years it had taken him to give birth to this new opera! After a gestation period of that length, the man had every good reason to celebrate, and who could deny him?

To my immense relief, I was greeted by Cosima Wagner, still in her nightclothes and robe and looking, as always, composed and graceful. But what about her husband? With a chuckle she replied, "I shooed him out of the house early this morning and ordered him not to return until he'd spent at least an hour with the barber ... not one of those German barbers who make men look like military recruits but a new barber whom my father recommends, a fellow from Seville of all places! I said to Richard, 'After this barber's done with you, you'll be writing operas and making money like Rossini!'"

Struggling to conceal my anxiety, I asked, "And your guest Henryk Schramm —?"

"He took his leave very early this morning saying he had an appointment with the wardrobe mistress, some problem about his knight's tunic needing refitting. Mind you, Henry Schramm could wear a shepherd's smock and look magnificent, don't you agree, Inspector?"

"You'd have to ask sheep about that, Madam." I said. "I take it he left his belongings here, then?"

"No, he insisted on taking everything. Said he didn't want to overstay his welcome. Accepted a cup of coffee, exchanged a few pleasantries with Richard and me, then — poof! — he was off. Wouldn't even let us arrange for a carriage. He did, however, take a moment to attend to this —" I took from Madam Wagner a small sealed envelope addressed to "Chief Inspector Hermann Preiss — Personal and Confidential." Excusing myself, I turned my back to her, tore open the seal, and read:

> Good morning, Preiss. No doubt the first thing you will do before the rooster crows is show up at the Wagners' house and find an excuse to search the room I occupied. You need not bother, however. I assure you that you will not find so much as a hair from my head. But do make a point of attending the premiere tonight. I wouldn't miss it if I were you.

The note was simply signed "HS."

I turned to face Madam Wagner. "I won't take any more of your time," I said. "I really must be off."

Eyeing me a little too sympathetically, she said, "Won't you stay? You *do* look as though you could use a hot strong cup of coffee."

"Thank you, no. Perhaps another time."

I started to leave when she called out, "By the way, Inspector, you disappointed us last night."

"Disappointed you? How so?"

In a gently chiding tone she said, "You have no hesitation when it comes to inquiring about — or perhaps I should say prying into — the private lives of others. But the least you could do, in return, is grant us a peek into your own."

"I am a public servant, Madam Wagner," I said. "As such I do not have a private life." I hoped this glib remark would close the topic.

"Not true, Inspector. Not true at all."

"I'm afraid I don't understand —"

"You ought to have brought along your friend, the cellist —"

"Helena Becker, you mean. Unfortunately she isn't here. She lives in Düsseldorf, you see."

"Now you're being coy, Inspector. Or simply dishonest. Friends of ours saw her earlier in the evening. They happened to be in the lobby of the Empress Eugénie and saw her signing the guest register."

"Your friends must be mistaken."

"Not at all. They recognized her from her performance recently with the Bavarian Quartet. But why do you go out of your way to keep her hidden?" She gave me a teasing smile. "I think I know why. The word is that men find her most attractive … with or without the presence of her instrument. Still, Inspector, it's not right that you should be so possessive. It does you no credit, you know. Treasures are made to be *shared*."

I smiled back through gritted teeth. "Obviously you are very generous when it comes to sharing your pearls of wisdom," I said. With a slight deferential bow, I added, "I will try to be a better man in the future."

CHAPTER FORTY-SIX

"*Helena, what the devil is going on?*"

"Why Hermann Preiss, what a *nasty* way to say hello!"

"Very well, I'll begin again. Welcome to Munich. Now what the *devil* is going on?"

Opening wide the door of her room, Helena Becker made a sweeping gesture, her arms extended invitingly, and curtsied like a ballerina. "Perhaps you'd like to step in … unless of course you want every single person in the hotel to overhear your ranting and raving."

I waited until she closed the door behind me. "Once more, then, Helena —"

"— just what the devil is going on?" she said finishing the question. "I'm here to attend tonight's premiere."

"Without so much as a word to me in advance?"

"I didn't know I required permission, Hermann. In case there's some doubt, I *am* a German citizen. Let me take your hat while you examine my papers."

"I fail to see the humour in all this," I said. "Nor do I have time for your charming little guessing games, Helena."

"Then I take it you won't be staying long," Helena said. "Well, perhaps it's just as well, seeing you're in such a foul mood, Hermann."

"You would be in a foul mood too if you'd been made a fool of."

"Are you suggesting that somehow *I* made a fool of you?"

"Apparently people who are total strangers knew of your arrival in Munich while I — I of all people — knew nothing."

"The way I hear it, Hermann, if anyone made a fool of you it was you yourself. It seems there were two things you couldn't resist last night: Champagne and Cosima Wagner. You indulged in far too much of one, and couldn't get enough of the other. In fact, as she was bundling you into a carriage for your ride home you embraced her so effusively even the *horses* snickered!"

"Nonsense. Besides, you weren't there, so you could not possibly know what —" I halted in mid-sentence. In the few moments of awkward silence that followed, I found myself staring at Helena as though she were part of a jigsaw puzzle whose pieces were suddenly and strangely falling into place. In a quiet voice I said, "*He* told you all this, didn't he?"

"Yes," she replied without hesitation.

"Are you *lovers* then?"

"Lovers? I'm not sure what that word means. Looking back on our past, yours and mine, I would say 'lovers' is impossible to define ... something on-again, off-again ... here today, gone tomorrow, who-knows-what the day after." Helena looked away, a wistful smile on her face. She seemed to be reflecting. "Remember that night at Maison Espãna —"

"I remember it all too well. Soon after, you said to me, 'He is everything you are not ... kind, considerate, charming, not to mention handsome.' Your exact words. Hard to forget. So now, Helena, I have acquired a new title: Hermann Preiss, Inadvertent Matchmaker. I suppose I have only myself to blame. After all, I did throw the two of you together. But I never dreamed it would come to this. It's all wrong, you know. The man isn't who he says he is. Worse still, he hasn't the slightest compunction about making promises and breaking them. He's a master of obfuscation. He's convinced his own moral code is all that matters. Hardly ideal credentials for a lover, wouldn't you say?"

"Say what you will, Hermann. The fact is all of us — even you — bend the truth from time to time when it suits us."

"So let's speak of the truth then. I suppose Schramm was honest enough to reveal all about the Vanderhoute woman, the one you were so incensed about the night he broke his appointment with you? How she was an obstacle lying directly in his path of revenge? And how very convenient for him was her sudden death?"

"I don't understand what you mean by convenient, Hermann. What are you saying?"

"I'm saying that getting rid of an obstacle is not what I would call bending the truth. In my circles it's called murder, pure and simple."

"And in my circles, Hermann, people are more concerned about the kind of brutality Wagner inflicted on Hershel Socransky's father. So whatever Hershel has done, allowances must be made."

"But he has no right to take the law into his own hands, Helena. None!"

Angrily, Helena said, "Please, Hermann, spare me your policeman's sermon about right and wrong, and especially those off-duty musings of yours about the artist being one thing and his art being quite another! There is *no* distinction! When will you ever learn this truth? If Hershel Socransky brings the opera crashing down tonight, then he brings Richard Wagner crashing down with it. The two are inseparable, and that is exactly as it should be."

"You said, '*If* Hershel Socransky brings the opera crashing down —' You mean *when*, not if, don't you, Helena? Crashing down can only mean one thing: in the final scene … the 'Prize Song' … the defining moment, according to Wagner … he's deliberately going to foul up the 'Prize Song,' sing it so badly that the entire opera will be turned into a laughingstock, and Wagner along with it."

With a coldness I had never before witnessed in her, Helena gave a contemptuous laugh. "Well, why not? Anyway, that hardly amounts to a crime. My God, Hermann, if singing a song badly were a crime, half the tenors and sopranos in the country would be in prison."

"I'm not an idiot, Helena. Of course ruining a song is not a criminal offense."

"Then why do you care what he does tonight? For God's sake, Hermann, let him be! Let him do what he must do."

"We're not speaking here merely about ruining an opera, Helena. If Socransky killed once as part of his mission here in Munich, he will likely kill again. This time his victim will be Richard Wagner. I'm sure of it."

"Then so be it, Hermann. Look at it this way: by leaving Hershel Socransky alone to do what he has to do, *you*, Chief Inspector Hermann Preiss, will actually be looked on as a hero in the eyes of the mayor and police commissioner. You complained to me not long ago that they had — as you put it — dumped the future of Munich on your doorstep, remember? Well, beginning tomorrow, perhaps the shadow of Richard Wagner will no longer darken Munich. And whom will the grateful population of Munich have to thank for this happy turn of events? Inspector Hermann Preiss! Who knows? Maybe they'll appoint you von Mannstein's successor. Commissioner Hermann Preiss ... how does that sound to you?"

"Very hollow. Very cynical."

"Don't pretend the thought doesn't appeal to you," Helena said. "That splendid office with the fine view of the city, the handsome desk and a carpet on the floor, heels clicking to attention as you pass your underlings at the Constabulary. Admit it, Hermann, it would be everything you've always yearned for."

"Am I ambitious? Yes. Can I stand by and leave your new hero free 'to do what he has to do'? I'm afraid not. Sorry to disappoint you, Helena. I must find him and there's not a moment to lose. If you know where he's gone, you must tell me."

"I have no idea," Helena said. "But even if I did know, I would not tell you, Hermann."

"A moment ago you painted a picture of my future if Socransky's mission were to succeed. Now let me paint a picture of *your* future. Let's say if he's *lucky*, he will be deported under police escort back to Russia because the authorities find it convenient to rid the country of him. So you follow him to Russia, to godforsaken snowbound Russia. I can see it now, Helena: you with a babushka on your head, dining on boiled cabbage three times a day, dwelling on a farm the size of a stable, taking your turn behind the plow, and fending off attacks by Cossacks. Is that what Hershel Socransky has to offer?"

Helena shot me a defiant look. "And what have *you* got to offer, Hermann? Years and years of on-again off-again?

And before we know it we're both too old and dried out to make love. So what's left for me? The thrill of watching you sift through the cinders of your career after you've retired? Thank you, no!"

"Then there's nothing more to be said?"

Helena handed me my hat. "Nothing."

As I turned to leave there was a knock on the door. A voice called out, "It's me, Helena, I've just arrived —"

I recognized the voice of Madam Vronsky. "I didn't know you were expecting company, Helena," I said.

"I'll get the door," Helena said quickly. Admitting Madam Vronsky, she said, "You must be exhausted, my dear. Hermann is just leaving —"

"I *am* exhausted. The night train from Düsseldorf, you know —" Madam Vronsky shrugged, as though shaking off a bad experience. "But Inspector Preiss, what a pleasant surprise!"

Helena planted herself between Madam Vronsky and me. "Yes, well the Inspector was just on his way out."

Madam Vronsky said, "What a pity. Oh well, I'm sure we'll see one another this evening."

"So you've come to Munich for the premiere?" I asked.

Before Madam Vronsky could reply Helen interjected. "Hermann, the poor woman is a wreck after her overnight journey. This is no time for interrogations. Go, and let her get some rest, for heaven's sake!"

"By all means," I replied. "But first, a question for *my* sake, Helena." Gently pushing Helena aside, I confronted Madam Vronsky. "Perhaps you can help me, old friend. I know it's been a while since you lived in your homeland, but they say 'once a Russian, always a Russian,' so tell me: if a Russian man wishes to get away from everything, to relax, maybe even to hide out for a bit, where does he go and what does he do?"

My question brought a mischievous smile to Madam Vronsky's face. "Are you suggesting that somehow I, Madam Vronsky, a humble piano teacher, have some special acquaintance with the dark side of Russian men, with their intimate habits?"

"Madam Vronsky," I said, "one of the reasons you are a *great* piano teacher is that you are a true woman of the world, a Russian one at that."

"Ah, Inspector, Russian women — unless they are peasants, of course — are raised in bird cages. We are not women of the world in the way that women are in France, or England, or Italy. But for what my knowledge is worth, if I were a typical Russian man and wanted, as you say, to get away from everything, there is one place I would go —"

"And that would be —?"

"To a Russian bathhouse."

"I beg your pardon. To *what*?"

"A place that has plenty of hot steam, boiling hot in fact, and pails of cold water. Russian men love to scald themselves alive until every pore in their bodies is screaming for relief. Then comes the pail of ice-cold water. Sometimes they do this for hours until their flesh is almost beet red. My own father was addicted to this routine. Spent nearly every Sunday doing it. My mother would pack him some bread, a couple of chicken legs, and a flask of vodka. 'There you go, Alexei, off to the cookery' and we wouldn't see him again until suppertime."

"I believe I know Munich from one end to the other," I said, not hiding my disappointment, "but I can't recall ever coming across a Russian bathhouse."

"Don't look so discouraged," Madam Vronsky said. "Think of the next closest place, then. There must be a public bathhouse somewhere in this city that offers similar facilities, surely."

Hastily Helena attempted once more to position herself between Madam Vrosnky and me. This time I placed a restraining hold on her arm that made her wince. "Madam Vronsky, I won't detain you another moment. You've been most helpful."

Smiling, Madam Vronsky piped up, "I suppose the Russian man you're speaking of is that handsome young tenor?"

"How would you possibly suspect that?" I asked, smiling back. "Now, if you will excuse me —"

Very nervously Helena said, "Where are you going in such a hurry, Hermann?"

I settled my hat carefully on my head. "*That*, my dear Helena, is none of your business," I replied.

CHAPTER FORTY-SEVEN

This being the first day of summer, I was expected to attend a noon-hour meeting of senior staff traditionally presided over by von Mannstein at the commencement of each new season. From past experience I knew what would be uppermost on the agenda. Fair weather never failed to bring to Munich's surface two things: flowers and crime. After hibernating like bears during the winter months, the city's underworld were in full blossom. Therefore extra duties were the order of the day, a decree that would invariably be met with stifled groans and rolled eyes. This would be followed by the commissioner's recital of unsolved cases and his recommendations for demotions among the lower ranks. Congeniality at these briefings was never in the air. On the other hand, protocol called for full dress uniform to lend pomp to the occasion, not that von Mannstein's arm had to be twisted when it came to sporting one of his beloved uniforms and his array of decorations (all earned in peacetime).

I knew — oh, how well I knew! — that the case of Richard Wagner would raise its Medusa head at some point, most likely in a private dressing-down afterward, for the commissioner still preferred that his and the mayor's strategy concerning the infamous troublemaker be carried out sub rosa for the time being. Faced with a choice — to attend or to be truant — I chose the latter. I therefore dispatched a note by messenger to Constable First Class Emil Gruber (whose gratitude to me for his recent promotion was still eternal) requesting him to inform the commissioner that I was indisposed due to a severe urinary infection. Von Mannstein possessed a special sensitivity about such male disorders, having exposed his own organs on more than a few occasions to extra-curricular risks and consequences, and could be counted on to feel a pinch or two of sympathy. This would leave me free to concentrate on what was at the very top of *my* agenda … the hunt for Hershel Socransky.

It was now well past noon and time was shrinking fast. I had learned that Wagner's new opera was longer than most, taking up some five hours from start to finish. The curtain would therefore rise earlier than usual, that is, at seven o'clock. Being a stickler for punctuality the Maestro would not tolerate even a minute's delay.

I was absolutely certain that nowhere in Munich was there to be found the kind of Russian bathhouse Madam Vronsky described. Granted Munich was a remarkably cosmopolitan city, its restaurants and bakeries influenced by the French, its gardens and parks influenced by the English, its architecture influenced by the Romans and Greeks, but one foreign influence thus far had failed utterly to take hold in Munich: Russian-style bathhouses.

Think of the next closest place, then … there must be a public bathhouse somewhere in this city that offers similar facilities …

I could think of only one — Müllersches Volksbad, on the banks of the Isar in the south part of the city, steps from Ludwig's Bridge and not at all distant from the opera house. A popular tourist attraction and highly visible thanks to its tall white tower with clocks on all four sides, it houses the most beautiful indoor swimming pool in the country. But was there somewhere in that imposing edifice anything even vaguely resembling a Russian-style steam bath?

Entering the main reception hall I spotted an information kiosk occupied by a uniformed attendant, his peaked cap sitting squarely on a massive head, which in turn sat on massive shoulders without the benefit of a neck, features typical of retired military veterans blessed in old age with government patronage. I knew such men to be invariably sour, bored, rude, and bullies to the core. This attendant turned out to be an exception; he had all of the aforementioned qualities multiplied by ten!

"I wonder if you can help me, sir," I said.

"What sort of help? You don't strike me as somebody who needs help. I suppose you're from the Office of Civil Service Administration, eh?"

"No, sir, I am *not*."

"That's what they all say. Tricky bunch, sending around inspectors disguised as ordinary civilians, checking up on us, writing their damned reports. That's how your type get promoted, of course. Well, go ahead, ask me what it is you need to know and let's get it over with."

At this point I realized I had been standing before him hat in hand like a suppliant. To repair my image, I adopted a harsh authoritative tone. "I'm not here to listen to your life story. I need to know if there is a Russian-style steam bath on these premises. It's a matter of great urgency."

"A *Russian*-style steam bath, you say? That's ridiculous. I've had some dealings with Russians. Never known a single one of 'em to take a bath, steam or otherwise. Anyway, what's so urgent?"

I handed the man my identification badge. "I am here on police business. If there is not a Russian-style steam bath here, is there anything of that nature available to the public?"

Regarding me with open disapproval, the attendant replied, "As a police officer, are you not ashamed to be involving yourself in that kind of business?"

"What kind of business?"

"*That* kind of business. You know as well as I do what goes on in such places. My God, what's society coming to when a chief inspector spends his time in a bath house? That's no place for a *real* man."

"I am *not* here to engage in 'that kind of business!'"

My protest was in vain; the man simply could not overcome his disgust. "Third floor," he snarled, "south end of the building. Supervised by a man from Sweden or someplace like that. You'll know when you're getting close; you can feel the heat."

He was right. I was met by an invisible wall of heat as I approached the entrance to the steam bath. I wondered why any sane person would want to indulge in such a punishing exercise on one of the balmiest days in months. I wondered, too, about my own sanity. Here I was, after years of pursuing bizarre people doing bizarre things in bizarre places, about to engage in the bizarre act of hunting for a suspect in a hellishly hot public steam bath on a warm day in June! Report this to von Mannstein and my next "promotion" would be to an asylum.

Behind a tower of thick white towels sat another attendant, small metal cash box at his feet, next to it a bowl containing bars of soap giving off a strong carbolic scent.

"You wish to take a steam bath, sir?" the attendant asked, speaking German with an inflection peculiar to Swedes. There was an eagerness about him which was explained when I glanced at the open cash box and observed a fifty-pfenning coin lying there in solitary confinement.

I presented my badge. "Sorry to disappoint you," I said. "I'm looking for someone, a young man who may be here —"

The attendant shook his head. "Young men seldom come here in warm weather. They prefer *other* places. Today I have only one customer, an older man, but he's been here almost one hour so I expect he'll be getting dressed and ready to leave." I must have looked skeptical for he added quickly, "You can go in and see for yourself if you don't mind the heat."

I removed my hat, loosened my collar, unbuttoned my jacket, and started through the narrow entrance. Not more than a half-dozen steps in, I halted and stood aside to let the man whom the attendant described pass on his way out. He was indeed an older man with an impressively full beard and a generous handlebar mustache that functioned like a bridge joining one cheek to the other. He wore sensibly light clothing, and on his head a broad-brimmed straw hat favoured by fashionable Italians in summer. He carried a satchel. We nodded to one another, he went his way, I went mine.

A search of ten private dressing rooms yielded nothing. As for the steam room, three tiers of wooden benches lay idle in the fog. I could feel beads of sweat forming on my forehead. Again I wondered why any man in his right mind would subject himself to this kind of self-inflicted torture. Mopping my brow, I mentioned this to the attendant as I was about to leave.

"Odd you should say that, Inspector," he said. "The fellow who just left complained that the steam was not hot enough and the water not cold enough."

"Then he must truly be a mad man," I said.

"Or a Russian," said the attendant, winking as though he and I shared some measure of disdain for Russians.

Or a Russian —

That beard, the mustache, the satchel large enough to contain a complete change of clothing … who better than an opera singer would know about costumes and disguises? Such people lived day and night in a make-believe universe of costumes and disguises. The man behind the beard and mustache, his face partly concealed by that oversized Italian straw hat … he had to be Hershel Socransky.

CHAPTER FORTY-EIGHT

My second encounter with the attendant in charge of the information kiosk was no more genial than the first. "Oh, it's *you* again," he growled, squinting at me as though I were a tax collector. "What is it now?"

"Did you happen to see a man with a beard and handlebar mustache wearing a large straw hat and toting a satchel pass by on his way out?"

The attendant cast a frowning glance from one end of the main reception hall to the other, the place swarming by this time with people coming and going, many with bundles of swimming attire tucked under their arms or carried in satchels. Throwing up his arms, he said, "Look around you, for God's sake. I probably see a *hundred* men who fit that description on a warm day like this."

"I mean in the last minute or two —" My mind added, "you idiot."

"This *is* some kind of test, isn't it?"

"*Yes or no* —?"

"Yes, damn it!"

"Yes *what* —?"

"There *was* a man … stopped by to ask me a question. Said he was a visitor to Munich and could I recommend a good hotel."

"A good hotel where?"

"Some place close to Schloss Nymphenburg. Said he heard the castle and grounds were especially nice this time of year. I used to be a guard there. Told him there are any number of decent tourist lodgings in that district."

"Did you recommend one?"

"No. I suggested he try Romanstrasse or Prinzenstrasse. There's at least a dozen inns and hotels within walking distance of the castle."

Nymphenburg ...

In that blink of an eye when we passed each other it would have occurred to Socransky that my turning up at the baths — of all places — had to be more than mere coincidence. Never mind how or why I found my way here. What mattered was how to throw me off his trail. Figuring (rightly) that I would question the old attendant, what better way than to plant a false inquiry about hotels in a section of Munich far west of the National Theatre and Müllsersches Volksbad, indeed almost at the opposite end of the city. An amateurish ruse? Probably. But then again, if by the slimmest of chances he were serious, what then? At this busy period of the day a journey across the city would be no easy accomplishment. A search of numerous hotels and inns, not to mention the palace and its surroundings park, would exhaust what few precious hours remained until curtain time, a gamble I could ill afford.

Once outside the Volksbad I paused. To Nymphenburg, or not?

My thoughts flew back to that initial visit to the studio of Sandor Lantos ... to sketches of two costumes for Walther von Stolzing: one consisting of a plain workaday blouse and breeches; the other a dashing black tunic with silver trim and a matching cap; with both costumes a long slender ceremonial sword, its ornate handle protruding from the scabbard at the knight's left flank. Knowing Wagner's passion for authenticity, the sword would be a real weapon. No fake. No plaything. I pictured "Henryk Schramm" inspecting Lantos's drawings with approval, gloating inwardly. *Motive. Opportunity. And means!* The gods — not Richard Wagner's but Hershel Socransky's — were smiling favourably upon his plans.

I could see it unfolding:

It begins with the tenor mangling the "Prize Song," both the melody and the lyric, reducing Wagner's masterpiece to a grotesque pile of musical rubble. The audience is momentarily stunned. Seconds later there's an eruption of derisive laughter that rises from the main floor to the uppermost tier. Even the walls seem to be shaking with laughter. Thousands of glinting crystals in the enormous central chandelier rattle with laughter. On stage the cast are motionless, dumbstruck. The orchestra sit lifeless at their places in the pit, their instruments frozen in their hands. Mouth open in disbelief, the conductor stands limp at the podium, baton at his feet. Backstage there is utter chaos. Orders and counter-orders are shouted back and forth: Bring down the curtain! No, leave it up! …

In the wing, stage left, the composer works himself into a state of near-collapse, railing and wailing against the perfidy that has destroyed his work, his hopes, his dreams. Shepherded off to his private lounge, an anxious Cosima hovering over him as a mother hovers over a stricken child, he demands that the errant knight be brought before him at once. If there is a hell beneath the hell to which ordinary sinners are consigned, may Henryk Schramm descend to that lower purgatory before this hour is out! …

The young tenor is duly summoned. Does he resist? Not for one moment. Indeed, he heeds the summons with a willingness that borders on alacrity! …

Now they are alone in Wagner's private quarters, just the three of them, Wagner, Cosima, and Hershel Socransky, the singer still in costume. At his side the ceremonial sword. This is Hershel Socransky's time, his moment when all of his stars are aligned in vengeful confluence, when his plan will wax to its full malignance and the ghost of his aggrieved father will finally be laid to rest …

To Nymphenburg then?

No.

Sooner or later "Henryk Schramm" would have to make his way back to the opera house, and avoid being seen by me. That much, and only that much, was certain. I would have to figure out how to recognize him among the masses of cast and theatregoers thronging through the doors of the National Theatre.

CHAPTER FORTY-NINE

"Why would Germans build an opera house that looks like a Greek temple? Is it because the operas are Greek as well?"

Constable First Class Emil Gruber (outfitted in civilian garb as I had specified) was taking a moment to study an edifice which, though it is one of Munich's foremost landmarks, he'd paid little attention to until now.

I shook my head. "Gruber, when was the last time you attended an opera?"

"To be honest, there's never been a *first* time."

"Then let me enlighten you, Gruber. Germans compose operas. Italians compose operas. So do the French and Russians. Once in a while the odd opera trickles out of Scandinavia, the Low Countries, even tiny Lichtenstein. But Greeks? They give us colonnaded façades, Corinthian pillars, sculptures of Apollo, also fish and olive oil. As for music? Not one single note!"

"It doesn't make sense," Gruber said, looking troubled.

"Gruber, you are a good loyal German," I said, "but you are young. You will learn that the older you become the less *any*thing makes sense. *That*, Gruber, in a nutshell is what wisdom is all about."

Staying clear of the Constabulary this day, I had sent for Constable Gruber to assist me in what I feared would be an almost impossible task: to apprehend Hershel Socransky before he could gain entry to the opera house; almost impossible because, having gone to great lengths to disguise himself earlier in the day, no doubt he would don an even more ambitious disguise in an attempt to slip through unnoticed.

Despite the enormity of the National Theatre, only two points of entry were available: the public entrance consisting of a row of massive bronze doors at the front of the building, and the stage door at the rear through which staff and artists came and went.

I assigned Gruber to maintain a lookout at the stage door, "You saw the man once," I told him, "the morning you ushered him into my office when he announced Karla Steilmann had been murdered. But don't expect him to look the same, of course. God only knows how he'll turn up. My only advice, Gruber, is to keep a sharp eye for anyone who looks even the least bit suspicious. You'll likely come across a security guard there, big as an ox with a personality to match. Identify yourself to him; otherwise make yourself inconspicuous. I will patrol the throng as best I can here." I glanced at my watch. "It's going on five o'clock. By six they will start pouring in."

Looking troubled again, Gruber said, "With all due respect, Inspector, shouldn't you have sent for more constables for surveillance?"

"I'll explain later, Gruber," I replied. This was not the time to reveal to him Commissioner von Mannstein's hostility to any plan aimed at eliminating risk to Richard Wagner's life. "I repeat: anyone who arouses a shred of suspicion, get back to me."

As though obeying some invisible yet irresistible signal — or perhaps out of a habit of high society so ingrained that signals are superfluous — the advance parade of operagoers began to arrive at the stroke of six, decamping from an endless stream of gleaming carriages drawn by horses groomed as smooth as headwaiters. Women, many with brightly coloured gowns encircling their corseted figures like spun sugar, floated by, each leaving in my nostrils a whiff of her favourite perfume from Paris (thank God I'm not allergic!). Wickedly charming junior officers escorted the younger women so attentively and protectively one would think bullets were about to fly. Older women made do with aged retired officers, crusty men smelling here and there of cigar smoke, their bemedalled formal wear witness to days long past when backs were like ramrods and stomachs were more disciplined. Everywhere there was jewellery. Everywhere women's eyes darted back and forth checking one another's finery while mental charts were reviewed to determine who was wearing the same gown for a second or third time.

A perfect summer evening, the air filled with excited chatter of people of influence in Munich, a pleasurable sense of occasion and anticipation. What more could Richard Wagner ask of his gods?

The flurry of activity, the hearty commotion, the hustle-bustle which patricians feel privileged to indulge in … everything came to a sudden standstill. A hush fell over the assembly as they caught sight of the approaching carriage bearing King Ludwig, a midnight-blue jewel, its rooftop royal crest glowing gold as if Ludwig owned the sun. And suddenly, there to greet his monarch and benefactor, appeared Richard Wagner, Cosima at his side. It was no surprise to me, as I watched close by, that Wagner made no effort to rein in his taste for effusive utterances and movements when it came to the king. Such conduct, of course, is natural and expected in the grandiose territory of opera, but with King Ludwig himself on the scene Richard Wagner's celebratory gestures were on show in their fullest flower, even bordering on vulgarity. As the trio — Ludwig, Wagner, and Cosima — moved toward the bronze doors, the crowd parted like the Red Sea to grant them a clear path.

A second wave, well turned-out though less patrician, soon followed; then a third, the last-mentioned representing the "infantry" of opera, that is, those hardy folk who, lacking gold and glitter, made it to the National Theatre on foot, then faced a climb of five long flights to their seats in the uppermost tier.

It was now a quarter of seven. The ushers, under Maestro Wagner's standing orders to show no mercy to latecomers, slammed shut the heavy doors, at the same time foreclosing any hope I held of catching "Henryk Schramm" mingling with the surging patrons. Not one man gave me reason to think he was here under false pretenses, although several times I was compelled, as the crowd filed past me, to steal an extra glance at someone's face to satisfy myself that a beard or mustache was genuine, or at someone's paunch to be certain that the fellow was truly overweight and not concealing a pillow under his tunic.

Hoping that Gruber had better luck, I made for the stage door only to find him shaking his head and shrugging.

"No sign of him here either?"

"None," Gruber said. "Not so much as a hair out of place on anybody. Not a nervous twitch, not a stammer, nothing."

"Did you ask the guard to let you inspect his roster?"

"His roster?"

"Part of his duty is to check everyone as they enter … he has a list of the company staff, chorus, principal singers, orchestra, stagehands, everybody connected with the production."

Gruber's face reddened. "Sorry, Inspector, I had no idea —"

The guard, recognizing me, was not pleased when I commanded him to hand over the list. "It's all in perfect order," he said, his tone belligerent. "Only thing missing are the mice that live in the basement. You'll have to get their names yourself."

As I expected, the roll was long, taking up three pages and containing some two hundred names all carefully sorted according to their departments and specific occupations. Members of the orchestra were grouped according to their instrumental sections. I ran a finger down the list page by page. It seemed the guard was right after all. Everything appeared in perfect order.

Until my finger landed on the section of the orchestra headed "Double Bass."

I turned to the guard. "Since when are there nine double basses in the orchestra?"

"What do you mean nine? There are only eight."

"Exactly," I said. "I've been here often enough to know there are always eight. Your list shows *nine*."

The guard thought for a moment. "Ah, I remember. There *was* an extra double bass player … showed up almost at the last minute. Name's there … Horst Schmidt. Said the Maestro hired him because the music called for more sound from the double basses. Showed me a note signed by Maestro Wagner himself."

"So you admitted him?"

"Of course. Why not?"

"He carried a case for his double bass?"

The guard gave me a look of disgust. "Well what else would he use to carry a double bass, a snuff box?"

"You inspected the contents of the case?"

The guard took a deep breath. "Now why would I do a thing like that? I'm not in the habit of poking my nose into people's instrument cases. God in heaven! I suppose next thing you'll want to know is whether I make sure their instruments are *tuned*."

"What did he look like?"

"About your height only in better shape, I'd say. You know, you have to be strong to handle a double bass. Wore one of those French-type berets. Spectacles too, the kind with silver rims. Evening clothes like all the others, white bow tie and so on. Oh yes, he had a flaming red beard and mustache. If I hadn't known better I would've said he painted them, that's how red they were."

"Did you happen to see where he went from here?"

"Where everyone else in the orchestra would go, naturally. There is a large chamber down below ... I mean just under the pit ... where they get ready, tune up, whatever they do. When it's time, they go up a set of steps into the pit and wait for the conductor. I expect you'll find who you're looking for there."

I reached the players' chamber just as they were beginning to file up the narrow set of stairs leading to the pit. Not one among them even came close to fitting the guard's description. I spotted, propped against one wall, a row of double bass cases. I counted eight. My eyes fell on the rearguard inching their

way toward the steps, the bass players, their bulky instruments
and thick bows in hand. There were eight.

Gruber said, "He must be in the dressing room putting
on his costume."

"No, Gruber, that is one place he *won't* be. I guarantee
you he carried the first of his costumes in the instrument
case, sword and all. His other costume, the one he wears in
the very final scene, must be set aside in the dressing room.
He's probably deposited the case in one of the dark corridors
in the basement with his suit of evening clothes."

"Then he must be in the wings by now, waiting to go on,"
Gruber guessed. "Maybe there's still time —"

From the pit rose the familiar sound of the oboist's
piercing "A," the various sections of the orchestra tuning
one by one … violins, violas, cellos, clarinets, horns, a pair
of tubas gruffly clearing their throats … a swelling mélange
of tones and half-tones … the players swooping up and
down scales to warm up or fleetingly rehearsing yet again
a handful of bars here and there that were especially tricky.
Next a shower of applause from the audience, which meant
the conductor von Bülow was threading his way through
the first violin section en route to the podium. Any second
now he would give two or three sharp raps of his baton
on the music stand before him, extend his arms wide as
though embracing his players, nod solemnly, and the opening strain of the overture would settle majestically across
the silenced house.

"Maybe there's still time, Inspector," Gruber urged.

"No, Gruber, it's too late," I repeated. "Our man appears in
the very opening scene. As we speak he's already in his place on
the stage, ready the minute the curtain goes up. Get yourself

up to the wings, tell whoever is in charge there that you're on police business but say no more, just stay put and don't let Socransky out of your sight, especially whenever he's off stage. I'm off to the first tier. Word has it that Wagner and his wife are seated with King Ludwig in the royal box. I'll stay as close to the Maestro as possible, even during intermissions when he'll be mingling with the high and mighty in the lounge."

I took the stairs to the first tier two at a time only to be halted at the top by a pair of splendidly uniformed captains from the king's personal guard who, examining my police identification, and informed that I bore an urgent message for Maestro Wagner, allowed me to pass without further delay. A long carpeted corridor led to the royal box located at the centre point of the tier. Approaching the door to the box I noticed that it was slightly ajar, which I thought strange given that the king and his entourage customarily warranted absolute privacy. Strange too was the absence of additional guardsmen outside the box. Better to close the door, I thought, and I reached out intending gently to close it when a voice behind me said "No need to trouble yourself, Preiss. Just leave it —"

I swung about and found myself face to face with Commissioner von Mannstein. Next to him, wearing the medallion and sash of his office, stood Mayor von Braunschweig.

"You may consider yourself relieved for the remainder of the evening, Preiss," von Mannstein said. "His Honour the Mayor and I are personally taking charge of Maestro Wagner's security. You may go now, Inspector."

Both wore expressions that made it clear they would brook no nonsense.

I took no more than a half-dozen steps on my retreat when von Mannstein called out, "By the way, Preiss, tell Constable Gruber he too is relieved. See to it that you both leave the house at once."

CHAPTER FIFTY

I obeyed Commissioner von Mannstein's order to discharge Constable Gruber, said to myself, "That's more than enough obedience for one day," and proceeded without wasting another minute to find for myself a shadowy out-of-the-way cranny under the first tier balcony, not the most comfortable observation post from which to carry out a five-hour watch, but ideal for my purposes. From this vantage point I gained not only an unobstructed view of the performance onstage but the equally important performance in the royal box. I suffered only one disadvantage here: it was impossible to eavesdrop on whispered conversations as people across the aisle and beyond stole glances at the occupants in the floral-draped box where Cosima Wagner, in blinding white, her upswept hair fixed into place by a diamond-studded tiara, was ensconced in one of the throne-like chairs, looking more regal than any trueborn queen. Of course the topic of the moment would be her desertion of von Bülow, her union with Wagner, the king's rumoured disapproval, as well as the disapproval of her father Franz Liszt. But on this sparkling night, although the great Liszt chose to be conspicuously absent, King Ludwig apparently chose to let bygones be bygones. Let the prim and the proper gasp; there sat the controversial couple now anointed with their monarch's approbation.

A few minutes past seven the sconces and chandeliers began to dim, their brilliance reduced to a pale glow playing softly off the brocaded walls. In an instant the audience fell silent. Not a stir could be heard, not so much as a rustle of a program page being turned. It was as though everyone sensed that the eyes of Richard Wagner were upon them, that he was daring them to clear their throats, to cough, even to breathe! In the pit von Bülow's baton rose above his head, came down slowly like a magician's wand, and the majestic opening theme of the overture rolled like a gentle tide across the rows of hushed men and women. Before long the crimson and gold curtain lifted to reveal the interior of St. Catherine's Church in old Nuremberg. Eva, the heroine, was seated to one side; Walther, the hero, stood nearby, the two exchanging glances in the midst of a church service. Entranced by Eva's beauty, the young knight, in a voice pure and clear as crystal yet warm with desire, sang his first words: "Stay! A word! A single word!" …

As the curtain began its slow descent at the end of Act One there were a few seconds of hesitation, then a scattering of applause and murmured hints of surprise, followed here and there by cautious "Bravos." These gave way to less restrained applause, the "Bravos" grew more enthusiastic and widespread, and very soon it became clear that the audience were intrigued, even excited, by this new Wagner, this Wagner who could mix the serious and the comic and make it work, this Wagner whose every musical phrase and motif came to life at precisely the right moment in every twist of the plot.

Hardly had the curtain begun its descent at the close of Act Two when the audience, from the main partèrre all the way up to "the clouds" in the fifth tier, sprang to their feet cheering, demanding that the principal singers return again and again for curtain calls. And whenever the Franconian knight — this previously unheard of tenor by the name of Henryk Schramm — stepped forward for a solo bow, women of all ages tossed aside their fans, discarded their dignity, and unabashedly threw kisses in his direction. And when "Schramm," responding to his final call, brought a hand to his heart, it looked to me as though at least half the women in the theatre were on the verge of fainting with indescribable pleasure!

Up in the royal box King Ludwig too stood applauding, the tall benefactor smiling benignly down at his favoured beneficiary. At first Wagner remained rooted to his chair, seemingly overwhelmed. When finally he slowly eased to his feet, his exhibition of gratitude smacked of prior rehearsal: dramatically deep bows, hands modestly at his sides, chin buried deep in the ruffles of his shirtfront, eyes shut. Had I been closer I might have spotted a tear or two. I certainly would have bet anyone in the house that he'd practised these gestures days in advance before a mirror in the privacy of his bedroom.

The program explained that, due to the extraordinary length of the opera, the two intermissions would be shortened to ten minutes instead of the customary twenty, leaving barely enough time for women to tug their bodices and bustles back into shape while their male escorts grumbled about insufficient time to visit the bar. With Act Three about to begin in minutes, one option only was open to me: I would have to desert my place of concealment, find my way quickly backstage, and attempt to waylay Hershel Socransky.

According to the program, the Third Act would begin with the lengthy prelude which I'd heard in rehearsal, followed by Scene One during which Walther's mentor Hans Sachs, the town sage, broods about the state of the world and yearns for an era of enlightenment. Walther would make his next appearance in Scene Two. This would give me the opportunity I desperately needed to confront the tenor.

But confront him how? And with what?

An appeal to reason? *Look, Socransky, you have nothing to gain by deliberately mangling the "Prize Song." And less than nothing to gain by making an attempt on the life of Wagner. Say you succeed in achieving revenge ... then what? You leave your own future in ruins! ...*

Or what about threats? *Carry out this plan of yours, Socransky, and I will have no choice but to arrest you. Every law I can muster will come down on your head. On what charges? you ask. Fraud. Public Mischief. Willful destruction of property. Those are mere legal frills. Threats to Wagner's life. And then there's that business with Cornelia Vanderhoute, don't overlook that. I'm speaking of murder. You could be facing years in prison, years! ...*

There was one other card to play, one that I would play with great reluctance, a last resort that would be painful for me and leave me with a lifetime of self-disgust. But play it I would if necessary. *Helena Becker, Socransky ... Helena Becker is in love with you. Carry out this plan of yours and the two of you will never see each other again except through prison bars! You and she are perfect soulmates. Deprive yourself of freedom and you deprive both of you of years of happiness! ...*

With the house lights dimming in anticipation of Act Three, I started out for the area backstage where I was certain Hershel Socransky would be awaiting his cue. In the darkening theatre I kept to the least visible passageways, feeling with all this stealth like a bit of a criminal myself. I found my way to a set of steps, the final approach to backstage, and was about to mount when what I caught sight of just beyond the upper step stopped me in my tracks. There, with her back to me, stood Helena, alone. But where was Socransky?

CHAPTER FIFTY-ONE

"Helena! But how did you —"

"Slipped in at the last minute by way of the stage door," she explained, looking quite pleased with herself. "He arranged passes for Vronsky and me. She's up in the second tier. I preferred to be here, backstage."

"Then you must know where I can find him," I said. "I need to talk with him … urgently."

"There is nothing you can say to him, Hermann, that he hasn't already said to himself."

"Good. Then I take it you've succeeded in driving some sense into his head."

"I've done nothing of the sort," she shot back, as though what I had just said was preposterous. "Whatever happens in the next hour, let it happen, Hermann, and be done with it once and for all."

"Out of the question!" I began angrily, prompting one of the stage managers to rush over. Dishevelled and perspiring, he had the look of a man born to worry. "Please!" he said in a loud whisper, addressing the two of us, "we need this space clear." He pointed to an out-of-the-way corner where stage properties from other operas, draped in white dust covers, huddled together in silence and darkness like a gathering of ghosts. "You can stand over there if you wish," he said, "but you must keep your voices *down!*"

Helena and I complied but before I could continue she said, "It's pointless for you to stay here —"

"She's right, Inspector. It *is* pointless —" These words came at me from a disembodied voice. Then, out of the shadows, as though he were a spirit materializing before my eyes, Hershel Socransky emerged. "I hate to be inhospitable, Preiss, but you really are not welcome here." He was wearing the costume for his appearance in the song contest, the black and silver cape and matching cap, the long sword. Every inch the perfect Franconian knight. Every inch the personification of Richard Wagner's vision of a German hero.

"I don't give a damn whether I'm welcome or not," I said. "You've given me the slip twice today but now you've run out of luck."

He raised a quizzical eyebrow. "Twice, you say?"

"At the public baths, that *was* you with the red beard and the large straw hat, of course. And tonight … the extra bass player with the forged note."

Socransky smiled, his expression one of mordant amusement. "And here I thought I was making life so very interesting for you, Preiss. After all, you must be sick to death of dodgers who lack imagination."

"We haven't time for smart chit-chat," I said. "Give up your plan. If Wagner has committed a crime you believe needs punishing, it is up to me, not you, to deal with it."

"Preiss, my friend," Socransky said, "there isn't a police force in the world capable of bringing Richard Wagner to justice for the crime he committed against my father. That is a special mission for me, and for me alone. I would not let that maniacal woman Vanderhoute stand in my way. Nor will I let you!"

Back came the stage manager looking more upset than before. "My God, what is going on here? *Please,* we cannot have this!" To the tenor he said, "Herr Schramm, you are due for your entrance in exactly one minute!" Socransky nodded curtly, tugged at his cape and tunic to make certain they were snug, checked his cap to make certain it was centred, leaned forward to brush a kiss on Helena's cheek, and said quietly to her, "Wish me luck." He started to move forward in the wings in readiness for his next appearance on stage.

Hastily reaching out, I managed to take a firm hold of his shoulder and spin him around. "Listen to me, Socransky. You're right. You and you alone can mete out the right punishment. But let me tell you how. Sing the 'Prize Song,' sing it as brilliantly as you can. Turn the evening into a total triumph for Wagner —"

"Are you *mad*, Preiss —?"

"Be quiet and listen to me. As soon as it's over tonight, and Wagner is basking in all the glory … when it seems that all Munich is at his feet … no, *all Germany* … then tell him who you are, who you've been all along … Hershel Socransky, Mastersinger from Minsk. Let him know that a Jew was responsible for his success. Do as I say, I beg you!"

The stage manager beckoned frantically. "Herr Schramm, *now* —"

Shaking loose from my grip, Socransky said, "I must go."

CHAPTER FIFTY-TWO

A ny moment now the curtain will rise on Act Three. Backstage, my presence no longer challenged by the stage manager thanks to my police credentials, I keep one eye on "Schramm," the other eye on the royal box with the aid of opera glasses commandeered from the prompter (who has no need of them anyway in his mouse-hole). Nearby, though just out of reach, stands Helena maintaining her distance from me as though I am a leper. As for Commissioner von Mannstein and Mayor von Braunschweig, I have to rely on my imagination. I have visions of these two stalwarts posted outside King Ludwig's box, ready at a moment's notice to stand aside and look the other way should anyone — *anyone at all* — make a move to assassinate Richard Wagner.

Disaster, I am certain, is now inevitable. Yet through the glasses I see the composer and his wife, their hands clasped together on the railing of the box, exchanging jubilant looks, nodding as though saying to each other "Yes!" again and again.

At last, four hours and forty minutes since the opening strain, comes Scene Five, the final scene of *Die Meistersinger*.

The foreground is transformed into an open meadow, a narrow river winding through it. In the background lies the Town of Nuremberg. Suddenly the atmosphere is thick with festivity. From gaily decorated boats artisans represent-ing various guilds disembark with their wives and children.

Each guild displays its banners, waved to and fro boister-ously by standard bearers. To one side a raised stand is erected bearing rows of benches to accommodate the jury of Mastersingers. Dead centre stands a mound about which flowers have been strewn. Here the two competitors for the prize will sing. The Mastersingers' youthful apprentices lead the merrymaking decked out in ribbons and prancing about with slender wands which they twirl high into the air and catch like circus acrobats. Now the principal guilds — Shoemakers, Bakers, Tailors — take turns parading across the stage proclaiming their contributions to the good life of the town's burghers. All of this is sung and danced in high spirits. Colour is everywhere: in the set, the costumes, the lighting. I think to myself: if only Sandor Lantos were alive to savor the fruits of his labour.

Now Eva, led by her father, takes her seat near the judging stand. The apprentices call for silence. Hans Sachs, magisterial in the flowing blue and gold robe of head Mastersinger, declares in his authoritative baritone: "Let the Song Contest begin."

First to the mound is Beckmesser, by all appearances the unlikeliest candidate for the hand of Eva Pogner. Still, as an accredited Mastersinger he is entitled to his turn before the jury. Having earlier stolen the poem written by Walther, but lacking the slightest idea of the music to which it is to be sung, Beckmesser nevertheless plunges into the piece impro-vising a tune at best unoriginal, at worst silly. Immediately it becomes apparent he hasn't the slightest understanding of the *words* either.

The jury of Masters is confounded. "What's this?" they murmur to one another. "Is he out of his mind?"

Beckmesser plods on, his performance growing more grotesque by the minute, making a complete and utter fool of himself. Outraged by what they've just suffered through, the jury wants no more of this outlandish piece of work. But Hans Sachs persuades them to be patient and give the young knight who wrote it his chance. Skeptical, they nonetheless agree out of deference to Sachs.

On stage there is silence again. Sachs calls out, "Herr Walther von Stolzing, come forth!" Dazzling in his black and silver costume, Walther steps firmly onto the mound. The moment is ripe with expectancy. The orchestra offers him an introductory note played serenely by strings and harp. But Walther stands motionless, his lips sealed. He looks up at the royal box where King Ludwig has leaned forward in his throne-like seat, his hands folded on the railing of the box as though he can scarcely wait for the opening words and music of the much-talked-about "Prize Song."

From the royal box, Walther, still not uttering a sound, lets his eyes roam across the vast audience in the main partère. Then he glances up, up, up, one tier at a time, until his gaze is fixed on the uppermost tier. His lips part slightly, but still no sound.

Wagner too is leaning forward in his seat. Cosima is biting her lip. At the conductor's podium in the pit von Bülow clears his throat noisily. He raises his baton and, at his bidding, the orchestra replays the introduction. But the tenor is indifferent to the cue and remains mute. Here and there throughout the audience an uncertain chuckle can be heard. Perhaps this is yet another comic turn in the opera?

Wagner's face darkens. What is happening down there? Has his heldentenor forgotten the words? Or mistaken the cue? Or worse still lost his voice?

For a third time von Bülow lifts his baton. For a third time the strings and harp deliver the opening note. Only then does the tenor seem to find his voice. But the "Prize Song" begins uncertainly, the melody wavering, the words muffled. The unimaginable is happening!

In the royal box Wagner has gotten to his feet. Cosima tugs at his elbow urging him to sit, to calm himself.

Falling silent again, Walther stares pensively down at von Bülow. After what must be an agonizing pause for the entire cast and orchestra, "Schramm" calmly nods to the conductor. Von Bulow taps his music stand once again with his baton, bringing it down loudly this time like a drumstick. The orchestra repeats the introduction. The singer pulls himself erect. He takes a deep breath. His lips part. And he begins:

> *Shining in the rosy light of morning,*
> *the air heavy with blossom and scent,*
> *full of every unthought of joy,*
> *a garden invited me to enter*
> *and beneath a wondrous tree there*
> *richly hung with fruit*
> *to behold in a blessed dream of love,*
> *boldly promising fulfillment*
> *to the highest of joy's desires —*
> *the most beautiful woman:*
> *Eva in Paradise! …*

Here's a very different rendition! The jurors are impressed. As for "Henryk Schramm," standing poised and proud, his right hand clasped over his heart, his left hand lightly cupped over the handle of his knight's sword, he is now in full command. His singing is exquisite, transcendent even; so fervent one moment, so delicate the next, that at times it sticks in my throat.

A second stanza and the crowd on stage is abuzz with excitement. The hall begins to swell with the music, and the space seems barely able to contain the sound.

The third stanza brings the "Prize Song" to a thrilling conclusion. I tell myself this will be chiselled into my memory until my dying breath. Forgetting myself, I exclaim in a loud whisper, "Schramm's done it! The bastard's done it!" To which the stage manager, disregarding my police credentials, stamps his foot angrily and hushes me as if I'm an unruly child. Disregarding the stage manager, I turn to Helena and repeat in the same loud whisper, "The bastard's done it!" But Helena's face betrays no emotion. I cannot tell whether she is pleased or disappointed.

Of course the prize goes to Walther. One final tribute to German art is sung by Hans Sachs. The orchestra reprises the triumphant opening chords of the overture as the finale. The curtain begins slowly to descend on *Die Meistersinger* and a tumultuous ovation shakes the National Theatre to its foundations. In the royal box the king shoots to his feet applauding vigorously and motioning Wagner to rise. Of course Wagner holds back, playing the role of reluctant genius modestly declining to don the garland, but very soon he too is on his feet, lifted out of his seat by his persuasive monarch, bringing a fresh roar of approval from the house.

Now the curtain rises. First on stage come the chorus, followed by secondary characters, all bowing and smiling as applause washes over them. Then the principals come from the wings for solo bows at centre stage: Hans Sachs, Beckmesser, Eva, each greeted with unrestrained cheering, clapping, foot-stamping. This is more than applause; this is an outpouring of love!

And now the winner of the prize appears for his solo bow centre stage. I wonder whether the architect who designed this opera house took into account the effects of sustained thunder on a structure of this kind. Will the ceiling fall? Will the walls collapse? Will the floors crumble? Here and there voices call out, "Henryk Schramm!" and before long the tenor's name is shouted in unison throughout the house. Time and time again he bows low, accepting humbly the acclaim showered on him. In the royal box, Cosima, on her feet too, throws him kiss after kiss while Wagner, beaming, tosses him an informal salute.

But unlike his fellow cast members, the tenor (whose name repeatedly pounds across the apron of the stage like a tidal wave) is not smiling. The expression on his face is difficult to define. Serious, yes. But is there a touch of sadness too? His mouth has a resolute set, the lips sealed. His eyes appear to be focused on some object beyond the confines of the opera house. He seems to be here and elsewhere at the same time.

"Henryk Schramm!" the crowd chants, but the young man has stopped bowing. He raises his arms, the palms of his hands toward the audience, as though he is pleading for silence. At first the audience ignores his plea, but after a minute or two the shouting dies down. The house goes quiet. The young tenor looks directly at the royal box, at King Ludwig who has taken his seat, at Cosima Wagner who has taken hers, at Richard Wagner who remains standing.

"My performance tonight," he announces in a calm clear voice which easily carries throughout the hall, "is dedicated to the memory of the late Simon Socransky. Perhaps his name is familiar to you, Maestro Wagner?"

Wagner shrugs as though he hasn't the faintest idea what the young man is talking about. "I'm sorry, but the name is not familiar to me, not at all. In fact, I've never heard the name before," he replies, treating the question with indifference. He shoots a glance at the king and shrugs again. He is the picture of innocence.

"Let me refresh your memory, Maestro," Socransky calls back. "Simon Socransky was a member of the symphony orchestra in St. Petersburg. You were a guest conductor there … in 1862, yes?"

Wagner is suddenly all smiles, eager to make light of this. "Ah yes, St. Petersburg, yes indeed. I believe I taught that band of balalaika players a thing or two about music on that occasion." His quip is met with the odd discreet chuckle here and there, much less than the outbreak of laughter he expected.

Socransky whips off his cap and flings it aside. He steps to the edge of the stage, the silver buckles of his shoes glinting in the light. He slips his ceremonial sword from its sheath and lets it drop to the boards beside him, but all the while his eyes never leave Wagner. "Simon Socransky was no mere balalaika player, Maestro Wagner," he says. His tone is defiant yet he is firmly in control of his emotions. "On the contrary, Simon Socransky was a great violinist."

"The name means absolutely nothing to me, I tell you," Wagner says, a note of irritation creeping into his denial.

Now there is a stir in the audience. People turn to one another shaking their heads as though wondering if this is some kind of ruse. After all, Richard Wagner has never been above resorting to theatrical antics, no matter how bizarre, in order to gain attention. Limelight has always been his favourite form of illumination, even when what it reveals may turn out to be less than praiseworthy.

Socransky becomes more insistent. "But you *must* remember him, Maestro. You were responsible for his dismissal from his position as concertmaster of that orchestra *on that occasion —* "

A weak smile on his face, Wagner says, his voice becoming a bit hoarse, "My dear fellow, you are mistaken —"

"No, Maestro, I am *not* mistaken. It was you who caused him to be dismissed. It was you who *killed* him."

"*That's a lie! He killed himself!*" Wagner blurts out. Then, in a voice barely audible, he repeats, "He killed himself." He turns stiffly to the king seeking the monarch's endorsement, bending slightly toward him, almost beseeching. But King Ludwig has no stomach for what is rapidly giving off a strong smell of scandal. Abruptly he rises and without waiting for so much as a syllable of explanation he makes a hasty exit from the royal box, leaving Wagner and Cosima stranded there, strangely isolated in the midst of the attendant throng. An eerie silence falls across the theatre, disturbed only by the shuffling of feet as row upon row of operagoers leave their seats and begin an exodus. They seem to move mechanically, as though in obedience to some unspoken royal command. The cast on stage has already evaporated.

The orchestra has quietly vanished from the pit. The house stands deserted ... except for three people who occupy that immense space now: Richard Wagner, Cosima Wagner, and the heldentenor they thought they knew.

"Why? Why have you done this?" Wagner shouts, his voice echoing throughout the empty house. "Why should Henryk Schramm give a damn about an obscure fiddler from Russia?"

"Because my name is not Henryk Schramm. It is Hershel Socransky. Simon Socransky is — *was* — my father."

"Then rot in hell!" Wagner says. "No ... better still ... if there is a hell beneath hell, rot *there*!" Almost roughly, he takes Cosima by the arm and the two of them start from their box.

At centre stage, Hershel Socransky, hands on hips, watches their departure until they are out of sight. Only then does he leave the stage, moving with the confident stride of a man who believes he has finally completed what he set out to do. Yet when he approaches Helena and me, there is no air of satisfaction about him. Behind him the shards of Wagner's great new opera lie scattered throughout the grand auditorium. On the young tenor's face I see only the sour aftertaste of revenge.

Ignoring me, he speaks softly to Helena. "I need a place to stay tonight —"

Helena needs no time to consider the request. "Of course," she replies.

CHAPTER FIFTY-THREE

"I suppose you are eager to return to Russia as soon as possible now that you've accomplished your 'mission,'" I said to Socransky. It was the next morning and we were in the lobby of the Empress Eugénie. Socransky had just set down a lone piece of luggage and was folding an overcoat which was too bulky to be packed. "That coat will come in handy back home even though it's summertime," I joked. "Fortunately the travel documents I took the trouble to obtain are still valid, and there's a train leaving tomorrow night —"

He shook his head.

Puzzled, I said, "I don't understand. I would have thought you couldn't wait to get back. I can't believe you plan to remain here in Munich!" As I said this I happened to look over at Helena. Something about the expression on her face told me she knew something I didn't know. Quietly I asked, figuring one or the other would respond, "Does this mean you … I mean the *two* of you … have plans?" Even as I put the question to them I felt as though suddenly I had become hollowed out, as though from this moment on the core of my own existence would consist of nothing but an empty cavity.

Helena and Socransky exchanged quick glances, each inviting the other to speak up, both hesitant. I said, "For God's sake, somebody say *some*thing!"

At last he spoke up. "The fact is, Preiss, I cannot go back to Russia, much as I wish to. Russia and I have parted company, you might say."

I had difficulty taking his answer seriously. "You're joking, of course. Don't tell me you're some kind of revolutionary. What? Are you conspiring to get rid of the Czar?"

"I wish it were as simple as that," Socransky said, looking, I thought, too sober.

"Well, at least you haven't lost your sense of humour despite all that has gone on," I said. "I can see the headlines now: JEWISH TENOR BRINGS DOWN IMPERIAL DYNASTY. You know what they say, Socransky: Revolutionaries don't burn down palaces; they move *into* them!"

I thought this would bring a laugh or at least a smile. Instead he looked almost melancholy. He paused, seemingly on the edge of making some pronouncement, then, looking me straight in the eye he said, "The reason I cannot return to Russia is that people like me are now considered undesirables."

"Why? Because you're Jewish?"

"No, being Jewish has nothing to do with it."

"Then why?"

"Because … because I happen to prefer the company of men."

"Now I *know* you're joking. You are a born actor, Socransky. A comic actor at that! Anyway, I've seen how women react to you … the effect you have on them. Mind you, Socransky, for a split second there you almost had me —"

"Stop, Hermann! Just stop … *please!*" Helena interrupted. "This is painful enough. You're only making it worse."

"Helena, you mean you knew about this? And you said not a word to me about it? But I thought all along —"

"Don't blame Helena, Preiss," Socransky said. "She has kept my secret."

"Since *when*?"

Helena filled in the answer. "Since the night I visited him in his rooms. Remember, Hermann? The wine? The cake? The letter?"

I stared at Helena for a moment, then at Socransky. To him I said, "But I thought you were in love with her?"

"I do love her, yes. As a dear friend. The person with whom I *am* in love lives in Russia, a young composer. Perhaps you've heard of him? His name is Tchaikovsky. Peter Tchaikovsky. We met when I was a student and he an instructor at the Conservatory in Moscow. Unfortunately, people like us … well, need I say more, Preiss?"

I turned to Helena. "I had a vision of myself standing alone on the platform at the Ostbahnhof waving goodbye to the two of you."

To Socransky I said, "Where will you go then, if Russia is out of bounds?"

"I leave today for Paris. I have friends there, also refugees from Russia for the same reason. The atmosphere in Paris is a little more friendly for us. My ticket is already arranged, but I could certainly use those travel documents, if you'd be so kind."

"But can you get work there? Can you earn a living? It's a gamble isn't it?"

"If you are a Jew living in Russia every day is a gamble. Will they leave us be? Will they come after us? We are born gamblers. My coming to Munich was a gamble. What if Wagner had chosen someone else to sing the role?"

"And if he hadn't chosen you, Socransky, would you nevertheless have found some way to kill him?"

Socransky's face broke into an inscrutable smile as he thought of an answer. Finally he said, "What do *you* think, Inspector?"

"Damn it, Socransky! There you go, answering a question with one of your own!" I shouted back.

The young tenor took a step forward and gently said to Helena, "Give me your hand —" Taking hold of it, he placed her hand in mine, folding the two hands together ceremoniously, like a priest. "There now," he said. "With the powers vested in me by the God of vast improbabilities, I hereby declare the two of you inseparable."

I thought I saw tears forming in the corners of Helena's eyes but a moment later a faint half-smile played about her lips, and in her eyes I caught what looked like a flicker of surrender.

Could she possibly be resigning herself to yet more of *me*? I wondered.

NOTE TO THE READER

Several of the principal characters in this novel actually existed and were part of the rich tapestry of classical music in the Germany of the mid-1800s. Other characters, and the plot and subplot, are purely fictitious. I acknowledge with gratitude the following research sources which enabled me to blend historical facts with invented people and events:

Michael Steen, *The Lives and Times of the Great Composers*
Ernest Newman, *Stories of the Great Operas*
Nicholas Slonimsky, *Perfect Pitch: A Life Story*
John Culshaw, *Wagner: The Man and His Music*
Rosamund Bartlett, *Wagner and Russia*
The Diaries Of Richard Fricke, *Wagner in Rehearsal*
Barry Millington, *Wagner*

In a sense the story of Richard Wagner has continued long after his death on February 13, 1883. I therefore acknowledge as well many pertinent essays and articles that appeared during the writing of this novel in newspapers including *The New York Times*, *Globe and Mail*, and the English-language

Forward, a New York newspaper which, in both its Yiddish and English editions, has been an essential part of my family for two generations.

As always for their advice, encouragement, and assistance, my thanks to Beverley Slopen, Joanne DeLio, Henry Campbell, Malcolm Lester, and my editors Sylvia McConnell and Cheryl Hawley.